# No.1 Akashganga Lane

# No.1 Akashganga Lane

The First Novel about the Gig Workers of Kolkata

Ashoke Mukhopadhyay

Translated from Bengali by ZENITH ROY

THORNBIRD
NIYOGI BOOKS

Published by
NIYOGI BOOKS
Block D, Building No. 77,
Okhla Industrial Area, Phase-I,
New Delhi-110 020, INDIA
Tel: 91-11-26816301, 26818960
Email: niyogibooks@gmail.com
Website: www.niyogibooksindia.com



Editor: Sucharita Ghosh
Design: Shashi Bhushan Prasad
Cover Design: Antra K

ISBN: 978-81-992494-3-1
Publication: 2026

This is a work of fiction. The names, characters and incidents portrayed in it are the work of the author's imagination. Any resemblance to actual persons, living or dead, events or localities, is entirely coincidental.



Printed at Niyogi Offset Pvt. Ltd., New Delhi, India

*To*

*Millions of Gig Workers*

*Surviving On Dreams*

# Foreword

The app-based order delivery business – with food delivery often called ghost kitchens – has grown so rapidly since the pandemic ended, that watching it happen feels like a history in the making. The appeal of online ordering (of food) changes depending on age, from variety for the younger groups to balancing family and work for middle-aged professionals to the convenience of choosing diet-specific foods for older people. But it has been strong and sustained for everyone. Covid pushed the industry towards inventing user-friendly apps, and AI promises to add more personalisation to the ordering system. Technology and consumption have progressed at breakneck speed, each strengthening the other. Worldwide, the food delivery market was valued at roughly USD 60 billion in 2024. The value will touch almost 200 billion by 2033.

Will it? No business in history has involved so much uncertainty for the suppliers and the workers as app-based delivery. Once the app is ready and a workforce is available, it is, in theory, an easy-entry business, meaning it is also an easy-exit one. Little fixed capital is involved except for transport, which the workers usually own. Fierce competition has driven profit margins to low levels, increased marketing costs, and made it more difficult to build customer loyalty. Competition has led to a concentration of the business in fewer hands, which is not good news for the workers.

Facing such competition, the business has thrived only partly by innovating. It has thrived also by shifting the risks and the costs on the workers. This is a 'gig economy' with neither employment contracts nor salaries. A hundred and fifty years ago, Karl Marx defined capitalism as a new economic system where workers no longer owned the means of production. The gig economy has turned capitalism upside down; the workers own the physical means of production, and the capitalists own an app, a virtual means of production.

Workers sign up with the companies owning the apps to receive delivery requests through apps. They can choose their working hours and accept or decline orders. Payment is per-delivery, sometimes supplemented by tips. Gig workers are responsible for their expenses, such as fuel, food, and vehicle maintenance. The company saves on labour costs, and the workers have flexible hours. There is more. Unlike most traditional businesses, much of the burden of customer service and communication failures is passed on to the workers.

A world of work has been created around us in a breathtakingly short time that is nothing like we have known before. In a city like Kolkata, which has seen a retreat in the manufacturing industry, delivery is one of the largest employers of young working-age people. It is a world that gives opportunities to earn where opportunities are scarce and gives freedom and flexibility in working, all bought at the cost of brutal hours and high insecurity to property, safety, and even life. Business statistics will not tell us what this world means to the people inside it. What will? Ashoke Mukhopadhyay has an answer.

At one level, *Ek Number Akashganga* is a story of relentless economic hardship redeemed by friendship and ambition. Shiuli struggles to support her family, Sriman navigates the challenges of his profession while dealing with personal and familial issues, and Somnath offers competition and camaraderie. Ashoke Mukhopadhyay brings his characters to life with sensitivity and plain good writing. But beyond the fictional plot, which is a timeless one, there is a story of breathless change. The ageing city is remaking itself with consumerism. High-rises appear in the ashes of old quarters, and the roads and common spaces are more crowded, busier, and chaotic than before. The professions that the book's protagonists join are a big part of the city's reinvention. The book is a powerful and sensitive human drama and shows how well the background of the gig economy helps to make sense of the lives of the youth in a transforming city.

**Tirthankar Roy**
Professor of Economic History
London School of Economics and Political Science

# 1

Nature once had its own melody, its dulcet cadence. That is gone now. The seasons have lost their poetry and the traits that defined them. One of the alarming fallouts of this phenomenon is the exponential rise in incidences of lightning. Twenty-seven casualties in two consecutive days of lightning across the state of West Bengal. The annual average of lightning-related deaths, which is on the rise, is a marker of an alarming trend. The crisis, blamed on global warming, is exacerbated by the rampant decimation of greenery.

Kolkata used to be so fascinatingly green even a few years ago. Most of it has been destroyed. Old houses and porticos are being demolished to make way for multi-storeyed apartment buildings. Scanty spaces punctuated by rickety pillars of sky-high constructions are crammed with cars.

Raja Dinendra Street, very close to Shyambazar, is one of those rare localities that sustain the charm of old-world Kolkata. Houses with porticos can still be seen here, providing sanctuary from rain to stray dogs, cows, cyclists, beggars, and students hailing mostly from the decadent middle class. Even flies hate to linger in the rains for long. Like wayward children, they take frolicking turns at bothering the portico-sheltered strays and humans.

Sriman Kundu had taken shelter motorcycle in tow beneath one such portico as soon as the rain began its rampage. The downpour that had been raging since noon was like a misplaced clef in a sheet of notations—untimely, discordant—throwing the rhythm of the day into disarray. The obstinate torrent was refusing to budge even after one and a half hours. The sky seemed to be determined on wringing out the last droplet before yielding itself to the embrace of a resurgent sunshine.

Sriman was one of those Kolkatans who traversed the length and breadth of the city from 10:30 in the morning till 11:30 at night on a regular working day. He was perfectly conversant with its nooks and their safe havens which could shield his bike from unforeseen calamities. With a scruffy rag from his toolbox, he had dried his valued scrambler thoroughly alongside the company-provided squat, black box strapped to the back of his two-wheeler. While bringing out the water bottle for a quick sip, he rechecked his satchel for the usual: biscuits, mobile phone charger, the spare yellow vest provided by the company. Sriman was mindful of keeping the motorbike spick and span, particularly because it was a borrow from Bablu-da and must be returned to his garage every night.

Sporting a yellow t-shirt and blue denims over a pair of loafers, Sriman was on the wrong side of twenties. At five-eight his robust build was defined by a dusky complexion, headlined by a crew cut that his helmet camouflaged. The yellow tee was the working attire from Yellow Shirts, the app-based food-delivery company he worked for. Both the tee and the jeans had, thankfully, escaped the pluvial ambush. Sriman had wiped the moistness off his hair with the hand towel. Somewhere in between performing these chores, his eyes grazed poetically over the mesmeric verdancy of the park across the street.

Looking back at the park, Sriman could sniff the impending chill despite the rain. Delivery riders like him, who crisscrossed the city on two-wheelers, savoured an intuitive familiarity with its motley-spirited whims.

With the rain subsiding a little, people were coming out. Bytes of conversations had begun to waft in the air like dialogues from an unfamiliar play. Sriman caught the angry strains of a young female voice. 'Why shouldn't I answer his call? He was calling from 300 km away! … we had a hell of a showdown over this last night … why does he call you? How did he get your number? Why do you talk with him for hours on end? Why does he call in the afternoon? … He was bloody grilling me … I told him repeatedly that they work in shifts;

he calls in the afternoon because that's when his morning shift ends and he takes the colony-bound bus—'

The conversation stopped abruptly. Turning his head, Sriman located the speaker—a young woman, pacing the lane in self-absorbed frenzy, venting her innermost rage into the hand-held phone that was wired to her ear.

'Okay, I admit Tapan had been courting me before marriage,' the girl had resumed her livid argument, 'but I had refused each time. Rajesh knows it, yet he won't accept … same old story … distrust and grilling … I too lost my cool …Why shouldn't I speak with him? … Rajesh suddenly started thrashing me, that was the limit … my back is paining, yesterday—' A four-wheeler went past, its raucous horn making the girl inaudible. 'Son of …' Sriman swore clenching his teeth.

'Oh yes! He was just seeking an excuse to pounce upon me … lecherous beast …' Sriman heard the girl say. She was closer now. A thirty-something; frail; a scurfy, swarthy face, mole near the chin; smudged hint of crimson at the parting of her hair. She was wearing a nightie over stockinged feet ensconced in walking shoes. Strange choice of time for a promenade, Sriman could not help thinking.

Those who deal with people day in and day out are generally seasoned judges of the human character. But this girl defied stereotypes. Was she a housekeeper in some rich businessman's employ? Such people usually have a daylong routine of toil. Their days begin early with a couple of hours' respite at the most, typically around 1:30 to 2:00 in the afternoon. Though a round-the-clock job, her employer surely let her off after dinner. That explained her heated exchange with the husband.

She could be from the canal side. One of those windowless, tin-roofed tenements with curtained doors, where the oven simmers endlessly and the eternally blaring TV adds decibels to the inmates' quotidian narrative of cacophonous chaos. They may be long-term tenants in one of the houses on the southern fringes of Raja Dinendra Street. The actual owner being untraceable, they possibly shell out a sum of Rs 150 or so every month to live there with the blessings of the local political bigwig.

The notification alert on his phone nudged Sriman out of his trance. An order had arrived. He had already delivered five moderate orders since morning. Kolkatans were stuffing their faces with biriyani and Chinese fare. This too must be a similar order. Apart from a relatively less squalid air and a mostly clear sky, the Covid-19 pandemic in Kolkata had brought about a surge in demand for doorstep delivery of food.

Serving a profession that thrives on incessant dynamism, Sriman couldn't afford the luxury of staying rooted to a spot for long. He had been stuck here for almost a couple of hours. Two hours of inactivity cost him four trips which amounted to the loss of Rs 200. The crepuscular sky offered no hope of the rain stopping anytime soon. He should have realised this earlier. Sriman chided himself for the unpardonable stupidity of wasting time by eavesdropping on other peoples' conversations.

Sriman took out the raincoat from the box attached to the bike. Bishan-da had gifted it to him. That reminded Sriman of Bishan-da's request to watch the western sky today post sunset. 'The crescent moon will hang like a smiley at the bottom of the western sky. Venus will be a little above, Mars on the left. The two planets have lately drawn unusually close. Leo will be visible overhead. Even if you miss it today, you must watch it tomorrow,' Sriman vividly recalled every syllable of what Bishan-da had said.

The smiley thing was typically Bishan-da. The imagery brought a smile to Sriman's face, an incongruity beneath the humourless sky, despite the raincoat. It was an ordeal to work in such attire, which easily drenched him in sweat. Once the raincoat was soaked, rainwater dripped down the shoulder, soaking the shoes and socks and weighing down the raincoat. Damn it, how could anyone rush from place to place in wet clothes? But he could not delay any more. The sizeable loss he had already incurred would keep mounting as long as he prolonged this immobility.

The intensity of the rain reduced as soon as he brought the bike out. Sriman glanced gratefully at the sky to convey respectful thanks to God. Key already in the ignition, Sriman muttered, 'Let's get going, baby!' Sensing the response, he fondly patted the petrol tank and stepped on the gas.

Sweet nothings of this kind were a commonplace between Sriman and his darling bike, a diminutive monster that effortlessly ran forty-two to forty-five kilometres on a litre of petrol, charged by a 160-cc cylinder. The bike belonged to Bablu-da. Sriman had to return it every night to his garage. It was an unwritten arrangement between both of them that Sriman would pay whatever he could every month. Once that amount equalled the price of the bike, it would become his. There was no dearth of swanky bikes in the ritzy showrooms. But Sriman would never part with this darling. It may be a bit old, but it had been his loyal companion through ups and downs.

At once, a small four-wheeler, painted with the Agarwal Motor Training School logo, came to a halt on his right and the nightie-shoe-stockings girl jumped in. Sriman was stumped. She was not a housekeeper then? But time was of essence and Sriman could not waste it on useless speculations. As he shifted gear, the four-wheeler upped its momentum. Callers on his number now would be greeted by the initial lines of a catchy Jubin Nautiyal song.

On reaching the restaurant from where he would be collecting the parcel, Sriman quoted the last four digits of the ten-digit order code. Though a familiar face, he was known by the code of every new order that brought him here. Even in Yellow Shirts, he was merely a cypher: two letters and six digits. All his personal details—name, parental identity, face—appeared on the screen when the code was typed in the company's database.

Likewise, the restaurant too would know what the order entailed—biriyani, rezala, or reshmi kebab—once they typed in the order code. Two plates each of chicken biriyani and chicken chaap along with two firnis—the items of the order—arrived in three minutes in polythene packets bearing the name of the eatery. Sriman had to rush. A rupee would be deducted from his earnings for every minute of delay. Generally, he earned Rs 40 for delivering each daytime order from Monday to Thursday and 50 for nightly deliveries. From Friday to Sunday, he earned Rs 50 for each daytime delivery and 65 for the ones at night.

The bike vroomed back to life, in the direction of Chiria More. The sun's golden hue smeared the statue of Subhas Chandra Bose at the Five-point Crossing at Shyambazar. A similar glow must have daubed Bose's upright frame when he had given the call for the Delhi-bound expedition in Kohima, Sriman imagined. Absorbed in such thoughts, Sriman reached Baghbazar. He would be taking the Chitpur Bridge to reach B.T. Road from where his destination would be a brief northward drive. The virtual map on his phone would lead on the specifics of the delivery location. Programmed in a sequence of mathematical symmetry, the entire cycle of his actions, from picking up the package to the final delivery, was an obedient conformity, an unconditional surrender, to the design predetermined by an invisible arbiter, just like yielding oneself to the hairdresser's mercy at the salon.

What does she do? ... That nightie-shoes-stockings girl who got into the training vehicle? Sriman's musings brought the temperateness of a summer afternoon to his mind. He had barely reached B.T. Road when a bus taking a sudden, stupid turn from the right nudged him to the left. He had signalled his right turn with both the indicator and a hand gesture, but public buses in Kolkata are hardly bothered about other vehicles. Goaded by the bus's belligerence, the two-wheeler had rapidly slithered towards the footpath on the left. Its front wheel edging over the causeway, the bike had slipped into the gutter, while Sriman was thrown off onto the ground by the impact. The bus had left the spot with the professional nonchalance of a hired assassin after doing away with a target. Sriman was grateful that the grey SUV immediately behind had pulled the brake at the right moment, screeching to a halt barely a foot away.

Was the bike intact? That was the first thought that came to Sriman's mind once he regained a semblance of composure. His left elbow had been bruised and he felt a piercing pain in his left knee. But he must steady the bike first. He could see petrol dripping from the tank. As soon as he sat up, a gentleman rushed towards him from the SUV behind. 'That was a close shave!' the fair-skinned gentleman tried to buck him up with a reassuring grin. 'Are you alright?' Sriman was too dazed to figure out whether he could he call himself 'alright'. Yet, he nodded, trying to put on a courteous smile. The sharp pain he was experiencing would not let him do that.

The pepper-haired gentleman had steadied the bike at one pull. Luckily, it had not suffered any discernible damage, except the cracked mirror on the right. Sriman had fallen on his left yet the right-hand mirror had broken. Sriman shook his head in disbelief, scattering his glance over the shards of glass strewn on the road. The service centre would definitely hand him a hefty bill.

Sriman stood up somehow, holding on to the gentleman. But the pain in the knee was too sharp to let him stand for long. Kolkata has not yet run out of good samaritans completely. A gangly specimen of that scanty species surfaced from among the crowd, fetching him a dry outer shell of a car battery to sit on, the kind roadside fish sellers sit on while vending their wares.

'Have a glass of water,' a female voice pleaded. The speaker was standing close to the flaxen-complexioned gentleman. She looked uncannily familiar. Sriman refused politely with a shake of his head. 'Then have some tea,' the lady insisted with a smile. Although in considerable pain, Sriman observed the lady minutely. Elegant, grey-haired, dimpled cheeks. Tea arrived in a white polystyrene cup. The resourcefulness of the couple suggested they were out on a long drive. They must be carrying cookies too. 'Can I have a cookie?' Sriman heard himself saying. He was ready to tackle the embarrassment with a hint of a smile in case his assumption proved wrong—a strategy he had loaned from Bishan-da. The lady, eager to oblige, scurried towards the car, leaving Sriman with no doubt that he had hit pay dirt. She returned with a packet of cookies.

Everything these days is as temporary as jobs. Same was true about Sriman's pain. With its intensity losing its edge, he tried to rub his injured knee to diffuse the awkwardness of the situation. It obliged. 'Good,' the gentleman sounded glad. So, the bones were intact. With a little more effort Sriman stood up holding the gentleman's extended arm. Accidents on Kolkata roads tend to attract a sizeable throng of curious bystanders, each a doctor in their own right as far as offering suggestions is concerned. 'Tetanus is essential,' someone said. Someone else recommended a tincture iodine dressing. Another voice ruled these diagnoses out and mentioned Betadine.

'Feeling better now?' the gentleman enquired softly.

Sriman smiled at last. A spontaneous smile, tinged with embarrassment. The couple was watching him intently. He gestured that he would be okay in no time, followed by a categorical 'Thank you'.

'Bye, take care …' The couple left.

To the edgy mob, habituated to large-scale, critical accidents in the city, Sriman's incident was bland in its uneventfulness. The bus did not hit the bike. The car coming behind too had braked at the right moment. The helmet intact on the driver's head had ruled out any major injury. The disheartened crowd gradually melted away.

What to do about the delivery, Sriman wondered. He rang Somnath.

'Out with it,' Somnath responded curtly.

Sriman gave him a quick lowdown.

'Somnath, please help me with this delivery,' Sriman said in a tone of helpless urgency. 'I promise I'll help if you get into an accident.'

'So, I need to be in an accident to get your help? … You are incorrigible!' said Somnath in jest. 'Be there in five minutes.'

Sriman felt buoyant on Somnath's arrival. Somnath extracted the parcel from the Yellow Shirts bag. 'Forget about all other assignments today. Go straight to Dutta Medical. Get the injection and all that done …' Sriman nodded in assent. 'Don't worry, I will take care of the delivery, bye …' Somnath said hearteningly before rushing towards his motorbike. For delivery riders, even the few moments to regret a personal loss or an injury is a luxury. Sriman was grateful that Somnath had allotted him precious time from his constricted schedule in this hour of crisis.

A new message for another delivery chimed in as soon as his wound was bandaged. He had incurred quite a heavy loss since morning. It was time to compensate. He could afford no lapses from his single-minded commitment to perform as many deliveries as possible through the rest of the day.

Sriman returned home past midnight. By that time, the pain had dulled, thanks to the painkiller given by Haru-da of Dutta Medical.

Sriman never forgot to perform a couple of essential chores before going to bed. He went to the terrace to meet Bishan-da.

Bishan, as always, was absorbed in watching the sky. 'Come, look at the southern sky … this is incredible!' he said, on hearing Sriman's footfall, without taking his eyes off the telescope.

Glancing into the eyepiece, Sriman found the dazzling Elder and then, the Scorpion. 'Fabulous!' he exclaimed. The brilliance of the stars seemed to be piercing into his consciousness. He gave a thorough account of the accident to Bishan-da even as he maintained his celestial gaze.

'You won't need to work hard once I find a different planet.' Bishan-da, at times, could be so bizarrely obscure.

Usually, Sriman spent at least an hour with Bishan-da before going to bed. But tonight, he was yearning badly for the comfort of his bed. He came down sooner than usual. Both dada and ma were fast asleep when he stepped into their room downstairs.

Turning turtle on the mattress, a pillow tucked below his chest, Sriman started writing the day's details in his diary by the light of his mobile phone. A quick peek into his diary would acquaint the reader better with the individual called Sriman.

'Woke up at 8:35 this morning. Rushed to queue up for the loo. Soon after, with the daily ablutions done, sat down to drink lemonade prepared by ma. Had barely completed drinking it when Sidhu-da yelled he was going for his bath. My turn comes immediately after him. Proceeded for my bath with towel and soap. We bathe at the roadside tap where water is available at specific hours, from 6 in the morning till 9:30 and again from 3 in the afternoon to 6:30 in the evening. After bathing, I rushed to the neighbourhood grocery shop and returned with two laddus. Ma hurriedly baked four chapatis. Had them with the laddus. Got ready. Took the key to fetch the motorbike from Bablu-da's garage, which is a few houses away. Brought the vehicle to our door. Tied the Yellow Shirts bag to the rear seat along with the extra bag I carry—drinking water, vehicle documents, biscuits, mobile phone charger, charging cable. And, yes, a sanitiser and an extra mask too.'

Writing thus far, Sriman remembered his second dose of the Covid-19 vaccine was due in five days. He saved a reminder on his phone.

'Put on the shoes, wore the mask, and left. Ma, as always, wished me "safe travel". Set out for the Mughlai food joint at Hatibagan, where our *adda* zone lies. We delivery riders based around the area assemble there and disperse for our respective restaurants (I no longer say "resturant" ever since Bishan-da corrected me) to collect the consignments once the orders arrive.

'It began to rain as soon as I was done with the delivery. Was stranded beneath a portico for quite some time, switching my mobile off. Switched it on when the rain ceased. A new order had come. Met with an accident on way to the delivery. Thankfully, it was a minor one. Somnath was of much help. The world still has some good souls left.

'Returned home after getting the wound treated. Was home for some time following lunch. The sky had cleared up by then. Set out at 5:45 in the evening for Hatibagan again. Opened the app, received a new order. Bumped into Shubhamoy at the food joint. He is also a delivery boy with another company. He had skipped going home for lunch, was working all along in the rain in his raincoat. He was on his twentieth order of the day when we met, while I was on a miserable seventh. Felt desperate. Resolved to deliver at least twenty orders by 11 pm.

'Since then, I have delivered whatever order came, rushing madly, manoeuvring the crowds. When I wrapped up at 11, I had delivered twenty-four orders. Less than Shubhamoy's daylong feat of thirty-five, but fairly good in terms of the shorter span in which it was achieved. At the end of the day, I am happy. It was 11:30 by the time I started for home. Went to the garage to return the bike. Water is not available at the roadside tap at that hour, so ma preserves a bucketful for me. Changed, washed, and sat down to have a meal of milk and chapati. Went out as usual on the street to take a drag. Came back and gulped down a bottle of water, as always. Visited Bishan-da before going to bed. Found him in one of his typical, mad moods.'

Sriman lay down on his back, turning out the torch on his phone. Sleep was merely a few sighs away. Suddenly, the image of the nightie-stockings-shoes girl venting angrily into her phone emerged. He had forgotten to mention her or the graceful lady and her male companion in his diary. He had not been able to locate her yet. Could she be Jnuiphool Roy Corbyn, Bishan-da's friend? Sriman sat up in excitement. Jnuiphool was married to Mike Corbyn, the famous French table tennis player. She toured villages all over the world in search of folk tales while her husband travelled all over the world playing matches. She may have come to India in pursuit of the same.

He must tell Bishan-da. Sriman tottered up to the terrace in sleepy steps.

Bishan-da was watching the star-spangled sky with his telescope and scribbling things in a notebook kept on a low stool lit by a reading lamp. The austere ambience left Sriman in two minds whether to part with the information. Suddenly, Bishan-da turned towards him and said, 'Whatever you have come to tell me can wait till tomorrow ...' He turned back to the telescope while muttering, 'Strange, very strange ...'

'I met your friend Jnuiphool today,' Sriman chipped in.

'Oh yes, that will be our name for the planet once I find it ... strange, very strange, looks like a nova ...' Bishan kept murmuring.

He would never understand this man.

Sriman started descending the stairs.

# 2

Sriman lived in one of those ancient houses of north Kolkata that still retains a distinctively musty charm. 1 Akashganga Lane, the house that initiates the locality, is aptly named after the indigenous equivalent to the Milky Way. No one can say for sure whether the neighbourhood was named after the house or the other way round.

Every morning, while stepping out for work from the sun-kissed eastern room on the ground floor of this house, Sriman romanced over its illustrious past. The decrepit pillars of the tabernacle, the pallid enormity of the age-old windows, the past growing in soot and grime inside the locked rooms, the lofty crevices reverberating with the cooing of pigeons, made Sriman feel he had been living an existence steeped in history. Being a denizen of this eminent house instilled in him a sublime dignity which did not allow him to stoop to any mundane baseness that could tarnish the prestige Bishan-da and his family commanded in the locality.

Akashganga dates back to the Calcutta where Gobindaram Mitra was a formidable name. Deputy collector of Calcutta and better known by his nickname, the brown zamindar, Gobindaram commanded a lot of clout. Three things had earned popular notoriety in the streets of the then Calcutta—Gobindaram's cane, Banamali (Sarkar)'s den, Omichand's mane. Gobindaram's mansion was among the most magnificent in the city, the *nabaratna* temple its crowning glory. One of its turrets, the tallest in the city at 165 feet, was devastated in the cyclone of 1737.

One has to sift through many a sepia page of history and return to Siraj ud-Daulah's siege of Calcutta of 1756 to rediscover the specifics of Akashganga's Gobindaram connect. Siraj's ravaging siege, the Fort William its epicentre, was purportedly strategised to teach its British occupants a lesson for ordering unauthorised fortification of the premises. The siege forced many denizens of the city to desert it. The nawab returned to Murshidabad after entrusting the charge of the Fort to one of his officials. The very next year, the Battle of Plassey led to Siraj's defeat and death. Mir Jafar became the new nawab. The East India Company made Mir Jafar pay the compensation for Siraj's siege. The Company administration decided to pay a part of that compensation to those families which had been loyal to it and had held ground in the city despite Siraj's infarction.

Gobindaram Mitra and Shobharam Basak were assigned the responsibility of earmarking the loyal families and distributing the largesse among them. For Gobindaram and Shobharam, both masters of embezzlement, this was a golden opportunity to fill their personal coffers with the lion's share of the funds. Flashy and flamboyant, both men maintained their respective retinues of dependents who were also allotted shares of the grant. After all, the social standing of these babus depended largely on the patronage of their menials. Among the subordinates of the generous Gobindaram, on whom he lavished a substantial share of the largesse, were his three concubines—Ratan bai, Lalita bai, Moti bai—at whose places he spent most of his bohemian nights.

Bishan-da had told Sriman that Akashganga was built on Lalita bai's money. Bishan had no clear idea how his forefathers came to own this depleted vestige of aristocracy from Lalita bai's adopted son. People say, his grandfather, Ratikanta Basu, knew the whole of it. Bishan had no recollection of his grandfather except his shaggy moustache.

But where was Bishan-da this morning, one of Sriman's rarely early ones? Sriman, as usual, had begun this rare day with a purifying glance at the Ganga from the terrace, though the scanty opening between the two buildings ahead does not allow more than a sliver of the river. The terrace exuded the sacred aroma of inviolate sanctity in these early hours. Sriman dug these immersive dips into serenity that endowed him with the vitality necessary to survive the day. He, however, was uncharacteristically restless this morning. Last night, he had not been able to adequately apprise Bishan-da on the chance encounter with Jnuiphool madam. Sriman peeped into the second-floor balcony while pacing across the terrace. Bishan-da was not there. This man would always be an enigma. He went to bed in the wee hours of the morning only to wake up at 6 sharp every day, to go bathing in the Ganga. How did he manage this feat?

Bishan-da was the only member of his family to be presently living in this house. Three rooms on the first floor, including a toilet and a kitchen, comprised his humble moiety. Sitangsu Chakraborty, the priest of the Radhakanta Jiu temple in the southern block of the house, was the virtual caretaker of this property. The absentee parceners sent their contribution for the upkeep of their respective portions to him. Electricity bills as well as all essential repairs were met with that money.

It was Bishan's mother, the revered *mejoma* of this household, who had given shelter to Shiuli Barik, Sriman's mother, in the minuscule room in the sedate eastern corner of the ground floor. The house then was a virtual matriarchy, ruled by the triumvirate of widows—*badoma*, Uma, the widow of Bishan's uncle Amiyabhushan; *mejoma*, Gauri, Bishan's mother; and *chhotoma*, Lakshmi, the widow of his other uncle Binoybhushan. After their death, Bishan-da's cousins and nephews staying in the house shifted base to Delhi, Bengaluru,

London, New York, and other places, leaving their respective portions under lock and key.

Barely was Sriman back home with the laddus from the neighbourhood shop when his mother handed him a piece of tattered cloth warmed in the earthen kiln. Soothed by the steamy touch of the fabric on his wounded foot, Sriman felt thankful that his injury was not severe. His company had a health insurance policy of five lakh rupees in place. It was meant to address the eventualities of major medical expenditures. Despite this, an unsettling apprehension perturbed Sriman. Even if the cost of the treatment was managed with the money, how could he compensate the loss if the accident had rendered him bedridden for days and nights on end? Had the accident resulted in his death, would his mother get the money?

While his mind was engaged in such morbid thoughts, Sriman's eyes were surveying their room, which despite its quotidian mundaneness, differed from the middling familiarity of the typical Bengali middle-class habitat. The walls evinced a marked dearth of images or idols of gods or eminent personalities. Instead, the wall on the north documented a humble specimen of Shiuli's artistic skills, an anonymous maxim embroidered on a tapestry:

> Stay honest,
> To master thy fate.

With an upright spine,
Your home becomes a shrine.

Ma had told him that she had sewn this during the heady post-marriage days, much before his father had deserted her for another woman. Sriman was in his mother's womb then.

Your worries shall be gone,
If you surrender them to The One

read the message sewn on another embroidery on the wall close to the south-west corner. Shiuli had made this when she had tided over the initial trauma of the desertion. To her, the heartening messages sewn in these self-crafted artistries were nothing less prophetic than an oracle.

Apart from these, a photo of his parents, taken shortly after their marriage, hung on one of the walls. Sriman had often thought of discarding it but curbed his angsty urge lest it hurt his mother's feelings. He did not want to have truck with anything that was even remotely connected with his father. One of these was his paternal surname. He preferred Barik, his mother's surname, instead of Kundu, the cognomen inherited from his father. Sriman refused to be cowed down by the dead weight of the memories of a man who had left his mother pregnant with her second child and never bothered to come back. The father never came to visit his second son. Did he not feel for once the fatherly urge to see his own child in the last twenty-seven years?

'How could he? He was in jail!' His mother's skewed logic infuriated Sriman. Actually, Shiuli couldn't think of any stronger justification. She was more or less her husband's conduit to attain orgasmic bliss. Besotted with the man, she was blithely heedless to his shady past of drug trafficking and opium trade and his identity as a jailbird. A shrewd dissembler, he kept manipulating her with his ostentatious flamboyance. Shiuli was too naïve to suspect anything.

Those days, they were living in a tile-roofed tenement near Baghbazar Park. The man's youngest sister, Champa, used to live with them. Srinath was born first, Sriman two years later. The man went to jail a couple of months after Srinath was born. Champa herself had warned Shiuli that something was off about her brother. The unsuspecting Shiuli, who had begun to sniff something fishy by then, became more cautious with Champa's warning. When the police picked up the man from Kidderpore, two months after Srinath's birth, it was found that he had been involved in drug trafficking big time on the pretext of going to work at the hosiery mill.

Ever since his release, which happened remarkably early on that occasion, Shiuli and he would be at loggerheads. Shiuli often tried to reason with him, urging him to mend his ways.

But wise counsel was lost on him. The man was a smooth talker. His pretentious protestations of love would often make Shiuli go weak in the knees. Months later, Shiuli was pregnant again. The man was taken back to prison soon after.

He was acquitted the day Sriman was born. People credited it to the auspiciousness of the birth. But Shiuli knew very well that it would not be easy for her to live with him once he returned. She resolved not to allow him to exploit her again. Strangely, the man never came back.

In spite of everything, Shiuli couldn't vouch even to this day that she would really have discarded him. A long hiatus often made the resplendent gloss of a heady yearning camouflage unpleasant memories. It took away the edge from acrimony, however strong it might be.

That was a critical time for Shiuli. She was working in four households yet what she was earning proved inadequate to feed four mouths: herself, Champa, and the two kids. Champa's earnings from her sewing machine, though slight, helped. She would also look after the two kids while Shiuli was out on work.

It was in such circumstances that Shiuli met *mejoma*, Bishan's mother, popularly known as Gauri Ma. Having performed her early morning ritual of bathing in the Ganga, she came up the stairs of the ghat. Shiuli had developed the habit of spending a few tranquil moments at the ghat before yielding herself to the chaos of daily chores at the houses she served. When the magnanimous lady, in course of offering alms to the beggars assembled there, came to Shiuli, the latter said, 'Ma, I don't need money. If you can, please employ me at your house.' Gauri Ma was stunned at this unusual overture. 'I can't, at this moment ... Sorry, dear ...' she had politely refused, but told her that she would need one a month later. Shiuli had told Gauri Ma everything about herself. The intervening month was one of eager anticipation. She arrived at Gauri Ma's door exactly at the beginning of the next month. The lady did employ her.

So, one fine day, the three of them—Shiuli, Srinath and Sriman—had shifted to 1 Akashganga Lane. Champa did not come with them. She was missing for the last few days. Days later, someone had left her on Galiff Street, ravaged and grievously bruised. Some kind soul admitted her to R.G. Kar Hospital. Champa died there a couple of days later.

Sriman had heard all this from his mother. Sriman retained the remembrances of his childhood at Paramanandapur, a village near Jayrambati. He recalled heady afternoons of play that used to culminate into evenings when he sat down to study along with dada. Their mother, busy making rotis in one corner, minutely monitored the brothers' dedication to studies. The ruddy glow from the heated kiln complemented the coppery hue of their mother's face, enhancing the rare interplay of workaday practicality and the warmth of affection.

Ma continued to make rotis with their eternal full-moon rotundity and served them with the same dedication till this day. How had she maintained this flawless precision? Did not this unflinching dedication ever bore her, Sriman felt tempted to ask, but he knew what ma's response would be. She would simply ask him whether he was bored of having the same roti and laddu every morning. Sriman had often tried to think it out, but an apt retort had always eluded him.

Sriman was having his second roti with molasses when Srinath entered. Srinath had bought a vehicle under government subsidy on monthly instalments. The exorbitant price of petrol and the proliferation of app cabs had drastically reduced clients for government-run cabs. The client base had reduced further due to the lack of clarity regarding the procedure of booking such vehicles. In such a scenario, Sriman seriously doubted whether Srinath managed to pay the instalments every month. Dada was a good man, but indolent to a fault—he could not do without a sound post-lunch siesta. Whenever ma sought money from him, Sriman realised that dada must have defaulted on paying an instalment. But he could not refuse her even if he was in a crunch. They understood this very well and fully manipulated his inability to say no.

Sriman often thought of taking his mother and brother to the famous joint nearby for a sumptuous treat. He anticipated the pocket pinch to be to the tune of Rs 2000. But each time he managed to save the amount, some or other unforeseen expense gobbled it up.

'Pintu is getting married. *Badomama* had phoned me. He insists we go,' informed Srinath. 'When is it?' Shiuli's eyes exuded excitement. 'Sixth of next month.' Their faces told Sriman that both were eager to attend the ceremony.

The reference to the phone call rekindled old memories in Sriman. Those were days of innocent bliss. He was in the eighth standard. As on previous occasions, Sriman had accompanied ma and dada to his maternal uncles' place at Paramanandapur. But what made that particular trip different was the heartrending imprint of sadness on ma's face when she and dada were about to return to Kolkata without him. Sriman was clueless as to why ma looked so pensive while bidding him adieu.

Sriman was admitted in a local school by his maternal uncles. Together, his two uncles owned nearly fifteen acres of arable land along with a pair of oxen and three cows. The land, regarded auspicious for its fertility, yielded a rich harvest thrice a year. Sriman learnt to till the land with the oxen, milk the cattle, and even sell the milk. On holidays, Sriman would accompany his cousin Pintu to work in the fields: six to eleven in the morning, four to six in the afternoon. He shared an intimate bond with Pintu who also taught him to drive a motorbike. In that respect, Sriman owed his livelihood to Pintu.

'Why not?' Shiuli asked Sriman after he had stated his inability to attend Pintu's wedding. 'It's the wedding of your dear cousin … you two were so close …' How could he tell ma that his decision was occasioned by a quick mental calculation? The ceremony would be nothing less than a four-five-day affair, including the journey to Paramanandapur and back. For Sriman, it would amount to the loss of around Rs 3000.

'Think over it,' Shiuli persisted. 'Impossible, Ma … so many things to do …' Sriman was firm in his refusal. 'Give me another roti,' he said, 'getting late.' This unusual demand for the third roti was Sriman's ploy to please his mother who seemed rather miffed at his firm declaration of inability to join them on the trip to Paramanandapur.

Sriman was about to leave when Somnath rang. What Sriman gleaned from Somnath's hasty blabber was that Russell, another delivery worker and their mutual friend, had been arrested by the police for allegedly slapping a girl. 'Come to Bartala police station immediately. I will join you there,' Somnath said. 'Okay,' Sriman replied without emotion. However, on making another quick mental calculation, Sriman decided to do a few trips before going to the police station. He could not afford to begin the day with loss.

At Hatibagan, he bumped into Somnath who was on the way to a delivery.

'You were supposed to meet me at Bartala PS!' Sriman sounded irritated.

'Felt like messing you up a little ...' Somnath responded with his annoying grimace. 'What if I had taken you seriously and missed deliveries?' Sriman felt his anger rising. 'How many deliveries have you done since the morning?'

'This is the third ...' Somnath smirked before vrooming off.

Sriman dwelt over the discontent with his work. Everything was so mechanical about it, allowing not even a semblance of creativity. He was not involved with the preparation of the food he delivered. The delivery worker was an utterly self-centred individual who could not bond with his co-workers because the delivery worker was always running short of time. The gig worker was a hopelessly mercenary fellow who must always guesstimate the potential monetary loss before taking any decision, even that of attending a ceremony in the family.

Even his earlier stint as a worker in a hosiery mill, while studying in a Kolkata college on passing the Higher Secondary examination from Paramanandapur, gave him the pleasure of being productive. He would feel a deep contentment while caressing the vests made with his own hands.

The delivery location of the next order was in the vicinity of Bartala police station. On reaching the spot, Sriman was directed to the cell where they had kept Russell. Russell burst into tears on seeing Sriman. 'Believe me, I haven't done anything!' Russell patiently narrated the entire episode to Sriman.

'Did you inform the company?' Sriman asked.

'Yes. But will they do anything?' Russell sounded cynical.

'Certainly, don't worry … I'll speak to the inspector in-charge,' Sriman assured him.

'Sir, my friend is a decent boy …' Sriman said to the IC, pointing at Russell.

'He has the gall to manhandle girls … your friend behaves like a bigwig … "decent" indeed!' the IC reacted with utmost rudeness.

'There must've been some misunderstanding. Russell is not that type, sir. He comes from a Bengali Christian family of devout churchgoers. He can't stoop to such levels.'

'Good boy, my foot! He slaps girls … "good boy!"' the IC said with a suggestive smirk while twirling the paperweight on his table.

'He didn't grope the girl, sir. Please listen to him once,' Sriman pleaded.

Caught off-guard by the bluntness of Sriman's remark, the IC thundered, 'What did you say? "Didn't grope"? … Scoundrel, how dare you?'

Sriman ignored the officer's unwarranted attack and said, 'Just think over it, sir, had he any indecent intention, he would have touched the girl lewdly. Isn't it? The customer accuses that he had slapped her. Why would a delivery worker do so when that would simply result in loss? … Please listen to him once, sir.' Sriman pleaded with utmost earnestness.

'Okay, let's hear what he has to say,' the officer responded in a tone mellowed down by Sriman's entreaty.

Russell had gone to Jorasanko on a delivery. Puja Mehta, the girl who had ordered the food, was annoyed at the delay. She had called customer care and demanded the package be delivered free of cost. Russell had informed the company beforehand that he was stranded in a massive traffic snarl and despite that he was trying to deliver it as early as possible.

'Sir, she raised hell simply because I was late by five minutes,' Russell said.

'You didn't point that out?' the officer wanted to know.

'I did, sir. But she wasn't ready to see reason, she kept insisting that the package be given to her free of cost … I told her I couldn't do that and that she needed to speak with the company … she kept arguing and threatened to lodge a complaint against me …' Russell stopped.

'What did you say?'

'I said, please go ahead. To that, she took off her sandal to hit me …'

'Bitch!' The officer had no better term to describe her.

'Then she slapped me. She was about to hit me again, but I ducked … the moment I side-stepped, she lost balance and fell. The bruise on her lips is probably because she hit the edge of the table while falling … I didn't hit her, sir. I never raise hands on women …' Russell said.

'Bravo! Grandfather Bhishma is here,' the IC jeered.

A little later, he drafted an FIR, slapping Articles 355, 341, 504, and 506 of the Indian Penal Code on Puja Mehta. The allegations included physical assault without provocation, unlawful detention, insulting with the motive of instigating a person to break the law, and more.

Russell signed the FIR.

***

Somnath had done eight deliveries by the time Sriman reached Hatibagan with Russell. Sriman had missed orders amounting to at least Rs 300. He decided to deliver as many orders as possible for the rest of the day, even at the cost of forgoing lunch at home.

# 3

A star was continually gaining in glow with every new day. The senescent star appeared to be on the verge of exploding. Bishan was pretty thrilled that the rare spectacle had been captured in his telescope.

'This must be a nova, a new nova … we have found it at last, Sriman!' Bishan squealed in excitement. 'We'll call it Jnuiphool Corbyn, or simply Corbyn … what say?'

'Let me take a look,' Sriman said. He glanced through the eyepiece. 'Where is it? I don't see anything! … Has it exploded?'

'The outer part of the star will dislodge itself from the inner,' Bishan was elucidating the phenomenon in the layman's lingo, 'the larger part of the star's mass will stay in the centre and gradually regain its earlier appearance and brightness, while the detached part …'

A twinging pain in the right side of his abdomen stung Sriman so sharply that he could not hear the rest of Bishan's illuminating discourse. The pain had been asserting its presence since the afternoon, when Sriman was at the club. Though intermittent, it had been affecting his movements. Sriman somehow suppressed it and placed his eye on the eyepiece. 'Where is the bright star ...'

'Strange!' Bishan exclaimed, looking through the telescope. 'Where did it go? It was there just now! ... No problem, it's Monday, you will be home, I will call you as soon as I spot it again—' Bishan said while fine-tuning the telescope.

'You must have imagined it, Bishan-da,' Sriman said. 'By the way, Corbyn is a better name for a star than Jnuiphool. It has an exotic twang.'

'Are you kidding? ... There's no dearth of stars with Bengali names, alongside their English equivalents ... Chitra-Swati-Rohini ...' Bishan elaborated. His eyes were still mooning over the dreamy encounter with the mysterious star. At the same time, they were brimming with the nostalgia of the canopic Rajnagar sky of his childhood.

Bishan was barely ten or eleven. Gajen uncle of Rajnagar had taught him skywatching. The sky over the semi-urban Rajnagar spread like a canopy from one end of the horizon to the other. At night, it was studded with stars. Teaching him to recognise the Orion, Gajen uncle had said, 'My relationship with the world, dear, is exactly like that of the Sirius—there yet not there ... Always maintain a self-effacing lightness of being, my dear.'

Bishan came to decipher this conundrum later. This stoical insouciance perfectly suited Gajen uncle, who was concerned with the greater good through his involvement with the Tebhaga Movement in Kakdwip.

Everything about those days was almost elfin in its innocent simplicity. His mother, *mejoma* of this house, was the queen of that fairy-tale past. Bishan watched his mother converse with the trees in their courtyard. It was her way of filling up the void left behind by the demise of his father. Bibhutibhushan Basu, a self-proclaimed Netaji aficionado, had left home to join the Naval Mutiny. The little Bishan, then barely ten or twelve, had gone to Kakdwip with their family physician, Binoy Roy. Bishan vividly remembered Binoy uncle tending to the wounded under the dim glow from an earthen lamp, surrounded by the ebonite darkness of the night.

Bishan pointed at the northern end of the sky. 'That's the Pole Star. Can you see it with bare eyes?'

'Crystal clear.'

'The light that you see is coming from 430 years ago,' Bishan smiled.

The strange things Bishan-da said often made Sriman laugh. But tonight was different. Though Sriman had restricted himself to a mild laugh, he could not escape the searing stab of pain it brought, too agonising to be suppressed.

That brought Bishan's attention back on Sriman. Watching his face contort with pain, Bishan anxiously asked, 'What happened?'

'A terrible pain …' Sriman winced.

'Where?'

Sriman gestured towards the right of his underbelly.

'Lie down in the Lunar Pod and watch the stars. Let me check you.'

Lunar Pod was Bishan's fond nickname for the attic where the telescope occupied place of pride alongside the upholstery. The owner of the telescope liked brief spells of relaxation in bed between the stargazing sessions.

Bishan was at home with the situation at hand. Though he had retired as a travelling ticket examiner with the railways, he was an extremely well-read jack of all trades.

Bishan lightly pressed on a point on Sriman's underbelly. Sriman squirmed in pain. 'Too much pain … it's suffocating …'

'Since when have you been feeling it?' Bishan asked in a serious tone.

Sriman initially believed that the pain had begun while he was in the club. But with a little nudge to his memory, he recalled it was already there when he had gone to the club. He tried to recollect the day's events in their sequence to locate the initiation of the pain.

It being his day off, he had woken a little later than usual. Did he feel the pain on waking up? No, but there was a hint of discomfort in the abdomen along with heartburn. The discomfort had lessened after he had gulped consecutive glasses of water. The pain was not there on Sunday night, Sriman was sure. While returning from work last night, he had heard someone taunting him, 'Look at the rascal. Delivery boy with the airs of a film star ...' The taunt had left him seething in futile rage. The ones mocking him were at least twenty years his senior.

'I felt like battering their heads,' Sriman had told Bishan-da during his post-dinner visit to the terrace.

Bishan-da had smiled. 'Forget it. Only a stinking bile would come out of that batter. Look at the sky. See, a new light is kindling our galaxy. This mystery light is coming from 30,000 light years away.'

The pain had not begun when Bishan-da had been explaining all this. So, it must have started in the morning. After a sound siesta, he had gone to the club in the afternoon. In the swanky interiors of the club, courtesy the magnanimous largesse from the government, Sriman found his friends engaged in games of carrom and cards. Sriman loved playing carrom, but he hardly had the patience to trudge on with a game of cards. He preferred watching cricket on TV.

'Day off?' Mathuresh asked.

Sriman nodded. 'Yes … Is it a busy season?'

'Yes, dear. Orders are pouring in from Chicago, New Jersey, Montreal ever since Covid ended … Will finish the overseas orders first and then take up the local ones,' Mathuresh replied with a pleasant smile.

Mathuresh's father Gurakesh was a renowned idol maker. It was impossible for him to tackle the barrage of orders alone. Mathuresh had been helping him for the last couple of years. He too had made quite a name for himself.

Sriman had learnt the art of making idols from Mathuresh's father. Being a quick learner, he rapidly mastered the tricks of the trade under Gurakesh's tutelage. Gurakesh taught him that the nature of the soil can be altered by adding pieces of straw and jute to it. Sriman had even funded a part of his educational expenses with the proceeds from selling idols of Goddess Kaali he had made. Gurakesh once told him that the soil from which idols are made bears all the sixty-four components needed in making them. For a sculptor who has an intuitive bonding with the soil, idol-making is a labour of love. Later, he would cite Sriman's instance to people. He knew Sriman's Paramanandapur background. 'Do you like this delivery job?' Sriman was caught off-guard by Mathuresh's question. 'Not as much as making idols, but not bad either. I meet so many types of people from dawn to dusk …' Sriman replied.

Sriman did not feel the pain while speaking with Mathuresh. Done with speaking to him and exchanging pleasantries with his friends, Sriman was about to leave, but a stinging bout of pain on the right of his underbelly made him sit down again. He got up a little later, having drowned the pain in his enthralment with the suspense-filled cricket telecast on the 80-inch LED TV. Must be indigestion, or diarrhoeic pain. Almost all his delivery colleagues suffer from gastric issues—diarrhoea and acidity. Sriman trashed his preoccupation with the pain into the mind's dumpster of expendable thoughts.

Returning home, Sriman gulped three spoonsful of an antacid. He was fast asleep by the time ma returned from her daily regimen of cooking at three houses.

'In bed at this hour? Feeling unwell? Hope it isn't Covid,' Ma said worriedly resting her palm on his forehead. 'Thank God, you don't have fever.' She sighed with relief.

'Just a little stomach pain … probably acidity,' Sriman said.

'If it's indigestion, it's due to your habit of eating too fast, especially before leaving for work,' ma complained.

'I am okay now.' Sriman got up. The pain resumed as he took the stairs to the terrace.

Bishan listened to Sriman intently. Then he asked, 'Did you feel it as long as you were talking to me?'

Sriman was surprised. True, he had not felt the pain so long.

'No, dear, it doesn't look like acid reflux. I suspect appendicitis,' Bishan-da continued with no-nonsense probity. 'Antacid won't work. Go to the doctor ASAP.'

'My God!' Sriman was not prepared for something serious.

Heeding Bishan's advice, Sriman went downstairs. At times, Bishan-da was so normal, so perceptive, so full of concern. Sriman remembered he had forgotten to ask Bishan-da what to do in case it was really appendicitis. Absorbed in these thoughts, he dozed off.

Sriman woke up to a blissfully painless morning. But vis-á-vis what Bishan-da had told him last night, he knew he had to be careful. He followed the usual morning routine, except going out to fetch laddus. Sriman decided to stick to the safe option of having chapatis with milk for breakfast. But unlike other mornings, he had no appetite at all. One chapati, that is all he managed, that too forcefully. Something was seriously amiss.

The first delivery of the day was of everyday necessities to a location on Beleghata Main Road. Yellow Shirts had lately diversified into deliveries other than food as well. Aladdin was the name of its wing that managed the delivery of Mr X's package from Tala to Mr Y of Tollygunge. Delivery of such items were more in demand nowadays than food.

The discomfort, though within bearable limits, began as soon as he started the bike. But he could not afford to heed the pain, he had to make deliveries worth at least Rs 500 before he could visit the doctor in the evening.

Sriman chose the Beadon Street-Maniktala route to access the delivery location. The pain returned, and with a vengeance, when he was passing Karbala Tank behind Maniktala Market. When did it assume such intense proportions? Sriman somehow prevented himself from falling. Managing to bring the bike to a halt, he got off. But he could not steady the bike, it was leaning against him. He was having a tough time standing straight while he apprehended an imminent collapse.

He rang Mathuresh.

'What's up?' Mathuresh asked.

'I'm in severe pain, can't take it any more … I am going to collapse,' Sriman could feel the fear in his voice.

Mathuresh had a cool head. He asked, 'Where exactly are you now?'

Sriman was standing at the junction of Karbala Tank Lane and Beadon Street, an easily accessible point. Mathuresh sent his friends, Kajal and Raj, with his motorbike.

'Let's keep your bike somewhere nearby. We'll fetch it later.' Raj took hold of Sriman's bike.

For Sriman, staying away from his bike was unthinkable. He was more concerned with the safety of his bike than his pain. He asked, 'Where are you keeping it?'

'Inside the hostel,' Raj stated, pointing at the hostel at a distance.

'Will they allow it?' Sriman asked anxiously.

Raj gestured with his hand to not worry.

'But what about the delivery?' Sriman voiced his other concern.

'Chhottu-da will take care of it,' Raj replied reassuringly.

Chhottu-da aka Ravishankar Das had been working for Yellow Shirts ever since the company opened shop in the city. He was better paid than the others. Sriman wondered why Chhottu-da's name did not occur to him.

Kajal said, 'You are in pretty bad shape. Mathuresh has told us to take you to the hospital.'

Raj helped Sriman through the humongous crowd gathered around the Enquiry inside the hospital. Kajal tried to sum up the whole thing as briefly as possible to the staff manning the counter. 'Please arrange for a doctor to treat him … severe pain in the underbelly region … it's an emergency!' The staff handed Kajal a form accompanied by what sounded like an automated response: 'Fill up the form and get a ticket from the counter over there.'

The combined odour of medicines, chemicals, and phenyl suddenly nauseated Sriman. He felt a desperate urge to go out and relieve himself. In his attempt to rush out through the crowd, he lost balance and tripped on the floor of the lobby.

He vomited the undigested contents of his stomach and fell unconscious. The suddenness of the incident set the multitude in a tizzy. Somebody rushed in with a trolley.

Furious, Kajal lunged at the staff inside the Enquiry and grabbed his collar—'Motherfucker, didn't I tell you my friend is sick? Get him admitted immediately … you won't live to see the morning tomorrow if anything happens to him.' The man, catching sight of the firearm jutting out from behind Kajal's waist, was mortally scared. Everything thereafter went smoothly. No bed being available in the Emergency, a makeshift one was set up like many others on the corridor facing the section.

Sriman regained consciousness in ten minutes. By then, a catheter had been attached to his left arm to feed saline while a nasal cannula was supplementing oxygen.

'You won't get decent treatment in this goddamned country unless you raise hell. Don't worry, the doctor is on his way,' Kajal said hearteningly. He phoned Raj, 'Listen, bring Sriman's dada and ma along.'

The doctor arrived.

'What do we have here?'

'Severe pain in the lower abdomen,' Sriman stated in a feeble voice.

'Feeling nauseated?'

'Feeling it acutely now. It wasn't there yesterday or even this morning,' Sriman replied while groaning in pain.

'Where is the pain the sharpest? Here?' the doctor asked pressing a part of his abdomen.

Sriman shoved away the doctor's hand when the latter touched the spot. The pain was unbearable. He remembered Bishan-da examining him in exactly the same manner last night. He had correctly suspected it to be appendicitis, the doctor's diagnosis confirming it. Surgery at the earliest was the only option. The doctor prescribed a few medicines and gave necessary instructions to the nurse.

'When's the operation, doc?' Kajal asked.

Turning to him, the doctor said, 'We plan to do it later this afternoon … It could be done tomorrow, but there's no point delaying it, I fear it's already leaking inside …' The last part of his statement bore the twang of an ominous monologue.

'Should we arrange for blood? Medicines?' Kajal asked.

'Blood won't be necessary … and he's A positive, a widely available group … you may bring a few medicines … only if the hospital cannot provide it … sister, please explain the deets to him.' The doctor moved on to attend other patients.

The saline and oxygen made Sriman feel somewhat better. He took a good look at the nurse attending him only to be pleasantly surprised that it was the same thirty-something girl he had seen conversing over phone the other day from beneath the portico. Dressed in the nurse's livery, she looked charmingly affectionate. Sriman refrained from introducing himself to her lest she took it as a flirtatious attempt at small talk.

'By the way, relatives must sign a form before the operation. You seem to be his kin … let me get you the form,' she was saying to Kajal.

'I know you,' Sriman said with a forced smile, 'have seen you earlier.'

'Were you admitted here before?' she asked.

'I saw you from beneath a portico on Raja Dinendra Street. It was raining heavily … you got into the driving school vehicle.'

'By the way, do we need to arrange for some money?' Kajal budged in. He hated small talk.

'Can't say. You may keep Rs 5000 or so handy.' She was about to say something more when someone from the table at the centre of the ward called. 'Subhra, bed no. 10's temperature chart please.'

Kajal was worried. Though Rs 5000 was a trifle, it was beyond his means. 'Should I tell Raj?' he asked Sriman with a tone of confidentiality.

'You may,' Sriman replied. With a hand-to-mouth existence, saving money for the future is idle fantasy for people like Sriman. He rang Somnath. 'No problem. If ten of us can shell out Rs 500 each, we'll have the amount … I will be there by 5, don't worry,' Somnath assured Sriman.

Sriman, however, could not rely on Somnath. Sriman could not be sure he would be there before the surgery began. Nevertheless, Somnath's assurance boosted his sagging spirits.

Kajal came up with another piece of encouraging news. 'Raj too will definitely try to get the money. Your folks have also been informed.'

Would it be possible for ma and dada to procure the amount? Asking Bishan-da would be asking for undue favour. It might annoy him too. They were already indebted to him for allowing them to stay at his house. Though Bishan-da loved him a lot, it did not entitle Sriman to exploit Bishan-da's affection. Amidst such musings, the intimation came. The operation would start at 6 in the evening.

There was no sign of Somnath even at 5. But he rang Sriman a little later to inform him that none of their delivery colleagues at Yellow Shirts was in a position to provide any financial help. Somnath could cough up Rs 800. 'Can you send someone to fetch the money?' Somnath asked.

Sriman was preparing to send Kajal to Somnath when Raj arrived along with ma and dada. Dada gave him Rs 1000. And ma had loaned Rs 3500 from the families she cooked for.

Sriman looked at Kajal, 'No need of Somnath's money. What say?'

'No.' Kajal was relieved.

'Just convey it to Somnath. Will you?'

'Get on the trolley.' A hospital staff had arrived to convey him to the operation theatre.

Following the operation, Sriman was returned to a proper bed inside the ward, no longer the makeshift one on the floor. Back at the threshold of consciousness, Sriman looked at peace. He smiled at dada and ma.

Kajal asked, 'Hope you're out of pain.'

Sriman's lips trembled, but no sound came out.

'How's everything?' Subhra, the nurse, was asking. Sriman identified her even in his daze. He nodded to imply all was okay. 'I have got you the bed. What do I get in return?' she demanded, with a naughty smirk.

Sriman's lips quivered. 'Louder, please,' Subhra said while bringing her ear close to him.

'I will fetch a star from the galaxy to adorn your coiffure … the world will be mesmerised by its unearthly dazzle …' Sriman muttered in a poetical stupor.

'The doctor should have operated on your delirium instead,' Subhra said, beaming impishly once again.

# 4

'COVID generates a millionaire every thirtieth hour! Can you believe it?'

'Billionaire, not millionaire,' Bishan corrected Jnuiphool. 'You're referring to the "Profiting from Pain" report, right?'

'Yes … and every thirty-three hours, it drags ten lakh people into the abyss of inhuman misery.'

'Add to that the lack of livelihood and the surge in depression that compels many to commit suicide. I read a newspaper report about a mother poisoning her daughters before consuming the toxin herself.'

The reference to this heart-rending incident came up during a conversation between two individuals in the living room on the second floor of Akashganga. Although the worst of the pandemic was apparently over, the devastating aftermath was still a bleeding ulcer. The colossal loss of human lives it had left in its wake still had a stultifying sway over rational minds. Bishan and Jnuiphool were no exception.

'How was your Totopara experience? Any new findings?' Bishan changed the context to resume the conversation that had grinded to a grim halt.

Jnuiphool had come to India for a brief stint this time. She visited Totopara before coming to Kolkata. She had put up at Madarihat for a few days. But it was nothing short of an ordeal to negotiate three rivers and two springs each day to reach Totopara from there.

Jnuiphool nodded, 'Yes, I have memorised some of their lullabies ...'

'Good.' Bishan's unenthusiastic tone did not gel with the supposedly positive connotation of the interjection. But it was enough for his friend from his early days to discern that he wanted her to sing at least one of the songs.

*Gigi lei gigi lei*
*Aape ko*
*Ne tong ka gi paro*
*Ne tong ka gin sa*
*Hati ta ha ro*
*Tong che pu oui ro hang ta*
*Mung chang ga*
*Gigi ba ro...*

Jnuiphool sang and transliterated the lines before Bishan could ask her to—

Descend, dear moon, descend,
To the little girl who goes to the fair soon,
Will her friends fetch her the moon?

'This planet is a strange world, Bishan,' Jnuiphool said. 'But those roaming over it are even stranger.'

'The universe is a weird place, somewhat like women. Like them, it never ceases to intrigue. One can't resist its allure,' Bishan said with an enigmatic smile. 'How else can one explain the presence of the Centaur of classical mythology in the sky?'

'What's that?' Jnuiphool had never heard of this celestial body.

'It's either an asteroid or a small planet, moulding into a comet … we are witnessing how a comet is born,' Bishan explained. Jnuiphool knew better than to cut Bishan off now. If he was interrupted or made to stop, he would lose his cool and that rancour would linger for an infinity. 'The Atlas telescope on the high mountains of Hawaii detected this comet and its erratic movements a couple of years ago, in May 2020,' Bishan elaborated. 'This is one incorrigible itinerant, jumping axes every now and then in the last 200 years. It will take at least another forty-three years to become a full-sized comet.'

While Bishan carried on his elucidation, Jnuiphool's eyes surveyed Bishan's room. It was essentially a cocoon caught in a time warp. Two of its walls were choc-a-bloc with books, mostly antique. An entire shelf housed the complete set of *Encyclopaedia Britannica*. The true hue of the walls lay undiscernible beneath layers of age-old grime. In consort with the geriatric lethargy of the ceiling fan, the furniture too spoke to a hoary past.

Leaving Bishan's company, Jnuiphool tiptoed into *mejoma*'s bedroom. The steep bed with its tall bedposts that occupied the centre of the room was an antique that recalled a distant past. Had she married Bishan, this would have been her home. She would have loved it, Jnuiphool was sure. Circumstances were conducive to their conjugal union when they were studying in college. Both the families had accepted their relationship. So, what went wrong?

Jnuiphool may put the blame on Bishan that he did not insist, but she was aware that it was largely due to her. The relationship with Mike happened through the exchange of letters. He was her pen-friend. He helped her go overseas. Her decision to marry him was a token of gratitude from her end. Bishan did not complain. He simply gave up pursuing his master's and became a travelling ticket examiner (TTE) with the railways. A man destined to have a bright career in academia spent his life travelling across rail routes. Despite everything, Bishan had no complaints, no grudge. Whenever somebody asked him about the reason behind his choice of career, he gave the stock reply with a smiling face, 'Familial compulsions, you see … father died suddenly, there was nobody except me to run the family. Plus, the railway job had the guarantee of post-retirement pension.'

Bishan's choice of the TTE's occupation coincided with the birth of his interest in skywatching. Alongside this obsessive absorption with space, perhaps a manifestation of his disenchantment with ground realities, came the habit of making esoteric observations that would sound like deranged babble to the average listener. This Bishan, his insular isolation from the mundane world, deeply saddened Jnuiphool. It was for his sake that she spent the greater share of her time in this house, whenever she was in Kolkata. She returned to her hotel at night. Occasionally, she stayed over.

Bishan was telling Jnuiphool about the Comet NEOWISE when Sriman arrived at his doorstep.

'NEOWISE returned after six and a half millennia. We saw it with our bare eyes here. Can you imagine? A guest from the frozen frontiers of the solar system visits humanity in its final throes, before bidding adieu for another 6500 years.'

Sriman cleared his throat aloud to convey his presence at the door.

'Come in, Sriman,' Bishan said warmly. 'Fit like a fiddle, I hope?'

'Yes, much better, dada. Planning to visit the doctor next Monday. Hope to be back on the road from Tuesday,' Sriman smiled as he stepped into the room.

'Another four days, the loss of Rs 3000 at least,' Bishan murmured grimly.

Sriman nodded.

By the time Jnuiphool entered the room, enlivening the ambience with the fecund fragrance of flowers, the conversation between Bishan and Sriman had neared its end. Looking at Sriman, Jnuiphool smilingly asked, '*Nako ming hanga*?'

Before Sriman could express his confusion at the strange-sounding question, Bishan did the necessary introduction. 'This is Sriman. He is a delivery boy, a gig worker, product of the gig economy created by your first-world civilization.'

'Good ... *nako ming hanga*? What's your name? *Kung ming* Jnuiphool,' Jnuiphool said with a broad smile to Sriman with a hand extended for a friendly shake. Sriman responded by shaking hands with her.

'This "nako ming" thing ... is it the Toto language?' Bishan wanted to know.

Jnuiphool said, 'Yes.'

Sriman had been listening attentively. He replied, '*Kung ming* Sriman.'

'Good, very good!' Jnuiphool applauded with animated glee.

Sriman had seen Jnuiphool's photos in Bishan-da's photo album and phone gallery. Based on those recollections, he had confused the B.T. Road lady a few afternoons ago with her.

In the manner of a typical researcher, Jnuiphool tried to assess Sriman on the basis of statistics. 'Sriman, does your dear Bishan-da know that the number of gig workers is steadily increasing ... by almost 200 per cent per year?'

Sriman could not make sense of these statistics. He chose to stay silent. A delivery worker like him was aware that the gig industry was rapidly expanding. But the same increase had been counterproductive. The increase in the number of workers had reduced several old facilities. Earlier, with a lower number of delivery persons, there were many facilities: fixed pay, better incentives. Very few got the base pay. There was no Provident Fund nor any provision for footing monthly medical bills. Incentives were still there, but their quantum had been drastically reduced. Deliveries between 7 pm and midnight fetched better perks. Everybody, naturally, was desperate to utilise those hours to the maximum advantage.

Actually, this was not at all a job as such. As long as one was serving the company, as long as one's name appeared on its payroll, one's earnings would be duly deposited in one's bank account. Despite depleting facilities, the profession continued to attract a steady influx of new recruits. One probable reason was the precarious post-Covid shrinkage of the job market. There was hardly any opening in the government sector, while the private sector offered precious little in terms of jobs worth one's salt. Quite naturally, young aspirants were flocking to gig work despite the hardship and lack of job security it involved.

'The food-ordering market alone will see a 16 per cent growth and by 2023, it will amount to seventeen billion dollars,' Jnuiphool predicted. She had done some research on the gig economy.

Bishan said, 'Sriman, do note this, apart from food-delivering people like you or those who carry riders, the gig worker includes those who work in IT or engineering companies, salons, restaurants as well. Am I right?' He sought endorsement from Jnuiphool.

Jnui agreed.

This was Bishan. Cloudless like the blue sky in such rare moments of clarity, ready with solutions for all problems. Jnui wished Bishan to be this clairvoyant all the time.

'What are your plans for the evening?' Jnuiphool's abrupt question took Sriman off-guard.

'Why do you ask?' Sriman asked her in turn.

'I want to know what makes you the happiest,' Jnuiphool elaborated.

'I wish I could take ma and dada for dinner to the restaurant from where I pick up orders for delivery. For a change, we would give the orders and the staff there would serve food to us,' Sriman stated with a frank wistfulness.

Jnuiphool said, 'Bishan, why don't we make Sriman's dream come true tonight itself? Let's all go out for dinner.'

'No, it's my dream, and I would like to fulfil it myself.' Sriman was about to add something when Subrata's call came. 'I have lost everything!' he was on the verge of tears.

Subrata's frantic outburst, slurred in a torrent of emotions made mostly unintelligible by the uneven connectivity, was hard for Sriman to follow. The sum and substance he could unpack before the call dropped was that Subrata was in great danger. Sriman rang back while climbing down the stairs. Sriman gleaned from Subrata's incoherent burble that he had parked his motorbike somewhere at Burrabazar to go to a public toilet. When he returned to the spot, the bike was gone!

There was something remiss about what had happened to Subrata. Thieves generally spare delivery workers. Sriman himself had gone to public toilets in the Burrabazar area several times. Alongside requesting the parking staff to keep an eye, he too had been alert. Did somebody play a prank?

Responding to Subrata's distraught SOS, Sriman reached Satyanarayan Park in a jiffy. Subrata came running towards him and grabbed his hands. 'Only you can save me! It happened there,' Subrata pointed at the spot where he had left his bike.

'Let's have a cup of tea first,' Sriman said, in his attempt to ease Subrata out.

'I don't know what to do … yes, let's have tea.' That Subrata was harried was evident from his flustered speech. Sriman could not help feeling sad about the pickle his friend was in.

Sriman was savouring his cuppa when he espied two blue-liveried parking handlers on the other side speaking to each other and intermittently pointing at him. One of them appeared familiar. Sriman recalled him to be Tublu. He used to handle the parking space adjacent to Presidency University.

Asking Subrata to stay where he was, Sriman crossed over to face Tublu. 'Motherfucker, are you a mighty extortionist or what? Can't you let a boy earn honestly?'

Tublu smirked, 'What did we do?'

'Rascal, stop playing games with me. Give him back his bike,' he pointed towards Subrata. 'The boy has not earned anything since the afternoon, and you are kidding with him! Mess with a big shot, if you have the guts!'

The boy standing by Tublu was livid. 'We repeatedly asked him to pay Ganesh Chaturthi subscriptions … tell him he'll never find his bike.'

Sriman was left with no doubt that Subrata's bike was somewhere in the vicinity. They would have to shell out some moolah to get it back.

'Okay, I am getting the money, meanwhile you bring the bike.' Sriman crossed over to Subrata, 'You need to cough up some cash.'

'Cash? What for?'

'You won't get back your bike unless you pay Ganesh Chaturthi subscriptions.'

'Will Rs 500 do? I can't pay more.'

Tublu grumbled when Sriman gave him the money. 'The miser won't shell out more than 500 even in dire straits?'

'Stop being a scoundrel, tell me where the motorbike is,' Sriman demanded.

Tublu pointed at a bike covered by a black polythene sheet, about 100 metres ahead.

Subrata ran to lay his hands on his bike as soon as the polythene sheet was removed. He glanced at his mobile. An order had arrived.

'I have a pick-up at Beleghata, wanna come?' Subrata seemed to have come back to life.

'Not now. Somewhere else to go.'

Someday, he would walk to the farthest extremes of the world. A lonely boat, devoid of a rower, would be swaying to the serene cadence of a placid water world, waiting to take him beyond the bounds of this mortal world. Lost in these musings, Sriman was walking northwards.

'Let me see how you perform in bed.' The voice of a woman walking by him broke Sriman's trance. He realised he had reached Sovabazar.

The diminutive girl, who was speaking continuously to the much taller boy walking by her, had a rather rough-hewn body language. A few minutes after they had passed him by Sriman realised it was Somnath. Turning round to call out to him, Sriman found that Somnath was beyond earshot. Instead, he decided to follow them into the house he had watched them enter a fraction of a second ago. The house, to which he had often delivered orders, is one of those havens that have mushroomed across Kolkata lately. Workers with a moderate pay stay in these buildings paying a daily rent which varies between Rs 700 and 800. Food delivery agents know that the rooms are occupied by professionals from other states or traders from the *mofussils*. Sriman was getting the whiff of a shady deal.

As he followed the couple into the premises, he was stopped by the familiar guy seated at the reception. 'Delivery? Room number?'

'No, not on delivery today,' Sriman said, camouflaging his growing impatience with a smile.

The receptionist, if he could be called so, sensed the reason that had brought Sriman there. Pointing towards an indeterminate floor above, he said, 'The love birds are perched in one of the rooms. They'll stay there for a couple of hours, relish each other, and then fly away in separate directions. They come here frequently like many others … the house owner makes a fortune … 700 bucks per hour … for a bit of electric light and air from a ceiling fan … everybody is happy.'

Sriman was processing the sudden revelation as he walked towards Bagbazar. Somnath was shelling out hard-earned money for the pleasure of two hours. He was spending half a day worth of earnings for a couple of hours of carnal pleasure. Why? What does one gain from such transient gratifications, Sriman wondered.

# 5

Mrittika Sen's was a classic case of deceptive appearances. Her petite frame of five foot two might make her look ineffectual. But had her brittle shoulders not carried the onerous weight of a crucial chunk of this story, it would have crumbled like a castle of cards.

The first thing that arrested attention about her were the good luck charms she sported: a coral ring on the middle finger of the right hand, a topaz ring on the index finger, a sacred red-and-amber thread tied across the wrist. The array of auspicious amulets made the onlooker wonder whether the tabor-trident emblem on her elbow or the mysterious capital B tattooed a little above the wrist of her left hand were good luck totems too? A conflicting combination of contradictions, one must say—an educated and self-sufficient young woman of the twenty-first century yet a staunch believer in supernatural agency.

Although in her early thirties, Mrittika bore a deceptive girl-scout look, courtesy a crew cut and an almost rotund face. Apart from her appearance, there was something immaturely girlish about her inner person as well. Smitten with her own looks, Mrittika loved to begin her day with a besotted glance at her own reflection in the mirror. The shower she took before going out for work was a self-gratifying orgy. As she stood before the bathroom mirror, in full view of the svelte splendour of her swarthy nakedness, she fell in love with herself anew every morning, ending up planting a passionately prolonged kiss on the lips of the Mrittika in the mirror—a fangirl's infatuated oblation to her mortal goddess.

To satiate the mad hunger that took over her once she was done bathing, Mrittika emptied a glassful of *sattu*. Though it could not be called breakfast as such, the heaviness of the fluid worked, making her immune to the pangs of hunger for long hours. By the time the dregs of the glass started their glide down her gullet, the moistness in the intimate echelons of her dainty anatomy dispersed. The latter was an indispensable chore for protection against fungal infection, a job hazard faced by every worker whose day was spent riding a two-wheeler. The next important chore, especially in the rainy season, was sprinkling an anti-fungal powder over every cleft and corner of her body. The final act, thereafter, was routinely monotonous: wearing the working garments—the pair of denims and the tee provided by First Move over it, topped by a light jacket. When going out on personal work, she simply wore a crewneck tee—a toss between azure and scarlet—over the jeans.

Dressed in the nondescript combo of bleached jeans and a crumpled crew-neck tee over a pair of rundown sports shoes, Mrittika was looking as unremarkable as she could possibly be on this particular Sunday morning. She had parked her scooter in one corner of the expansive atrium of Star Theatre, one of the prestigious remnants of the Calcutta of yore. The arcade saw sparse footfalls in the morning, even lesser numbers on a Sunday. A duo of Muslim tailors set their makeshift stalls on the portico in the morning. Mrittika addressed them as *bhaijaan* out of respect for their exemplary engagement in their job and discreet dignity.

That Mrittika relied on them was evident from the fact that she had parked her bike, as always, within their eyeshot. '*Bhaijaan*, please keep an eye, I'll be back in a tick,' she informed the seasoned seamsters before crossing the road to enter the lane on the other side. Her statement elicited a busy but condescending nod from both, while one of them peppered it with a knowing smile implying that she would not be back for at least the next hour or so.

Anybody, be it a casual bystander or a resident of the neighbourhood, could tell as much. For the rest of the story, one must depend on a few special insiders like Ramlakhan, the presser, who ironed clothes in the garage beneath the jaded apartment building.

Mrittika had activated the Fast Move app in the morning while getting ready after her bath. The first pick up was a man in his mid-forties. Destination: Kalighat Tram Depot. The fact that the next booking came in even before she had dropped off her first passenger could be taken as a marker of the growing demand for app scooters and bikes across Kolkata. With app cabs and taxis becoming too pricey and public transport too sluggish to guarantee timely arrivals, the app bike was the only cost-effective option. Moreover, these sleek vehicles could effortlessly navigate their way through even the most chaotic of traffic snarls and convey one to the destination much before a cab could.

However, the tireless rider who ferried passengers from one end of the city to the other, did not get to keep the entire amount of the fare. The company claimed the greater percentage, leaving a negligibly small portion for the rider. Fast Move took seventy per cent of the fare, Mrittika got the remaining thirty. Quick March, the other app Mrittika was registered on, followed the same arrangement.

Mrittika's second passenger was a young boy, headed to New Market. The third booking arrived within five minutes from that drop. Mrittika picked up the twenty-something girl in salwar-kurta from Chandni Chowk Metro station. There was a curious incongruity about her: eyes concealed beneath oversized dark glasses, but curves pronounced by the scanty kurta. Mrittika started her bike with a warning to the rider to tie up her veil, the careless handling of which was a cause of frequent road accidents.

Mrittika felt a surge of emotion while dropping this passenger off on B.K. Pal Avenue. The vicinity of this major street of north Kolkata made her nostalgic. She could not imagine leaving the area where she had spent a sizeable part of her conjugal life without meeting Bubka, her nine-year-old boy, briefly at least. The B tattooed on her left arm spelled the initial of the boy who was named after the legendary pole vaulter as he shared his birthday with the star athlete.

Mrittika's in-laws' place where Bubka lived was 150 metres into the lane. Mrittika was glad to find Ramlakhan ironing clothes in his workplace in the ground-floor garage where the lane took a righthand turn.

'Namaste, *Bhabiji*,' Ramlakhan greeted her with the usual courtesy.

'Namaste, how are you?'

'I am good.'

'Could you please call Bubka for a while?'

'Just a minute, *Bhabiji*.'

Some unwritten rules prevailed at Mrittika's in-laws', perhaps the only semblance of order in that anarchical household. She was barred from entry there. If she wanted to meet her son, she must send in Ramlakhan with the message. Malati, the maidservant, would leave Bubka in Ramlakhan's custody for a limited window of time. Bubka would sit on one of the stools in Ramlakhan's kiosk, Mrittika on the other, to have a heart-to-heart. If she brought anything for him to eat, he must have it here itself, he was not permitted to enter his home with it.

'*Bhabiji, aap baithiye na, turant bulata hoon.*' Ramlakhan was gone, asking Mrittika to wait while he called Bubka in a jiffy.

She sat there with bated breath. Having decided on today's meeting on the spur of the moment, she could not fetch the sumptuous treat she usually brought for Bubka except for a big chocolate bar and a chicken patty from a reputed eatery. Mrittika avidly anticipated the relish of feeding Bubka with her own hands. Each bite Bubka would place on the delicacies would sync with her ideomotor impulse of aping her son's mirthful mastication. She would follow it up by the repeated and impatient query whether the food was up his alley. At times, her persistent queries annoyed Bubka. 'Let me eat it first, Ma,' he said exasperatedly. She would eagerly wait for him to say 'just awesome'—those magic words—while his face would be glowing with delight. Nothing else gave her the contentment that moment brought.

'*Bhabiji, chachi ne bataya ki woh aaj nahin aa paayega.*' Ramlakhan returned with the heart-rending news that *Chachi* has conveyed through him—Bubka won't be coming today.

The information was too shocking for Mrittika to register initially. '*Nahin aayega*? He won't come?' she asked in a tone bordering on disbelief after moments of dazed silence, her deadpan stare fixed on Ramlakhan.

'*Haan, chachiji toh aisa hi bataya, aapko bolne ke liye.*' Ramlakhan reiterated what *Chachiji* had told him to tell her.

So, it was all about her mother-in-law, the sole arbiter who decided whether Mrittika could meet her son. Mrittika felt an acute paroxysm of anger rising within her, a mad fury that would be satiated only after she torched down that ramshackle one-storey house. But then good sense prevailed, making her suppress that incendiary urge as she realised Bubka too would perish in that fire. The effort brought tears to her eyes.

'*Thhik hai*, Ramlakhanji, *yeh packet Bubka ko de dena*, please.' Keeping the packet for Bubka with Ramlakhan she started leaving.

'*Zaroor, Bhabiji, aap nishchint rahiye*,' Ramlakhan assured her.

Despite knowing that she could not meet Bubka, Mrittika inadvertently started walking in the direction of the house on coming out of Ramlakhan's kiosk. She was following the prompts of her inner voice which was now instigating her to break into her in-laws' house. But soon sanity prevailed, and she somehow resisted the incitement.

Nevertheless, she ended up doing something impetuous. She called her son by his first name—'Akashdeep!'—while passing by the closed window of her son's room. She was about to call him a second time when the window opened and Bubka's smiling face beamed at her. 'Mummy, mummy!' he yelled in innocent glee. 'I have left a chicken patty and a chocolate bar for you with Ramlakhan uncle,' she told him as fast as she could before someone took him forcefully away from there. She left the spot at once with a sense of triumph.

Mrittika logged in to the Fast Ride app while walking back to the Star portico. The next passenger was a saree-clad Bengali. Destination, Sivanath Sastri College, near Golpark. Female riders are inquisitive by nature. They often pester her with queries: why are you in this job? Since when? Do you like the job? But this woman was uncharacteristically silent. 'It is difficult to balance myself. Can I hold your shoulders?' was the only thing she said. Mrittika consented at once.

Drivers of two-wheelers who ferry passengers across the city develop an instinct for sniffing the passenger's intentions from their intonation and body language. Once a male rider had wanted to hold her shoulders. It was a simple request devoid of any indecent motive. She did not refuse. On another occasion, she had sensed the passenger's motive soon after the trip began. She instantly made the passenger get down in front of Jadavpur police station. The SHO told the man to hail some other vehicle. The incident got press coverage, even appeared on television. She was a familiar face to cops of almost all police stations courtesy those reports.

Mrittika had acquired a motley miscellany of experiences in her years in this job. Once she was waiting for a passenger at the pick-up point on Rupchand Mukherjee Lane at Bhawanipore holding her helmet in her hand. The passenger exclaimed, 'A girl! Good God …' The frail gentleman in his mid-sixties looked like he had received the shock of his life. 'No, no, I can't ride with you, I value my life!' The elderly man's panicked face looked so funny! 'Why would I put your life in danger? Don't fear, come on.' Even the man's daughter sounded amused. 'Why are you so scared, papa? They are expert drivers.' The man finally gave in. Unsure about where to place his arms, he wrapped them tightly across Mrittika's waist. But there was nothing impure about the man's embrace. It rather reminded her of how her father had held her in a frantic embrace when his hosiery shop had been cruelly ransacked.

She conveyed the passenger at Sivanath Sastri College within half an hour's time. The incredibly fast arrival at the destination was occasioned by two reasons. One, the jubilant buoyancy generated from seeing Bubka. Second, the relatively vacant roads of the city. As soon as she had dropped the saree-clad rider in front of the college, she felt a foudroyant sting of hunger. The *sattu* sharbat she had had in the morning had long been digested. Though this was a posh locality, it had low-priced food stalls inside the alleys of Gariahat Market. This was what made Kolkata an amazing city with a large heart, Mrittika thought. It breathed the spirit of inclusion, it accommodated all.

Switching her mobile off, Mrittika procured flattened rice and banana—ingredients of a soothing summer lunch—from the market. Bringing out the utensils from the carrier of her bike, she had her lunch sitting in a corner of the stall of the familiar vegetable vendor. Carriers like her must stick to a healthy food regimen to sustain an unfatigued dynamism. Hence, the adherence to *sattu* sharbat, curd, banana and sundry nutritious items, and a firm abstinence from junk and spicy food. In fact, she typically ate less than required; a bit of a hungry stomach was conducive to agility.

The vegetable vendor, Sushil Saha, called out, 'Didi, wanna have a cup of tea?'

'Why not? But earthen cup only.'

'I know your preference, didi.'

Finishing the tea with a quick gulp, Mrittika logged into the app. Ramakrishna Mission Institute of Culture, the next pick-up point. The thirty-something man, clad in white shirt and trousers, was headed for National Medical College.

Mrittika had barely ascended the Gariahat flyover after making a half circle at Golpark, when a scooty from the left tried to overtake her. Mrittika usually spared such intruders, pitying the latter's pointless compulsion. But today's instance was rather interesting because the biker outpacing her was a girl and a delivery rider of Yellow Shirts. These folks are always in a mad hurry so that they can get trips back-to-back. Mrittika was amused. The girl driving past her in a desperate rush was unaware that she was trying to speed past a karate expert.

Another vehicle, a four-wheeler this time, wheezed past her while she was descending the flyover. The frenzied hustle of the driver made it evident that he was a novice. He got past the Yellow Shirts girl too, 150 yards or so ahead of Mrittika. At the same instant, the scooty took a sudden and somewhat left-inclined turn in order to avoid a large crater on the road. The four-wheeler lost control and collided against it; the Yellow Shirts girl fell off her bike. Instantly, the young man driving the car and the man sitting on the passenger seat swapped seats.

'Could you give me five minutes please? Need to …' Mrittika said to her passenger.

'It's okay, but please don't be long,' the man said courteously.

'Just two minutes.' Mrittika rushed to the rescue of the Yellow Shirts girl.

Mrittika held an arm and helped the girl stand. She had not noticed when her passenger, the gentleman in the white shirt, had followed her. 'No, the bones are intact,' he assured with professional wisdom, on checking crucial points along the girl's legs. 'The elbow has deeply scarred. You must get it bandaged with standard antiseptic, disinfectant, iodine solution, and get an anti-tetanus injection as precaution.'

'What's your name?' Mrittika asked the girl.

'Sampa … I could have died today … What would've happened to my kids?'

'Parents?'

'They stay in a village in Bardhaman.'

'What about your husband?'

'He does not live with me.'

Mrittika got the hang of the girl's predicament.

'Get someone immediately to deliver this order, and please text me your mobile number.'

Mrittika turned her attention to the driver of the car. 'How dare you make a learner drive! Show me your license!' She was seething with anger. 'Actually, I have left it at home,' the man responded feebly with the stock excuse of a delinquent aware of his misdemeanour.

Finally, it was decided that the two persons in the car would convey Sampa and her bike home.

'Sorry, sir. I took up a lot of your precious time,' Mrittika apologised to the passenger on returning to her bike.

'No problem. Actually, I've a patient to tend to,' the man said with embarrassed courtesy.

'You are a doctor?' Mrittika asked.

'Yes.'

Mrittika silently chided herself for not being able to guess this. 'I haven't seen a doctor riding app bikes,' she remarked.

'Why not? A doctor with a government job, surviving on a monthly salary, can't afford app cabs.'

The passenger Mrittika picked up from Kolutola after completing another couple of trips was a squat, paan masala-chewing middle ager, with nondescript looks. He was headed for Fariapukur. Soon after riding the bike, the man started spitting on the road. His breath reeked of alcohol. Mrittika felt a growing repulsion towards this passenger. To add to her woes, the man started yelling on his mobile phone.

'Gopalji … *kya bhaav chal raha hai* … what's the current rate?

'*Arre,* tell that fucker not to mess with our guy, *yeh hamara banda hai.*

'*Woh chutiya hai kya*? Does the rascal think he can fuck with our guy?'

The man was getting on her nerves. He was leaning against her. He had even touched her shoulders once in an inappropriate manner. She stopped the bike immediately after reaching the Fariapukur crossing.

'*Aap utriye!* Get down at once!'

'*Kyun? Kya hua?* Take this lane …'

'I won't take you any further! *Aap utriye!*'

A crowd had gradually gathered around them. After all, who does not love free entertainment? A biker too was watching from a distance, probably another delivery worker.

The man got down from the bike. He was wobbling and mouthing expletives with shameless abandon. '*Kyun nahin jaayegi?* I have paid you, haven't I? *Jahan boloonga jaana padega, jo boloonga karna padega … nachne boloonga toh nachna bhi padega!* So now you are bound to do as I say and as I please!'

Mrittika could not check her anger. '*Kya bola? Phir se bol!* What did you say?'

'I have paid for you … *maine paisa diya* … I own you … *jaisa boloon waisa kar* … do as I say!' the man snorted with a suggestive smirk. Now that he was in his locality, he thought he could get away with anything.

Enough of this distasteful thing. Mrittika had turned around, ready to leave the spot. She did not notice when the dastard had drawn close. She was startled when he spanked her hard. But karate had taught her to respond with a rapid reflex under even the most unanticipated attack. Using her right arm with the sharpness of a knife, she landed a shattering blow on his left jaw. The man immediately collapsed on the road, writhing in pain.

Mrittika started her bike in the direction of Central Avenue, via Shyambazar. Suddenly, the biker, who was watching the proceedings from a distance, appeared in her rearview mirror. The creep was trailing her! Well versed with the skills to keep her cool in such situations, she maintained normal pace and a straight course, avoiding lanes and arteries, which could be easier spots for her stalker to pounce upon her. She suspected him to be an accomplice of the lowlife she had just disciplined.

Crossing her path as soon as she had traversed Beadon Street, the biker stood a little ahead, blocking her path. She had rightly assumed him to be a delivery rider. He was wearing a Yellow Shirts tee. The boy was presumably younger than her.

Mrittika got down fast. Taking off her helmet, she stood battle-ready, prepared to land a powerful kick, if need be. But contrary to all her apprehensions, the boy greeted her with a smile while gesturing a thumbs up.

'Thanks,' Mrittika replied. But she was not overwhelmed by his gesture. Rather, she took him to be a member of the mute, cowardly multitude that enjoyed watching things as passively as a circus audience. They might applaud anybody who protested but would never stand up in protest themselves.

'The scoundrel completely deserved that punch,' the young man said with an appreciative smile. 'I am Sriman Kundu, I too would have joined you in teaching him a lesson, had I been my usual self. I have resumed normal activities today. Please keep my number, feel free to call whenever you need any help. I live nearby at Bagbazar.'

Mrittika nodded affirmatively while saving Sriman's number on her phone.

# 6

Humiliation is a serpent with poisonous fangs. The toxic teeth of an unjustified humiliation sting the victim with a particularly sharp edge, leaving him writhing in a pain that takes an eternity to heal, if it heals at all. The mind bleeds amidst groans of unbearable agony and futile rage. But often the worst thing about humiliation is that the person at the receiving end has to suffer alone, unable to share the anguish with anybody else. With time, the person learns to live with the trauma.

Sriman had been subjected to one such unwarranted indignity this morning. Despite his earnest efforts to come to terms with it, he had not been able to overcome it. What did he do to deserve it? The question rankling inside him ever since the occurrence of the incident had left him stumped. So much so that he had refrained from going out for work post-lunch.

Bishan Basu was Sriman's go-to person in all crises that indicated no potential closure. Sriman was now in Bishan-da's room. Sriman's account of the incident had stunned Bishan too.

A wild rage was simmering inside Bishan, ever since hearing about it. The fury was so savage that it could be satiated only if he could tightly slap the perpetrator on Sriman's behalf.

Jnuiphool returned a little later. Like most international academicians, she too bore an ambidextrous streak. A few days ago, she was working on a research project on lullabies while extensively studying the evolution of fairy tales among the Totos. In the middle of all this, she wrote and delivered a paper on a comparative discourse on Netaji Subhas Chandra Bose and Charu Majumdar at a sociological research institution.

Ever since being introduced to Sriman, Jnuiphool had developed a new research interest: gig workers. But Bishan had never intended to introduce her to Sriman in the first place because he was sure she would make Sriman a test case for another bout of arid theorising. 'Change the situation, if you can, don't waste time in dry discourse,' Bishan had told her. 'Sriman is not your lab rat. Your research won't make any difference to his situation,' he had warned her matter-of-factly.

Jnuiphool sensed the grim mood prevailing in the room as soon as she entered, right in the middle of Sriman and Bishan's conversation. 'What happened? Anybody ill?' she asked, to lighten the air. 'Yes, I am ill because I have written a poem after a long time,' Bishan chipped in, camouflaging the humorous thrust of the comment with a poker face. 'What!?' Jnuiphool had not expected such a bizarre reply.

Without responding to her stark surprise, Bishan started to recite the poem in a voice sacred in its sonority—

On her birthdays, I send her the ritual moon,
Moon-drops drip into her phone,
The smiley-moon is born, day and night;
With consistent precision, it wanes
And with a mystic muteness,
While our days
Oscillate between polar extremes!

The smiley-moon morphs into an icon,
Lighting her palm-peripheried utopia,
The moon of the first night glides
Across the mundane arc of mortality.
My palm slides the lucent moon,
Lending a glow to my pallid pocket.
As I descend to the edge of mist,
Step by step,
Life-saving drugs cost a universe,
And the world spits spasms of blood.

Too esoteric, the meaning of the lines eluded Sriman, but the melodramatic inflection with which Bishan pronounced the concluding line made him feel its visceral agony.

'Brilliant!' Jnuiphool was amazed. 'The smiley-moon ... wonderful! You should've continued writing.'

Bishan's response was a smile followed by silence.

By the way, this was not the first instance where Bishan had imagined the moon as a smiley. Sriman had heard him conjure the image earlier as well. But he refrained from pointing it out to Jnuiphool.

Jnuiphool had jotted down a lot of data from her interaction with food delivery riders of Salt Lake, Rajarhat, Barasat. She brought out her diary.

'Is this your field study?' Bishan asked.

'Sort of. It documents the genesis of a unique working class. I have spoken to fifteen of them. Dhananjay Bar of Keshtopur, Sameer Singh of Gourangapur, Sunita Agarwal of Rajarhat, Aloke Choudhury of Narkelbagan, Babu De of Sukantanagar. Their's a strange world where everybody labours from dawn to dusk. I found Marx's Alienation Theory at work,' Jnuiphool elaborated.

The obscure allusion to Marx's Alienation Theory was Greek to Sriman. He nodded in assent, nevertheless. Bishan understood Sriman's predicament.

'So, Jnui, you mean to say that Marx's theory of the detachment between the labourer and the product has affected these food delivery riders too?' Bishan's rhetorical question was designed to make things easier for Sriman.

'Exactly. The detachment infecting the shopkeeper has spilled over to the gig worker also; every single delivery rider complained of facing humiliation from customers. One of them even lamented there is none to care for them. They have nothing to do with the commodity they deliver yet they must bear the brunt. Hence, the alienation,' Jnuiphool said.

'There's a mismatch because the majority you have interviewed is from the suburbs or the villages, yet to attune themselves to the roads, lifestyle, dialect of the city. Not that they have none to care, they must look after themselves. They don't have any union either because the nature of their work makes unity impossible. Moreover, you won't find them on the official payroll of any particular company. Their relationship with the company is tenuous at the best,' Bishan explained the crux of the gig worker's predicament.

'Tenuous. That's the word. I couldn't have put it better. It's a loophole inherent in the capitalist society.'

'But, Jnui, repression will always lead to retaliation, it's the law of nature.'

Although he was minutely listening to the highfalutin exchanges between Bishan and Jnuiphool, Sriman was finding it difficult to come to terms with his disgrace. 'This insult is too upsetting to forget,' he suddenly blurted out, interrupting Bishan.

'Someone insulted you?' Jnui instantly asked. 'Tell me about it.'

Bishan had seen this coming long ago. He would not be able to protect Sriman from Jnuiphool any more.

Sriman rapidly went the whole hog again.

'Not so fast, I want to know everything in detail,' Jnui was all ears.

'Reaching near the delivery location, I phoned the customer, a young woman. I wished her good morning and said, "Madam, I cannot locate your address, please help." She rudely asked, "Why are you making a fuss?" "Madam, you've mentioned your flat number and the name of the road, but I need the apartment building's name and the apartment number. I can't locate your address," I told her. She—'

'Forget it, relate the conversation in its sequence, I will make out who said what,' Jnuiphool was getting impatient.

'You asked for it, Sriman,' Bishan warned with a smirk.

Ignoring Bishan's innocuous cynicism, Jnuiphool said, 'You see, Bishan, the customer expects decorum and courtesy. That's why delivery riders are taught greetings like "good morning", "please", "don't worry", "help". This is simply an attempt to commodify them as well as their interaction with the customer along with the food.'

'But, Jnui, most of them come from the underprivileged sections. Naturally, their behaviour will smack of their impoverishment. At times, they won't even engage in the essential pleasantries and that would put off the elite customers … go on, Sriman,' Bishan said.

'The lady said, "You don't know the location of Friends' Society? Don't you belong to the civilised world? This is a reputed residential society, movie stars live here … just mention my name at the gate, TV star Anwesha Deb, everyone knows me … uncultured brute!"

'I was at a loss. I requested, "Madam, please share your live location." The lady disconnected the call. I somehow reached the place by asking people. The gate was closed, no security guard in view. I rang her again. "Sorry to disturb, Madam, can the gate be opened?" "How dare you ask me to open the gate? Am I the security guard?" she yelled.

'The guard arrived and opened the gate after about ten minutes. The lady's apartment was on the tenth floor. They won't allow me to take the elevator without the customer's permission. I had no choice but to ring her again. "Madam, they won't let me into the elevator unless you tell them to." "No, our Society doesn't allow servants, salespersons, dogs in the elevator … how dare you show so much arrogance even though you are this late? Take the stairs … Asshole!" She hung up. I climbed all the way to the tenth floor, out of breath, throat completely parched. Despite that, I did not seek even a glass of water from her. She compared me to a dog, can you imagine? I have never faced something like this ever before—'

'Jnui, does Marx hint at any connection between capitalism and filthy language?' Bishan smiled.

'Stop kidding, Bishan. This filthiness is quite natural in a capitalist society, you know it very well. You were the first to teach me the essentials of politics, remember?' Jnuiphool said.

Bishan got up and stretched himself. It was obvious that he had run out of patience at Jnuiphool's undue investment in Sriman's episode. Moreover, it was in these late afternoon hours in spring, with daylight yet to disperse, that he began sky watching. 'It's almost evening, friends, let's get to work. The sky being clear, three stars of spring are visible.'

One could not reconcile the Bishan of the night with the Bishan of the daytime. Sriman was aware of it, but Jnuiphool learnt it the hard way, after getting a drubbing for disturbing him during sky watching at night.

Sriman asked, 'Which three, Bishan-da?'

'Bring me my notebook in which I had illustrated the night sky.'

Sriman was about to rush to fetch it when Bishan stopped him, 'You have gone through much since the morning, I won't scold you any more. I am telling you the name of one of the stars, let's see if you can recall the other two …

'Abhijit,' Bishan said after a brief pause.

'Shravana and Deneb,' Sriman remembered instantly.

'Good, you can spot them with the naked eye, but they look brighter through the telescope.'

***

Jnuiphool was invisible the following day. Same the next day. She wrote on Facebook about Sriman's humiliation at the hands of the TV star, Anwesha Deb. She cited Sriman's case as a pointer to how delivery riders are always humiliated in this country. Comments condemning the incident were pouring ever since from not only India but various parts of the world, including the US, France, and other countries. Many suggested bringing the matter to the notice of human rights organisations. The next morning's edition of a local daily covered the incident, in brief, though.

Anwesha had been trolled so heavily on social media that the TV channel which telecast her serials had taken them off air for the time being. Anwesha posted an apology three days later, but it was too little, too late. The tidal wave of condemnations was overwhelming.

Sriman, however, was quite happy at Anwesha's apologetic post. He had no idea of the massive reach and impact of social media. He had become a fan of Jnuiphool overnight.

In the meantime, there had been a new development. Sanjay had gone to pick up an order from Snacks Queen at Salt

Lake at around 11 pm. The staff of the eatery who were already drunk turned offensive when he requested them repeatedly to speed up the preparation of the food, as they were already behind schedule. When Sanjay protested against their high-handedness, they pounced upon him and lynched him until he started bleeding from his nose and mouth. They handed him the parcel only after that. Sanjay delivered the food first and then got his injuries treated at a Maniktala nursing home. One of Sanjay's friends wrote about the incident on social media. Jnuiphool read it out. 'When Sanjay, a delivery rider, protested against the repeated harassment of delivery riders by the staff of Snacks Queen, a Salt Lake restaurant, he was mauled by its staff. Let us not forget that delivery riders too are human. Let's boycott Snacks Queen.'

Jnuiphool had written in support of this post.

'All of us, responsible citizens committed to make this world a better place, should support this boycott call from delivery riders. Snacks Queen must immediately issue an unconditional apology and pay compensation to the particular delivery rider lynched by its staff. Snacks Queen must ensure that such things are not repeated in future. It must also open a helpline to redress customer complaints.'

Bishan sighed as Jnuiphool narrated the episode. 'Such things were unthinkable in this city fifty years ago. The owner of the restaurant would have shuddered to do such things.

Where are we headed!' Bishan shook his head in disbelief. 'Still, this is better than nothing, at least a flicker of hope,' he added after a brief pause.

"This is the age of lightning-fast communication, Bishan. News spreads like wildfire, so many TV channels, above all, the rapid growth of social media,' Jnuiphool explained.

'Well, Jnui, I am not quite conversant with this social media thing, but if it can penalise culprits, well and good,' Bishan acquiesced.

Snacks Queen could not be boycotted, but the number of its clients reduced significantly over the next few weeks. The management of the eatery sacked all its existing staff and substituted them with new recruits.

Bits and pieces of unpleasant issues came up alongside light-hearted conversations when Sriman and other delivery riders congregated close to the Hatibagan eatery. Subir, who once lived on Beadon Street and presently served the Salt Lake area, had told Sriman that they discuss the same things when they collect before Singhania Kitchen at Salt Lake, at about 8 every morning. The significant increase in the number of riders had drastically decreased the pay they used to get. There was a steady trickle of college and university students into the profession. They could not afford a motorbike and many of them performed deliveries on bicycles even. Though they got a paltry pay, it funded at least the cost of their studies.

Sriman was distraught to find that he had earned a measly sum of Rs 196 even after performing as many deliveries as possible, running madly from pillar to post right from the morning till early afternoon. What could he do with this paltry sum?

The world seemed to have undergone a drastic makeover while he was hospitalised for the appendicitis surgery. The emergency operation had imposed an additional financial burden on him of repaying the money ma had loaned for the surgery. Alongside, he had to pay the monthly instalments for the bike.

Ever since stepping out of the hospital, life for Sriman had become a restless routine of running around, so much so that it often left him out of breath. Yet, he dreaded the very idea of resting or relaxing because life had not been kind to friends who had failed to keep pace with its giant strides. It had discarded them in the dumpsters of time, as useless litter. Sriman could never think of being reduced to such expendable trash.

But what if he got injured in the bargain? What if a sudden accident reduced him to a vegetable? Even if that turned out to be his fate, he would not accept it. He would take the one drastic measure to put an end to all misery. Insecticides, phenyl, huge doses of sleeping pills—there is no dearth of means to self-immolation. It would be relief, instant and absolute. However, if Bishan-da located the new planet in the meantime, they would shift to that new address. He knew this was absurd wistfulness, but he loved to wallow in its luxury.

A package to be picked up at Chitpur Road and delivered to Bhowanipore. That was the first order to jingle itself into his phone in the evening. Sriman decided to take the easiest approach: snake through the lanes until gliding onto Red Road and then racing through the one-way along SSKM.

He was at the destination five minutes before time. The recipient of the package was so glad that not only did he beam a 'Very good!' but also tipped him Rs 200. 'Why the tips, sir? This is my duty,' Sriman tried to reason with the man embarrassedly. The fair-complexioned guy in a silk *punjabi* and a flimsy gold chain smiled, displaying betelnut juice-stained dentures. 'Brijnath, *aaja beta*!' he called out. A dark-complexioned boy in a dirty dhoti and vest emerged from inside the house. Handing the package to him, the man said, 'Take this inside and check whether it's one crore … *sau peti hoga*.'

So, he had just delivered a package stuffed with cash. Sriman had heard businessmen were using this mode of transporting money, but this was probably the first time he had been a conduit to this modern-day mode of monetary give-and-take.

Sriman accepted the tips reluctantly on the recipient's insistence. The next destination was Jadubabur Bazaar. He picked up a humongous consignment of fruits and spices and delivered it to Vivekananda Road. This recipient too tipped him, this time a fifty-rupee note. Sriman felt happy. Life is like this, he thought, a seesaw of ebb and tide. It does not matter if the ebb goes on indefinitely. Things are bound to change someday. Sriman drew sustenance from such cheerful meditations.

Sriman had initially planned to work till late tonight. But he had earned the day's target much earlier, courtesy the tips. So, he was home by 9:30. A text alert informed him that Yellow Shirts had deducted Rs 50 from his account based on Anwesha Deb's complaint. To hell with it, Sriman said to himself. He had earned quite enough through the day for the deduction to matter.

'Why would *you* pay?' Bishan-da was not ready to accept Sriman's reasoning. 'It was not your fault … *she* had given an incomplete address … *she* behaved rudely.'

'Bishan-da, I have earned handsome tips today, let them deduct fifty rupees …' Sriman tried to dissuade him with a pronounced joviality.

Instead of achieving the intended effect, the remark got Bishan-da's goat. 'That's not your honest earning, Sriman, it came free. But if you accept this punitive deduction, it will mean you are admitting it's your fault, and that's more humiliating … the amount deducted doesn't matter, what matters is that it is unjust. No two ways about that … Won't you protest? Have a straight spine, Sriman … people with compromised spines won't be allowed into our new planet.'

'Right, but would they revoke the decision if I protest?'

'Let's see …'

Sriman began jotting down the letter Bishan-da started to dictate. Each sentence, mentioning all necessary details, including the date and time, turned out to be a well-documented exposure of Anwesha Deb's misdeed and a stark condemnation of it. Sriman was surprised how the seemingly ineffectual Bishan-da remembered every single detail of the incident. Bishan completed dictating the letter, tweaking words here and there, replacing less potent expressions with more charged ones.

'Send it now …' Bishan said once he was done reading the entire letter.

Sriman e-mailed the letter with a pulsating heart, apprehensive of the probable fallout. Whatever the impact of it, he had to send it. After all, he could not disobey Bishan-da. But deep inside, he sensed the ominous foreboding that it was just the beginning, more such humiliations were in the works.

At the same time, he felt rather cross with Bishan-da's adamant insistence on sending the letter. Bishan-da had been in a government sector job, where one could afford to be whimsical, throw tantrums even. He would never appreciate that a job like Sriman's was a wholly different ball game. This job was a tightrope walk, a bit of a misstep and the worker would tumble into the void below. The worker must always be scared of losing the job at the drop of a hat. Here, one could neither be impulsive nor too sensitive nor hold on to self-respect. Otherwise, one fine morning, one's phone would tinkle to the dreaded e-mail, 'Your service is no longer required. You have served us well, thank you very much. Best wishes for your future.'

Sriman heard the notification alert of the incoming message even though he was engrossed in these thoughts. He sat on the terrace all by himself for quite some time, collecting the guts to open it.

He came down in the late hours of the night. Holding his breath, he finally opened the message before retiring to bed. He could not believe his eyes. The company had revoked its punitive decision of deducting the money from his account! They had credited the fifty rupees back to him. Sriman ran back to the terrace yelping, 'Bishan-da, they have accepted your point!'

He felt like embracing Bishan-da. But he checked his impetuousness at the sight of Bishan-da's meditative serenity. 'Just look at Abhijit, it appears fabulous tonight, like the three eyes of Goddess Durga ...' he said to Sriman.

Sriman placed his eyes on the telescope.

A little later, as Sriman lay in bed, he was mulling over the differences between Jnuiphool and Bishan-da. Jnuiphool epitomised grace and the rare skill of presenting even the most mundane thing in a mould so attractive that it could dazzle the onlooker. But Bishan-da was a delver of the deep. He navigated to the root of a matter, coming up with a lifelike montage, a monochromatic reality, devoid of veneer. If he gave you pictures of chivalrous riders, they would speak to the sighs of their desperate struggle for existence and their frantic attempt to survive the rat race.

Moments before giving in to the heady lure of a sweet slumber, Sriman's eyes hovered over a montage of faces and moments: Subhra, the nurse; Somnath and his old pocket transistor radio; Mathuresh, giving the final touches to the idol's eye.

At once, his phone sounded the arrival of a new message. 'Hello,' it read. Initially, he could not recognise the sender's name. Soon, he recalled, it was Mrittika, Mrittika Sen, the Karate Queen!

# 7

Sriman had come to meet Russell in his new office at Bagri Market on a delivery nearby. Russell had given up his delivery rider job and joined this east India-based pharmaceutical major.

'How much are they paying you?' Sriman had asked.

'Eight thousand.'

'Eight thousand! That's all?'

'Doesn't matter. I have a decent, desk-bound job, I work from an air-conditioned office. I was simply fed up with the running around,' Russell smiled.

Sriman agreed. Speed seemed to have infused into their bloodstream.

'Yet, I was persisting with it,' Russell continued. 'But I developed spondylosis carrying those fifteen-sixteen-kg bags continuously for twelve hours or more. Plus, accidents have increased, haven't they? I would surely have been bedridden with my bones in pieces.'

'Right. Doctors sagely call these occupational hazards!'

Russell erupted into laughter at Sriman's mock seriousness, mimicking the grimness of a doctor. 'You are right. Acidity, cold, headache, doctors blame every evil on our job.'

Sriman nodded, 'Thank God, we are at least better off than the miners who get silicosis.'

'Actually, I live with my parents, and I am the only earning member of my family,' Russell diverted the context. 'We'll starve to death if I don't work … this job provides a decent pay at least, low though …' Russell smiled.

Though Russell seemed to have a point, Sriman was hell bent on finding loopholes in his reasoning. He carried on the argument inside himself, destined to emerge the winner on the other side of the one-sided confrontation. 'The rider's job still retains great amenities. Earn as you sell, is our mantra. We can earn even Rs 20,000 a month if we work diligently. What would your new job give you? Nothing more than the fixed Rs 8000! You would be confined to the office daylong. How boring! Add to this, the harmfulness of a sedentary job. Above everything, the insecurity. You might be kicked out the moment you fall out of favour with the boss or if a more competent candidate comes by.'

Despite coming up with so many arguments in favour of his job, Sriman could not deny the fact that the crux of his grudge was his inability to bear the optics of Russell working relaxedly in an air-conditioned space, at peace with himself.

Sriman might not admit it, but he was actually feeling envious. His rather complacent sense of contentment with his job had been shaken.

In fact, the restlessness of a gig worker's job and the poise of a desk-bound worker's were utterly disparate things. Each had highs and lows of its own. One had to take up a job that suited one's aptitude. Sriman had often felt the idol-maker's calling was the bee's knees for him. Gurakesh uncle was quite impressed by his intense involvement when he used to work at his place, while in college. 'But making idols won't feed you,' Shiuli often warned Sriman. Hence the decision to run around in the Yellow Shirts livery. But later, after he had taken up the food delivery job, Gurakesh uncle had made a very revealing observation, 'You never really loved making idols, did you? That's why you could abandon it so easily. But that's understandable, you can't be a jack of all trades.'

Sriman had come to Beleghata on a delivery. Only after completing the assignment did he feel the cruel sting of hunger. He was yet to have lunch though it was quite late in the afternoon. Ma and dada still being at Paramanandapur, there was no provision for a decent meal at home either. The hangover of familial ceremonies lingered long. None could feel it more acutely than Sriman who had been surviving on the bland monotony of boiled rice and mashed potato for the last few days.

Sriman parked the bike at the spacious tea stall at the intersection of the three roads. He gulped a liberal amount of water from the bottle in his satchel before entering the stall. He wanted to have bread and butter, sprinkled with sugar. But the half-pound bread, the only option of it available at the place then, would be too much for him. Suddenly, he noticed another Yellow Shirts rider munching bread in a corner. Sriman ordered bread and tea and went inside.

Sriman sat down beside the other Yellow Shirts rider. Same company, same work, same age group. Circumstances were conducive to strike up an acquaintance.

The young man was Anup Manna, resident of Jotbhim, a 'village' near Biswa Bangla gate at New Town. Once a typical village, Jotbhim hardly had that rural feel any more. Like in other parts of the country, villages were fast losing their character in the face of the all-consuming surge of globalisation.

'A village is no longer a village once it starts selling mutton roll and spaghetti,' Anup remarked with a smile.

'The chefs of globalisation mix our pluralities, of language, manners, traditions, into one singular, tasteless broth in a giant melting pot,' Sriman observed wisely.

'Is there anything left to mix, dada? Yellow Shirts has taken care of everything. You and me greet clients the same "good morning", "good afternoon", "sorry, madam", "thank you, sir" and all. But globalisation fails to appreciate the fact that the me who greets a customer with a "good morning" and the me who is having a cordial chat with you are not the same person …' Anup confided candidly.

'Not just different, both these mes are eternally at war with each other. I am running to deliver food I won't be able to taste even once. It's so frustrating!

'Dada, we are like coins on a carrom board, rushing in whichever direction the striker shoves us. Can there be any attachment between the coin and the striker?'

Interesting, Sriman thought. Although it was his first meeting with Anup, it seemed they had met earlier as well, that Anup was an old acquaintance. Sriman was starting to like him. Anup's ideas jelled with his. Sriman was finding it difficult to have the entire half pound of bread, but he did not want to waste it either. He shared some of it with Anup. Anup brought out a longish fry from his bag and offered it to Sriman, 'Try this, dada.'

'What's this?'

'Take a bite, you won't regret it …'

Sriman obliged. Fried fish. No bones, yummy. Was it *bhetki*? Impossible, how could Anup afford *bhetki*?

'This is *lotte*, the poor man's *bhetki*, selling at Rs 80 a kilo where I live. Two hundred to two fifty grams, that's more than enough …'

'It won't be this cheap once globalisation enters your village,' Sriman warned.

'That's true,' Anup admitted. 'The shanties, "jhups" to the IT boys and girls, charge Rs 20 per piece of *lotte* fry …'

'Really? Why don't we set up a shop ourselves?'

'You can't be serious, dada! I have been planning one for a long time.'

Sriman and Anup, in their excitement about their new project, began considering possible names for their non-existent shop.

'Dada, the name has to be catchy enough to attracts clients. The food has to be of the best quality. Youngsters throng the shanties if the food is good.'

'Right,' Sriman concurred. Someday riders would be delivering food prepared by their shop. The shop would have a dedicated space for riders to eat. The arrangement and the food would be so impressive that the riders themselves would spread the word. Their shop would become a haunt for delivery riders to congregate and interact, just like the Hatibagan eatery where they gather now.

'But where would we set it up?' Sriman wondered.

'Dada, the name first,' Anup reminded him. 'Friends? Locally Global? Hungry Haunt?' he suggested.

'Not bad, but I think we could do with something more unique.'

'Dada, the point is, customers will come irrespective of the name, as long as the food is good … The Amherst Street eatery where I go has no name as such, everybody calls it Chachi's Hotel, but it is packed with customers in the afternoon, cab drivers queue up in large numbers,' Anup said. 'Can I suggest another name?' he asked, after a brief pause.

'Why not? Why the hesitation?'

'No, I mean, it might sound very traditional. We can we call it Anusri, combining Anu from my name with Sri from yours?'

'Beautiful name!' Sriman beamed. 'Perfectly suits the middle-class vibes of our outlet. Let's select the location on this auspicious day itself.'

'Yes, dada, it won't matter if we miss a few orders from Yellow Shirts,' Anup responded enthusiastically.

They were headed for New Town within the next couple of minutes.

Sriman had not seen New Town so closely before. Though officially an extension of Kolkata, it was so very different from the Kolkata Sriman was familiar with. Sriman realised the reason behind the difference. Kolkata had attained its present avatar through centuries of ups and downs, love and neglect, use and abuse. This new extension of the city was a mere mimicry of the grand, old city. Sriman hated the fact that this so-called 'newness' of the newfangled city was founded on audacious and pointless imitations of the old.

'Dada, wait till evening and you'll see delivery riders rushing through every block and delivering orders at almost every doorstep.' Anup gave Sriman a lowdown on the strange specifics of New Town.

'So, it's a posh haven of the moneyed elite?'

'Clans of private-company employees, many from the IT sector, real estate people too, have migrated here with wads of cash to spend. Come Friday night and long queues appear in front of liquor shops,' Anup tried to enlighten Sriman as best as he could.

'These real estate people … do they have to pay the political party honchos?'

'Of course, dada. It's a syndicate at work, you can't do any construction job without buying brick and mortar from them … crime rate too is quite high here.

'Another thing, dada,' Anup continued, 'many NRIs have built houses here only to sell them off later for astronomical amounts. They flock here in the winter, like migratory birds, as if obliging the city with their arrival. As long as they are here, they survive on food ordered on the food-delivery apps. They're too practical to waste money by eating out.'

'Very interesting,' Sriman smiled.

'These filthy rich NRIs think they can throw morsels at us and we would be obliged like stray dogs of a third-world country, born with insatiable hunger. I've had first-hand experience.'

'How come?'

'Once an NRI of AE Block, to whose place I was delivering food, handed me several food packets … chicken soup, pasta, and all … on returning home, I verified the expiry dates on a hunch. Know what? They were six months beyond the date of consumption … The bastard must have picked up those packets from some shop free of cost to distribute among poor people like us. They think we have no self-respect. I returned the whole lot as it is the next day.'

Anup was getting agitated while narrating the experience. Sriman liked this self-respect, this anguish born of an uncompromised spine. He at once resolved to introduce Anup to Bishan-da someday. Individuals with self-respect should congregate at 1, Akashganga Lane.

Suddenly, Sriman recalled what had brought them to New Town. He asked Anup whether he had any particular spot in mind. 'Exactly, dada, I was about to tell you this. We should pick a less crowded space, but with prospects of growth,' Anup said. 'I think we should set up shop at a spot where there is a demand for a square meal at cheap rates, preferably somewhere near the cancer hospital.'

'Not a bad idea, but whom should we approach if we want that land? How much must we pay him?'

'Let's approach Biplab-da … tell him everything … let's see what he has to say.'

Sriman was hesitating. Anup said, 'Shyness won't take you anywhere, dada.'

Sriman nodded. He must overcome this hesitation. 'Could you give a rough estimate of the cost of setting up a bamboo enclosure?' he asked Anup.

Anup nodded. 'Okay, dada.'

'By the way, who'll take charge of the cooking? I can ask my mother. You can ask your wife ... I don't think it would be a problem. We can appoint a cook later, depending on our funds,' Sriman said.

'Right, dada. There's a Chinese food joint opposite the cancer hospital. The Tibetan or Nepali cook there makes lovely momos. They sell like hot cakes.'

'Kolkata has a cosmopolitan culture. We must include delicacies of other states as well as continental dishes in the menu.'

'Right, dada. We should decide the menu right away. It should be a cosmopolitan composite, so that people are impressed right from day one. Should we go meet Biplab-da now?' Anup asked.

'What if he refuses?' Sriman was yet to overcome his shakiness.

'Let's try at least. But we can't go there in this Yellow Shirts uniform.' Anup's presence of mind impressed Sriman.

Heaps of sand, stone chips and bricks lying near the entrance of Biplab's four-storeyed house made it obvious that it was a promoter's house. One had to access the first floor through the spacious hall on the ground floor. Well-built young men, with hitman-like body language, were loitering inside the hall. A young man in a semi-supine posture, bearing the airs of a big shot, was speaking to a couple of people.

'Behave as if you own the property and nobody would dare ask you anything; don't look into anybody's eyes, they can sense your nervousness,' Anup warned Sriman. 'Avoid the sycophants on the ground floor as if they're vermin and climb up straight to the upper floor.'

Biplab ran his office from the second floor of his house. The first thing that struck Sriman was the eclectic assortment of photos of famous personalities on the wall behind Biplab, from Shri Ramakrishna to Karl Marx, Albert Einstein to Pt. Ravi Shankar. Immediately beside Subhas Chandra Bose's photo hung that of a man in a shaggy moustache and a cap. Sriman was trying to guess the identity of this unfamiliar face when Biplab spoke out, 'That's Keshav Baliram Hedgewar, founder of the RSS …'

'Biplab-da, have I ever demanded money or anything else from you?' Anup was at his persuading tactics best.

With brows rising up into the crookedness of a sickle, Biplab said, 'No, why?'

'Have I ever demanded what others do? A government job at a prominent government establishment?'

Biplab Ghosh was observing Anup quizzically, trying to figure out his real intent.

'I have attended meetings, processions, whenever you have told me to.'

'That's true,' Biplab replied while toying with his mobile phone. 'But what do you want now?' Biplab asked, voicing a patience that was running thin.

'Me and this dada of mine have decided to set up an eatery on the land beside the cancer hospital,' Anup had come to the point at last.

'Impossible. It's government land, moreover, it has already been allotted to a private institution,' Biplab clarified.

'At least ten eateries are doing business on that land, Biplab-da. What harm would the addition of the eleventh one do?'

'But you could be evicted later,' Biplab warned in a milder tone.

'Not evicted, rehabilitated, dada. Even if the government evicts anybody, it either offers ample compensation or relocates them. We would gladly accept either, plus, we have your blessings.' Sriman could not help being charmed by Anup's persuasive acumen.

'You've become quite the manipulator,' Biplab smiled. 'Okay, come next week, let's see.'

'Thank you, dada,' Anup signalled Sriman to get up.

'This man has everybody's photo. Strange, isn't it?' Sriman spoke out as soon as they had stepped out of the party office.

'The scoundrel's a master chameleon, mind it,' Anup said.

'Will he help us? What do you think?'

'Won't be easy, dada. But don't worry, I will persist. You just think over the menu, also how much capital to invest,' Anup said with a reassuring positivity.

'We've to generate the sum from what we're earning, right?'

'Right, we've to raise the amount by working harder and for longer hours in the next few days,' Anup answered.

'How long do you work usually?' Sriman asked.

'Noon to eleven at night. I will make up for today's loss by working till midnight to one tonight.'

'You won't be home before the dead of night,' Sriman felt sad for Anup.

'Actually, dada, we must fight it out to survive … we earn as we sell,' Anup winked as he quoted Sriman's favourite mantra.

'How much does it amount to at the end of the month?' Sriman asked.

'Around Rs 22,000, after meeting all dues and expenses …' Anup said, with a melancholic smile.

'How many members do you have in your family?'

'Wife and two children. Ma lives at Gourangapur, dada looks after her.

'What about your family, dada?'

Sriman told him what little there was to say.

'What about marriage, dada?'

'Forget it, brother. Marriage would be a liability considering the kind of job we do ...' Sriman said with a sigh.

'Never say die, dada, never say die. We'll carry on,' Anup said optimistically.

The dispiriting impact of the meeting with Russell dispersed by the time evening descended, thanks to Anup's pep talk. Anup's optimism had brushed off on Sriman. That conviction received a stronger boost from the prospect of setting up the eatery. The remaining deliveries of the day passed imperceptibly with Sriman absorbed in the thought of setting up Anusri.

On returning to Akashganga, Sriman learnt that Jnuiphool Roy Corbyn would be leaving for Paris in five days, to attend a seminar at the Sorbonne University. From there, she would travel to Columbia University for another seminar. Her calendar was choc-a-bloc with globetrotting schedules.

In the meantime, Jnuiphool had procured a new fairy tale from the Totos. 'It's somewhat like Aesop's fables. Toto grandparents tell these stories to their grandchildren,' she said, before beginning the story.

'Once upon a time, the wild fowl and the monkey were friends. They farmed together. One day, the wild fowl invited the monkey to her place. She hatched an egg and served it to him. The monkey had not tasted an egg before. He was so happy that he tilled the wild fowl's land throughout the day.

'Few days later, the monkey invited the wild fowl to his home. He wanted to surprise the wild fowl by offering her an egg. But despite roaming the forest the whole day, he could not find a single egg. "Where would I get an egg?" he asked the fowl. "Just light the oven and set the frying pan on it. Sit down on the pan when it turns red-hot and you'll produce an egg," the fowl suggested.

'Monkey sprung out of the heated pan, jumping madly in pain. "My backside is burning like hell!" he yelled. The fowl said, "Jump into the river!" But as he did not know swimming, the monkey began to drown. Lacking the courage to rescue him, the fowl helplessly watched the monkey drown. In the meantime, a tiger arrived in search of prey. "Save me!" monkey appealed desperately. Tiger agreed on condition that he would eat monkey up after rescuing him. Monkey, in dire straits, agreed.

'Tiger placed monkey on his back and brought him to the shore. He was about to eat the monkey when the latter said, "Wait. I am thoroughly drenched. Let me dry myself up first." Saying this, the monkey climbed on to a branch of a tree. A little later, the tiger said, "You've dried yourself, come down!" Monkey said, "But my feet are still wet." Saying this, he climbed further up the tree. A little later, the tiger again commanded the monkey to come down. Monkey said, "But my nails are wet." With that, monkey climbed to the topmost branch and from there to another tree and so on, until he was beyond the tiger's reach. Thus, the monkey saved his own life.

'*So, la-pan-leje*,' Jnuiphool smiled.

'What does that mean?' Sriman asked.

'End of the story,' Jnuiphool smiled again.

'Brilliant acquisition, Jnuiphool!' Bishan applauded. Turning to Sriman he said, 'So, Sriman, what's the moral of the story?'

Sriman did not know what to say.

'If the tiger symbolises adversity, the monkey represents us. Like the monkey, you too will have to think out ways to save yourself from the pitfalls of your job, your insecurities …' Bishan explained.

# 8

'New morning, new day. I am awake but have no plans to leave my bed any time soon. I locate my phone somehow, as if a blind person in a stupor. I sit up a little later. First things first, pay obeisance to my Gurudev (the wallpaper on my phone) and my deity Bholenath (my phone's back-cover image). A brief bout of playing Township, my favourite game. Two messages have come from Sriman Kundu. Have spoken with him three days ago, over phone. Nice guy, interesting too. I draft and send brief replies to his messages. Make a mental note of the topmost priorities of the day: buying Bubka's birthday cake and a shirt for him. Finally get up, freshen up and make tea.

'Some days, I have breakfast, skip it on others. Due to pressure at work, had my lunch today with dada and his family. I'm a tenant in their house. They live on the first floor, me on the third. These people are like God to me. They care a lot for me.

'Getting up later in the evening, around 7:30 or 8, I freshened up and had tea before leaving for work. Hit the road after a brief gap as I was a bit under the weather. Returned around 11:30. Boudi was waiting for me at the dining table. Activated Fast Move and Quick March while having dinner. A booking arrived soon after, Garia to Tollygunge. Accepted it and left home paying obeisance to Ma Durga. Bookings kept coming as I accepted one trip after another, while the night deepened. Witnessed the darkness of the night melt into the light of the morning. I was the usher of the new dawn.

'Though working the night shift involves a lot of strain, it has its own perks. Empty streets, smooth arrival at destinations. It was around 5 in the morning when I was back. Freshened up before going to bed. Surrendered gradually to sleep.'

That was Mrittika Sen's journal update for yesterday, which was a Saturday. Mrittika did not go out for work today, though Sunday was not usually a holiday. She had written a bit of the journal entry for the day till now.

'I was fast asleep as I had gone to bed after 5 in the morning. The first thing that knocks me out of drowsiness is the urgency to reach the gifts to Bubka. Did I hear the doorbell ring? Was too deep in sleep to be sure. The bell rang again, heard it clearly this time. Didi, who lives on the ground floor, was at the door, beaming at me with a breakfast of chholar dal and kachori. Though officially a Sunday, today was more of a funday because I had already got a few invitations. Had breakfast, managed a few domestic chores, played Township on my phone. Went out on some necessary errands. Had lunch on return. Fell asleep while watching movie on phone.'

Despite this, Bubka's mother did not forget to convey the gifts to him. Actually, the boy's birthday fell on a Monday this year, which was usually a particularly busy day for her. She might not have the time to take the gifts to him tomorrow. Hence, she delivered them a day earlier. The boy had demanded a smartwatch, but a standard smartwatch cost a lot. Finally, the cash-constrained mother zeroed in on a resplendent t-shirt bearing the graffiti, 'Get Going, Little Champ'.

Mrittika waited at Ramlakhan's until Bubka arrived. It was an out-of-this-world bliss for Mrittika to feed the cake to her son with her own hand! A thankful sigh to Bholenath came out spontaneously. Bubka was so happy to get the t-shirt that he not only forgot his demand for the smartwatch but put on the tee there itself. Mother and son clicked a selfie.

From there, Mrittika proceeded to attend the invitations.

Could a Sunday be better spent?

Monday morning. Mrittika picked up a passenger from the gate of Jadavpur University in the late afternoon. The drop location was near Girish Park. She had barely dropped the woman when a new booking came in. This time, the pick-up location was a reputed pharmacy on Vivekananda Road.

The drop location was an address she had never heard of before: Blue Moon on Mirza Ghalib Street. The original name of this street was Free School Street inspired by the school that taught the children of the British officers of the East India Company free of cost. The street branched out of Lindsay Street, which was named after Robert Lindsay, a double-dealing official of the Company. Like many other civil servants of the Company, Lindsay too worked for a meagre salary. Like them, he too was involved in shady deals to sustain a lavish lifestyle. Primary among these were hunting tigers and catching elephants. He used to earn a substantial sum by sending to the Company the annual inventory of the sixty-seventy tigers he slaughtered. The tuskers, on the other hand, were smuggled to the Company's military wing, which too paid him handsomely. Lindsay returned quite an affluent man to his country in 1787.

Free School Street used to be a dense forest of bamboo trees barely two and a half centuries ago. People, barring the exceptionally brave, used to avoid the wilderness. Pritiram Marh was one of those brave exceptions. He turned rich overnight by selling bamboo during the acute crisis of the same in 1780, so much so that he ended up establishing the royal lineage of Janbazaar. Free School Street, till most recently, was notorious as the haven of Anglo-Indian sex workers. Even today, a middle-aged man wandering the area might hear a wiry bloke's wary whisper, 'Seeking college girls?'

Despite negotiating the length and breadth of Kolkata for the last four years, Mrittika was blissfully ignorant of the existence of a building called Blue Moon on Mirza Ghalib Street. The rider too was weird, his face almost invisible behind a longish mask. It beat Mrittika whenever she was unable to see the face of her passenger. Though the pandemic had subsided, the health department had advised gig workers to stay alert. Fast Move too had instructed them to wear a mask while driving and interacting with customers. Thieves and people with indecent intent were using this to their advantage. The latter kind touched her inappropriately. In such circumstances, she made the passenger get off midway.

Let's take a hasty peep into Mrittika's past while she negotiated the route to her destination. She married Supriyo Sen twelve years ago at a time when she, a regular participant in state-level karate championships, was basking in the initial savour of fame. Supriyo, then sales personnel with an obscure ayurvedic medicine company, had come to watch one such championship. He approached Mrittika at the end of the tournament.

It was the first time that Mrittika came across a guy who was interested in meeting a girl practising karate. Men generally avoid such women because of their overtly masculine vibes. They probably suffered from the apprehensive insecurity of their manhood being challenged by the woman's machismo. Supriyo's out-of-the-ordinary interest in her impressed Mrittika. Since then, they met at the end of every tournament. Mutual fascination soon culminated in marriage.

A series of mishaps occurred in Mrittika's life prior to her marriage, beginning with her mother's cerebral haemorrhage. All their savings were spent in her treatment, in vain. Her father, Gopal Chandra, set up a hosiery shop at Garia. The business flourished and soon they were very close to compensate the losses. But one fine morning, they found that the shop had been looted. The tragic incident left their father shell-shocked, robbing him of his power of speech permanently. Mrittika and her elder sister Dharitri were too stunned by the sequence of tragic events to console their father. Dharitri was somehow wedded off. Mrittika got married a couple of months later, in a lacklustre ceremony. At peace after Mrittika's marriage, Gopal Chandra breathed his last within a couple of months. A month later, Mrittika conceived.

The mother-in-law had declared a bizarre whip. Supriyo and Mrittika must beget a son. In case the embryo was identified as a girl, it should be immediately done away with. The mother-in-law would foot the bill.

This gender discrimination was one of the manifestations of something alarmingly wrong about the people of the house. The house had another bizarre custom. Everything, including where a guest sat as well as anything along the trajectory of their movement, had to be scrubbed clean as soon as they left. Any inmate of the house walking into the ambit along which the guest moved had to cleanse themselves thoroughly.

All of this was the revered matriarch's despotic diktat. The lady ran a virtually autocratic matriarchy. Her neurotic obsession with cleansing herself was obviously an extreme case of obsessive-compulsive disorder. But nobody, be it the husband or her three sons, had the guts to oppose her or point out her excesses. The mother is a grossly overrated figure in India. A flesh-and-blood mortal with her fair share of faults and follies is most unjustifiably deified in Indian households. Mrittika had no qualms about saying this, even if it amounted to blasphemy or calls for ostracisation.

Living in the house became a claustrophobic curse thanks to these strange practices. Discontent brewed in Mrittika, as things became increasingly unbearable. Bubka was born into this milieu of autocratical anarchy. The birth of the coveted male heir found the Sen family in celebration mode.

Supriyo lost his job when Bubka was eight. The pharmaceutical company, struggling with severe financial losses, was downsizing its business. Supriyo's eldest brother, in the meantime, had shifted to another house. Supriyo's *mejda* was supporting the out-of-job younger brother's family. The mother-in-law gradually started making it apparent to her and Supriyo that they were the expendable members of the family. It did not matter to the spineless Supriyo, who simply kowtowed to his mother and brother. But it was too disparaging for the self-respecting Mrittika.

Dharitri, Mrittika's elder sister, whom she needed the most in such a predicament distanced herself from her younger sister. Mrittika was trying her best to turn back at any cost. She began vending homemade spices door to door. The spices, fresher and healthier than those available in the market, were selling well. But Mrittika needed a more powerful impetus.

Mrittika's attention was driven towards the job of delivery workers. Bucked up by the confidence of her cycling skills, Mrittika purchased a bike with her personal savings and by mortgaging the ornaments gifted to her on her wedding. It did not take her more than a day or two to learn the tricks of manoeuvring the two-wheeler, which ultimately motivated her to apply to Fast Ride for a job. They tested her in various ways. The company managers did not doubt her riding skills, but they had serious doubts about her capability of meeting the challenges of the job. She was a woman after all.

'Sir, women are proving themselves equal in every facet of life. Driving a bike and conveying people to their destinations is no challenge for a woman.' This was how Mrittika convinced the Fast Ride honchos to appoint her. She did not forget to mention her personal experience of carrying her father on a bicycle for twenty kilometres. She received the e-mail one pleasant summer afternoon that she had got the job. Mrittika had probably driven more than 2000 kilometres ever since.

Mrittika's resolve to move out of the house was bolstered by her new job and occasioned more by the concern for the future of her son than her own well-being. Soon after getting the job, Mrittika moved into a tile-roofed, rented house at Goabagan, not very far from her in-laws', and brought Bubka along. The one-roomed house was spacious enough for mother and son. The school had been complaining that Bubka was lagging behind in studies and growing increasingly inattentive. His studies were back on track once he started living with his mother, detached from the deleterious influence of that house. But things were down once again when Bubka was taken back to that house by his father. He was being badly pampered. His uncle was eager to provide anything he demanded. Obviously, the boy did not want to return to the humble life that his mother offered.

Supriyo was no longer the man Mrittika had married. She had once weighed the option of divorce. They had taken Bubka away. Whether it was her demand of divorce or the insistence on getting back Bubka's custody, they were bound to relent if she dragged them to court because the law was on her side. But she dare not take on the financial might of her in-laws with her meagre salary. Hence the decision of maintaining the status quo—keeping the divorce in abeyance, allowing them to keep Bubka, and limiting her interaction with him to the occasional visits.

However, a mother being a mother, Mrittika, staying in the proximity of her in-laws', started feeling restive about meeting Bubka more frequently. And whenever thwarted, the urge morphed into a mad impulse for causing severe physical harm to her in-laws. Each time, she had to douse this blistering urge with the composure karate and experience had taught her, and the cognizance that Bubka's well-being depended on hers. Ultimately, she shifted to a house on Garia Station Road, miles away from Bubka and that house.

***

It took Mrittika half an hour to reach Mirza Ghalib Street due to a traffic snarl. She slowed down so that she did not miss Blue Moon.

The Chinese restaurants that used to dot this street earlier had long closed shop. Bangladeshi restaurants had come up in their place, a few foreign-exchange outlets too. These centres of currency conversion thrived on the Bangladeshi tourists who put up in the lodges that had mushroomed in the area. But many of these visitors from the neighbouring country were medical tourists who came to India to avail better medical treatment. Blue Moon must be one such lodge, Mrittika inferred.

The GPS did not specify Blue Moon, though it directed Mrittika to a compound in the lane on the left. Three houses stood close to one another on the compound where a few cars were haphazardly parked. Evidently, these were old houses belonging to Anglo-Indians. Mrittika luckily spotted the rather discoloured signboard with the name Blue Moon on the building in the middle. The profession of the two women standing at the entrance was evident from their garish garments and audacious body language. So, Blue Moon was one of the shady hotels of the area.

The passenger got down. Mrittika checked her mobile and said, 'Eighty-nine rupees.' Her heart skipped a beat as the passenger took off the helmet she had given him and his mask. Supriyo!

The shock of the sudden meeting with Supriyo in these strange circumstances was too much for her to process. A little later, on regaining her composure, she decided to linger in the spot for a few minutes under the pretext of cleaning her bike. Mrittika was clueless why she fervently wished that Supriyo headed for another building though there was hardly even a tendril of a relationship between them. But he simply walked past the two ladies into Blue Moon, leaving her inexplicably devastated. The echo of his footfalls over the wooden stairs reached a stunned Mrittika outside.

But why did Supriyo need to come to this murky place? Who paid for these sexual romps? His *mejda,* as usual?

The Supriyo Mrittika knew was different. He would most rarely assert his virility. He would force himself on her with an uncharacteristic brutality on such occasions, irrespective of whether she was unwell or not in the mood. If Mrittika refused, he would cruelly make her get off the bed and sleep on the floor. Was it the psychotic streak inherited from his mother? Or were his carnal needs being taken care of in external locations of notoriety like Blue Moon? Did he feel the urge only during the interstices between those sex romps? Though she strongly believed an unambiguous 'yes' to be the right answer to all these questions, a part of her refused to buy it, despite everything.

But why was she bothered? Why was she agitated about the activities of a man with whom she hardly had a relationship any more? Was it insecurity? Or plain jealousy? Or was it because she was still possessive about Supriyo?

Mrittika felt helpless in her perplexity. She made several rounds of Blue Moon. At one point, she felt like entering the house to find Supriyo. But that would be more humiliating for her. On the edge, she kept scooting from one end of Kolkata to the other till midnight.

Mrittika was one of those people who surrendered themselves to the graveyard when sadness exceeded all bearable limits. She enjoyed the vacillating moods of the cemetery—busy, relaxed, noisy, serene, crowded, lonely, involved, aloof—beneath the pitch-black sky.

The sights and sounds of the graveyard—the moist miasma of the Ganga, the sweaty odour emanating from strangers straying along the ghat, people slumbering in canine curls—worked like an anodyne on her anguished mind. She watched pallbearers descending the stairs in silent austerity, to discard flowers and twigs that had been used to decorate the dear departed. A rickety rogue suddenly blocked their path, as if from within the bowels of the night, to demand alms. Initially reluctant, one of the pallbearers got rid of him with a measly amount. Instantly, the man's body language changed, his eyes assumed a jolly radiance as he shuttled meteorically towards some secret cove of intoxicating substances, whistling in raucous glee.

Mrittika longed to have a heart-to-heart with the river. Her restiveness would end only if she could disgorge the mass of her pain on the tranquil waters. Standing on the ghat, facing the river, she asked, 'Why is the life of a delivery rider so very inconsequential? Is a delivery rider the child of a lesser God?'

The urgency of bringing Bubka out of the clutches of her in-laws was the first thing to cross Mrittika's mind as she took a sip of her cuppa at the tea stall by the ghat. She must rescue her son before he turned into his father. But how?

What about Sriman? They had spoken with each other several times since that first meeting and met on several occasions too, briefly though. Only Sriman could probably replenish the sangfroid she had lost ever since seeing Supriyo earlier in the day. Her drooping spirits seemed upbeat at the thought of talking to Sriman. But would he be awake at this hour? He must be, because all delivery riders were working extra hours to avail the incentives being paid for each extra trip during this festive month. Plus, 'Only a delivery labourer would care for another,' Sriman had said.

As she placed the call, she was greeted by Sriman's caller tune. He must be driving. She disconnected and WhatsApped him instead: 'Please call when you're free. It's urgent.'

# 9

Sriman was back at Sonagachhi to deliver food after a long time.

Love—nakedly physical—was in the air that permeated these lanes and alleys of infamy. Sriman felt an affinity with the locals, most of whom were migrants from the villages of the South 24 Parganas, Hooghly, Midnapore, Bankura, as well as other states. Sriman respected these people because they were not squeamish about admitting that their livelihood thrived on humankind's most primal occupation and because theirs was a difficult survival. One of the other reasons why Sriman accepted delivery assignments to this area was the handsome tips he got from most of the denizens.

Each time he came to Sonagachhi, he remembered Bishan-da.

'Ever been to Sonagachhi?' Sriman had asked him once.

'You want to know whether I have visited the place or had sex with the women there?' Bishan was utterly blunt. 'If both, then my answer is yes,' he added without batting an eyelid.

'My God!' Sriman had exclaimed.

'Why? Does it shock you? I am neither God nor an inanimate thing, I am a flesh-and-blood human with normal desires and urges,' Bishan said straightforwardly.

'I mean, with these base women ...?'

'What did you say??? Base?' Bishan glared at Sriman. He controlled himself instantly and asked, 'So what, have I done something sacrilegious?'

Bishan had then explained the history and topography of the area to prove his contention. He read out relevant parts from books on social history.

'Three hundred years ago when the Mughal regime was in its dying days, absolute anarchy was raging over Bengal. Calcutta was witnessing the influx of a large number of Bengalis from the suburbs and villages, for livelihood and security. The population of the city had increased from ten or twelve thousand to four lakhs between early and mid-eighteenth century. It would leap to six lakhs in the next forty years. The majority of these outsiders were farmers, fishers, sweet sellers, washermen, gardeners, tailors, builders, small traders.

'Just like your folks from Paramanandapur, many people migrated to then Calcutta in search of security.' Bishan looked sharply at Sriman. 'Your friends, Somnath Bar from Jagatpur and Anup Manna of Jotbhim village, one a farmer, the other a fisherman. Their reason for migrating to the city and taking up the job of delivery rider was the same, the economic downturn in the country. The same reason that had brought about this city-centric exodus 300 years ago …'

Bishan's elucidation helped Sriman see things clearly.

'What about your hotel, Anusri?' Bishan-da was suddenly back in the present.

'We are location hunting. Once done, we'll seek permission from the authorities. The funds are also a concern, Bishan-da …' Sriman updated Bishan.

'That's it, never give up the courage to dream. It's not the destination but the journey that matters. Radha ran madly through the forest, only because Krishna had beckoned her. Thorns pierced her feet, they bled profusely, yet she ran. We too must stick to our respective determinations, our vision for reaching the planet of our dreams,' Bishan's baritone assumed a profound resonance, reaching Sriman as if from some interstellar space.

'The first emigrants to Calcutta three centuries ago had brought with them their own rural culture and the tradition of ritualised religiosity. The tone and tenor of those religious rites underwent a transformation based on the demands of the rich patrons of the city. These rituals were tweaked in accordance with the taste of the city people, leading to the birth of popular culture in Calcutta. The books being produced at Battala complemented the growth of this culture.

'The masses do not need the Battala books any more in the current ecosystem of easily accessible pornography or the ubiquitous Hindi film song,' Bishan-da added, briefly interrupting his discourse.

'Prostitutes of old Calcutta belonged to mainly three classes. The first comprised Hindu women of the upper classes, concubines of local aristocrats living a life of anonymity. Rare representatives of this category can be found today at Chitpur, Cornwallis Street, north Bagbazar, and central Maniktala. Prostitutes of the middle order live under the care of a landlord or landlady. The third and the largest section, Hindu and Muslim dancers living in Chitpur and its vicinity, mostly belong to the poor and lower classes, and cater to a cross section of clients.

'I used to know a rich, upper-class courtesan,' Bishan-da winked. 'The aged lady lived in Goabagan, close to where Cornwallis Street starts. Much of my anecdotes of the past are borrowed from her.'

'True stories … aren't they?' Sriman said.

'Well, that's what she claimed …' Bishan said with a hint of a smile before starting to relate a few of the 'stories'.

'When Swami Vivekananda's brother Bhupendranath was arrested by the police, the prostitutes of Cornwallis Street started pelting stones at them. The police were gobsmacked. The lady claimed she had witnessed the incident in her childhood. She had joined the processions and the singing choirs that collected donations during the floods in East Bengal. When she had placed those collections at Deshbandhu Chittaranjan Das's feet, he had blessed her … She loved to repeat this story … They had hit the streets during Gandhiji's non-cooperation movement as well.'

Bishan invariably raked up the story of that old courtesan whenever Sonagachhi was mentioned. 'Ms Chatterjee, the name she was known by, was above eighty then, but looked deceptively younger. She used to keep tabs on everything happening in the country. She told me about the clandestine romance between Motilal Nehru's daughter Vijaya Lakshmi and Syud Hossain, the son of a Calcutta-based nawab, about their clandestine marriage.

'Ms Chatterjee had devised a unique ploy to attract new patrons. Through her agent who was a watch repairer, she would entice rich and aristocratic clients to her quarters. Once those eminent people landed there, they had no choice but to surrender to her charm, ending up gifting her expensive jewellery or dedicating their magnum opus to her. She had even induced me to draft her autobiography for a few days,' Bishan had told him.

'Why did you give it up?' Sriman had asked.

She started to influence my entire being, I was incapable of any other work … Eventually, I managed to run away …' Bishan smiled.

'Good riddance!' Sriman heard himself exclaiming.

'Due to the Bengal famine near the end of the nineteenth century and the resultant collapse of the rural economy, many women from the overburdened and destitute families migrating to Calcutta were compelled to take up prostitution. The number of lower-class women started increasing in the brothels of the city in the 1860s or 1870s.

'So, you can't say they come from a "base" background,' Bishan rectified Sriman's misconception.

'I used to spend most of my afternoons at a prostitute's quarter at Sonagachhi while in the Indian Railways. Not an upper-class courtesan, she was from rural Birbhum. My ears were regaled by her flawless rendition of Tagore songs, while I downed glasses of alcohol, lying semi-supine on the easy chair in her room. One day, on reaching office from her place, I discovered that I had forgotten my gold wristwatch at her place. That watch was an heirloom; I got it from my father who had inherited it from my grandpa. I rushed off to Sonagachhi immediately, and knocked as hard as I could on her door. She was busy attending a customer. She peeped out in between and said, 'I knew you would be coming, here's your watch … You would have got it back even if you came ten years later,' she smiled kindly.

'Would you still call them "base"?' Bishan gave him a hard look.

'Actually, I did not mean to say it that way,' Sriman mumbled the evasive reply.

For Sriman, Sonagachhi had become synonymous with stories heard from Bishan-da ever since.

Today, he was there to deliver mutton biriyani, kebabs and mutton chaap to Lovers, a destination he had often supplied orders to. As always, he parked his two-wheeler beside Mishra-ji's paan shop.

Sriman knocked mildly on Kamala Mandal's door, following it with the declaration, 'This is Sriman from Yellow Shirts, here's the food you had ordered ...' Sriman waited patiently for the door to open. Experience had taught him that knocking a second time on this door when closed was taken as a mark of disrespect.

Kamala opened the door exactly three minutes later, in a dishevelled sari wrapped hastily around her body. Glancing over her shoulders, Sriman could see the half-lying form of a man on the bed, semi-naked, sipping liquor from a glass.

With Kamala gone inside, most probably to verify the content of the delivery, the interior of the outer room lay exposed to Sriman's scrutiny. The man's bare torso was quite clearly visible. The flimsy sheet, meant to cover his lower parts, accentuated them instead. The man with a scar on his cheeks was lying with half-closed eyes, the luxury of his recumbent bliss enhanced by the liquor he was sipping. About to lift the glass from the nightstand, he noticed Sriman, who had stepped into the room, unbeknownst to himself. Too late to run away, he stayed rooted to the spot, as if hypnotised by the brute charm of the stranger.

'*Kaun hai re tu*?'

'I am Sri-Sriman Kundu … Yellow Shirts … f-food delivery boy …' Sriman had suddenly developed a stammer. But he felt like playing a prank, '*Arre, aap hi ne toh andar aane ke liye bola* … you asked me to come in!'

The man was taken aback. '*Kamla, arre e Kamli, ghar mein kisko ghusaya? … doosra mard chahiye kya?* Not satisfied with me any more, eh?' he yelled in her direction. The frail cover shielding the man's shame fell off as he wobbled to stand up. Turning away from his monstrous masculinity, Sriman faced the wall on the left.

Kamala, after confirming that the food was okay and setting aside a little of it for herself, was coming back with tips for Sriman. She knew this boy. He had come a few times earlier too. His compassionate eyes made affection well up inside her. That is why she was always inclined to pay him a higher tip. She had hardly expected her patron to raise such an outcry in the few minutes she was away from the scene.

As she was walking back to Sriman, the sozzled figure of her client blocked her way. 'What's the matter? No longer satisfied with me?' With that, he pulled off Kamala's sari and shoved her onto the bed.

Sriman had no idea nakedness could be this brutal. He was shivering. He could not linger there for a single second. He ran down the stairs without waiting for the tips, head bent in shame. The humiliation was too much for Sriman to accept. Are delivery riders as insignificant as worms and insects that anybody could indulge in any bestiality in their presence! His entire being seemed to revolt. Instead of voyeuristic pleasure, the optics of a man and woman in the act left Sriman nauseated.

At once, his mobile rang briefly, followed by the sound of two consecutive incoming message. Two messages. Mrittika had requested him to meet her, but Sriman did not feel like it. The repugnant experience of the day had left a rancid taste. He decided to ring Mrittika and tell her that he would not be able to meet her tonight.

He could hear Mrittika's caller tune: *Pyaar humko bhi hai, pyaar tumko bhi hai, / Toh yeh kya silsiley ho gaye? / Bewafa hum nahin, bewafa tum nahin, / Toh kyon itne giley ho gaye? / Chalte chalte kaise yeh faasle ho gaye?...* (We were inseparable from each other, / Yet distances grew, / We parted ways even though we were walking together.) Mrittika did not pick up the call. She rang soon after, insisting that he met her at the tea stall by the ghat, close to the crematory. Despite the initial reluctance, Sriman finally agreed as the spot was not far from Akashganga.

Mrittika's account left Sriman stunned. 'What a coincidence! I was also returning from a similar place.' He narrated his experience in all its repulsive details.

'Ours is a dog's life!' a disgusted Mrittika exclaimed in revulsion.

'How can you be so sure that your husband, I mean, Supriyo babu, was visiting the prostitutes? Many small companies have offices in such obscure buildings there. He may have gone to one of them,' Sriman tried to console Mrittika.

'There's only one office, of a courier company, that too has closed down. I've asked people around. Supriyo had gone there to those women, I am sure,' Mrittika sounded utterly disgusted.

'I accept your point, but why bother? You are not staying with him, na?' Sriman could not see the reason behind Mrittika's irritation concerning a person she no longer had anything to do with.

'So what?' Mrittika looked sharply at him. 'I just can't tolerate the idea of that man caressing my son with the same filthy fingers with which he has fondled those women ...'

'So, what do you want to do?'

'I will bring Bubka to my place for good.'

'That will be great, but will they agree?'

'That's true, they wouldn't hand him over easily. They have never allowed me to keep him for more than a couple of days. Can you imagine what they would do if they got a whiff of my intention of keeping him forever?' Mrittika could not spell out the probable consequences.

'How will they find out?'

'I would have to bring all his books, a larger number of his clothes than I usually do while fetching him to stay with me … isn't it? It would be obvious.'

Sriman nodded. Mrittika had a point.

'I think the court would grant you his custody … you just need to drag them to the court …'

'But that's a question of patience and a lot of money too … twenty-five to thirty thousand or more.'

'That's true.' Sriman made a mental calculation of how many trips he would have to make if he were to raise that amount.

The apparent implausibility of the project silenced its two young stakeholders and veiled them in an impenetrable pall of gloom. The sense of frustration was exacerbated by the crematorium's melancholic milieu and the gut-wrenching wails of the kin of the departed and the faint stench of burning flesh. Complemented by the ominousness of the graveyard shift, it accentuated the despair in the hearts of the young mother and her compatriot who deeply felt her agony.

'I will make off with him on his way back from school,' Mrittika said with uncharacteristic determination after a brief contemplation.

Sriman was taken aback. 'Wait … you will need to do that only if they refuse to hand over Bubka to you, right? How can you be so sure that that's going to happen?'

'I have reasons,' Mrittika nodded at the river, lost in her thoughts. 'Bubka told me a few days ago that his father is consulting his lawyer. They'll go any length to keep him away from me … I was totally clueless that his custody case had come up for hearing in the court. They got the court rule in their favour, citing my absence. Akashdeep's father has owned his custody ever since.' Mrittika's eyes were brimming with tears.

'I've decided to abduct him and keep him with me forever. That's the only way out, let me see who takes him away this time.'

Sriman could feel the steel in her voice. He felt sad that it was a misplaced determination. Based on the experience he had earned from his exposure to a wide variety of people and their ways, courtesy his delivery assignments, he could very well foresee the gaping holes in Mrittika's misguided plan. But he could not afford to tell her that, for it would break her heart. Still, he made one last effort at dissuading her. 'They'll lodge a missing person's diary, set the police after you, what will you do then?'

Mrittika was silent, lost in her thoughts.

Whenever Sriman faced a crisis that had no easy closure, he did not allow a sleepless night to rattle him further. He simply yielded to sleep. He had seen that several innovative solutions occur to a mind refreshed by a sound slumber. 'Go home and get some sleep. Let's take it up tomorrow,' he suggested with a smile of forced positivity.

'You don't need to do anything, *I* will do whatever I can, after all it's about *my* son!' Mrittika exploded.

She keyed her scooter to start. The noise with which the bike returned to life, shattered the silence of the wee hours of the night. Within the next few moments, Mrittika had vanished into the night's heart of darkness, leaving Sriman stupefied.

# 10

Somnath Bar called at 10 in the morning. A call from Somnath, anytime of the day, meant trouble. He had left Yellow Shirts and was now with Horizon, an e-commerce company that sold almost everything under the sun. But he continued to nag Sriman whenever he found himself in a soup. Somnath was a sly soul who would drag others into his personal problems. Deep inside, Sriman believed that he must avoid Somnath, but he could not restrain himself from helping him whenever a crisis arose.

Sriman skipped the initial calls from Somnath. Ten minutes later, he rang again. Four calls within fifteen minutes! Must be a mighty predicament, Sriman thought and picked up.

'You must know Mintu Pal?' Somnath sounded agitated.

'Which Mintu ...?' Sriman could not recall anyone by that name.

'Your colleague from Yellow Shirts ... that lanky boy from Sukantanagar ... scar on the left side of his temple ... remember him?'

'Can't place him yet ... anyway, what about him?' Sriman could not check his impatience.

The sum and substance of what Somnath said was that Pal had probably been sacked by the company.

'Why "probably"?' Sriman could not understand why Somnath was not sure.

'He hasn't been able to access the company's app since this morning,' Somnath clarified. 'He can't log into his account or access his code ... Meet us at Hatibagan. We'll discuss it in detail.'

'Hatibagan?'

'Better come to Salt Lake, Sector II. We're meeting near Easy Breakfast.'

'Hmmm,' Sriman said to Somnath. A lot of fuel to burn, he thought.

Sriman had planned to spend the morning at home, then visit Mathuresh's workshop to watch the last-minute decoration of the idols. Saraswati Puja was round the corner; Kumortuli was in overdrive. He would go to the club from there as on other Mondays and play carrom. Somnath's call had upended his plans for the day.

Sriman sifted through Jnuiphool Roy Corbyn's messages from the previous night. She sent him enlightening inputs on gig workers from the world over. Courtesy her, Sriman had come to know that the gig economy was spreading its tentacles all over the world like the Covid-19 pandemic. Jnuiphool preferred to call gig workers virtual workers, a name coined by Bishan-da which she had appropriated.

Last night, she wrote to him about America's virtual workers, a class that had grown by 15 per cent in the last decade. 36 per cent of America's work force earned its livelihood through gig jobs. The number of gig workers had been growing exponentially in America since the pandemic, clocking a 15 times growth over other industries. Virtual workers contributed nearly 6 per cent of the American economy. Economists in the US predicted 52 per cent of its workforce would earn its livelihood from gig labour in the next couple of years.

Yet, like the gig workers of India, they too were grossly underpaid and also deprived of the amenities workers of conventional sectors were entitled to. But they were expected to meet all expenses, including rents, taxes, monthly instalments, with that measly pay. In the US as in India, the gig workers were worried that they might soon lose the resources necessary for survival. Like in India, male gig workers in America outnumbered females, who were a microscopic minority. The average age of gig workers in both countries ranged between eighteen and thirty-four years. Gig workers of both the nations were the precariat, staring at a bleak future.

Sriman studied the whole scenario minutely. Jnuiphool madam's painstaking research made Sriman feel an affinity with gig workers scattered across the world. He felt so excited that he wanted to share it at once with Bishan-da. But Bishan-da did not entertain intrusion when he was absorbed in studies in the morning. He behaved like a total stranger in those hours—cocooned impenetrably in a reticent remoteness. On afternoons, he ventured out, formally dressed, to places in the city that he had not visited for quite some time, perhaps to take stock of the changes they had undergone. If one wanted to meet the real Bishan, they would find him on the terrace of Akashganga in the dead of the night.

Stepping out of home this morning, Sriman took a lingering look at Akashganga. Badly in need of a fresh coat of paint for quite some time, the house resembled the wreckage of an ancient ship. A serious lack of care was tragically obvious in the scars dotting its primeval physique. The casual bystander could not even remotely assume that the house that lay lacklustre in its languorous somnolence all day, turned into a lively spacecraft at night, out on an astral odyssey. A curious affinity bound the spirits of 1, Akashganga Lane and Bishan Basu.

Sriman walked towards the temple of Goddess Kaali on the right of the house before bringing out his bike from the garage. This was Monday, his day for paying weekly obeisance to the goddess. Lanes and alleys of north Kolkata are replete with gods and goddesses. The southern parts of the city lack this variety. But why? Unlike Bishan-da, who would surely have given an academic answer to the question, Sriman would attribute this to the disparity between the demographic characters of the people of these two extremes of the city.

Once done with offering obeisance to the deity, Sriman glanced at Sanjeev Jain's construction materials shop close to the temple. Piles of sand, stone chips, and bricks had spilled onto the road. A dimly lit, nondescript shop barely five years ago, it now had assumed a sparkle, courtesy the soaring demand for construction materials with old residences along the lane being demolished to make way for plush standalone apartment buildings as well as apartment complexes. The rapidly changing character of the old neighbourhood was breeding a wide arc of rich-poor polarity in this once-middle-class precinct. The wealthy men living in these buildings and complexes appeared funnily awkward when they had to interact with their middle-class or lower-middle-class counterparts in the neighbourhood bazaar. The smarter among them rose earlier and splurged at the more upmarket and expensive bazaar at Shyambazar.

The garage where Sriman kept the bike faced the Ganga. Like on other Monday mornings, he walked over to the ghat across the Circular Railway tracks. Uncharacteristically lonely, the ghat appeared absolutely serene in these early hours. Rows of factories, their chimneys yet to emanate the dark fumes, lined the other side of the river. Sriman descended the stairs. A calming sensation spread over his system as he sprinkled a fistful of water on his face from the river. Sriman had been sensing a deep assiduity in everything he had been doing since the morning. The serenity provided him some relief from the insecurity that had been haunting him ever since learning of Mintu Pal's predicament. What if he too was sacked one fine morning?

Last night, Mintu Pal had eaten the food he was to deliver. Such incidents were heard of in Delhi-Mumbai-Bengaluru; Mintu had ushered it to this city, unknowingly. He was sitting on the trunk of the oak tree, his head lowered, surrounded by co-workers who were standing scattered under its shade. Somnath too was there, lending a patient ear to what everyone had to say, while toying with a piece of stone.

'Each of us may have a different take on the issue, but none of us supports what Mintu has done. We unanimously condemn his dastardly act. This maligns our image,' one of the boys surrounding him said.

'Absolutely,' someone seconded him.

'But why did you eat it?' one of them asked.

Mintu was silent.

'Out with it, Mintu … you must tell us why you ate the food,' the boy who had asked the question insisted.

'You all know I can't control my hunger. That's my problem. I feel hungry round the clock,' Mintu said without lifting his head.

'We all feel the same more or less, but that does not mean—' one of the boys said.

'I know it was wrong. I can't say why I did it. The scent of the food made me insanely hungry, as if I was fasting forever. I was under the spell of the devil,' Mintu could not give a better explanation.

There was absolute silence beneath the arboreal shade. Some had their eyes glued to the screens of their phones.

'He should apologise to the customer,' someone suggested.

'The customer would never pardon him,' one of them said, as if on cue. 'They are rich people; they don't know what hunger is!'

Another spell of silence.

'So, whom should he go to? Who would give his job back?'

By then, Sriman had formed a fair idea of what had happened. Yellow Shirts had blocked Mintu's access to their app as a punitive measure on receiving the complaint that he had eaten the food ordered by multiple customers.

Blocking. It was the modern mode of punishment. Though a virtual form of disciplining, it was much more ruthless than actual punishment. Somebody pulled invisible strings and one was instantly made extinct, rendered dead, practically, a ghost.

The very thought of it gave Sriman goosebumps, eliciting an unconscious sound of desperation. All the boys, including Mintu, were watching him. In order to evade the queasiness, Sriman addressed Mintu in the sermonising tone of a wisenheimer, 'You ate it as you couldn't control your hunger. Well and good. But you should've filled up the packet.'

'How could he?' Somnath chipped in. 'How many packets could he fill? … How many customers should he seek pardon from? The moron has eaten from several packets, bit of biriyani, a fish fry, nuggets of paneer.'

Though Somnath's mockery made everyone laugh, Sriman objected. 'We shouldn't be saying this. He didn't have the means to replenish the food.'

'In that case, he should've controlled his hunger. I have no sympathy for him,' Somnath said with obvious contempt.

Somnath was beyond Sriman's understanding. He had sounded so very concerned over the phone while asking him to come to discuss Mintu's predicament. But the same Somnath was now eager to wash his hands of the matter.

'You could've admitted your guilt directly to the customer before the latter lodged the complaint,' Sriman said.

'None of the customers has complained,' Somnath informed Sriman.

Sriman was surprised. 'Somebody must've snitched.'

'A girl recorded the whole thing from her balcony and posted it on the internet. It became viral within minutes,' Somnath stated before playing the video for Sriman.

Sriman could see Mintu opening the containers by cautiously removing the wraparound tape embossed with the Yellow Shirts logo. He was savouring the food inside and then wrapping the same with the tape carefully before opening another container with the same alacrity, so on and so forth.

'This does not end here. Just check out the deluge of comments. Some have said, "Yellow Shirts can't be trusted any more." Some have called it a crime, that the culprit should be severely punished. Others have expressed apprehension that delivery persons can even poison the food,' Somnath added.

'But we can't afford to wash our hands of it. We must think of a way out,' the boy seated on Mintu's right remarked.

'What's the delivery address?' a familiar voice asked. Sriman instantly recognised it to be Anup Manna's.

'You want to go there?' Sriman smiled.

'Yes, or else, I'll seek Biplab-da's help,' Anup replied.

'Don't make this political, Anup. We're capable of dealing with this,' Sriman asserted. 'Mintu, address please.'

Mintu's lips trembled, as if in a trance, but there was no sound.

'Speak clearly!'

Sriman's rebuff brought Mintu back to his senses. 'Three residential complexes side by side—Broadway, Paradise, and Basudhara Apartments,' he said.

'If all of us go there together, the customer might construe it as intimidation tactic. The important thing is that none of them has complained to the company. If we now tell them that they ate leftovers they might raise an outcry … besides, they have no sympathy for delivery riders …' Somnath reasoned.

'So, what's the way out?' Anup asked. 'Something must be done. Mintu has a family to feed.'

'What if we all request the supervisor to condone his first offence?' Sriman could not see any other option.

'That's probably the only way out, but just a consolation perhaps,' Somnath remarked. 'I don't think he would be able to do anything, but let's give it a try.'

The supervisor's line was busy, even on the third attempt. During the fourth attempt, Anup agitatedly pointed out the comment posted by the company beneath the video grab of Mintu's tactless peccadillo.

Somnath read it out.

'We at Yellow Shirts want to inform our patrons, restaurant partners, and stakeholders that we have taken these allegations very seriously. Yellow Shirts stays true to its zero-tolerance policy towards lapses and transgressions of any kind at its end. The delinquent employee was removed from our delivery ecosystem as soon as the deplorable act was brought to our notice. He is no longer a part of our company.

'The unfortunate incident, however, has been a learning experience. The company has already initiated measures to make the tape bearing its name and logo, which is fixed on the food containers, better and tamperproof so that once taken off, it cannot be re-fixed. Alongside, we have resolved to be more careful towards orienting our delivery partners on the do's and don't's and, based on the same, we would like to assure all concerned that there shall be no recurrence of similar instances in the future.'

The official statement issued by the company made it pointless to contact the supervisor or request him for a reprieve for Mintu.

Sriman spent his entire Monday outdoors. It was 10 at night when he returned home. He went to the terrace right away, to fill Bishan-da in on Jnui madam's updates from last night. Bishan-da made no reply.

'Look into the telescope, see how stunning the early winter sky appears!' he said a little later.

Sriman looked.

'Look eastwards. There's a bright star. That's the Sirius. What do you see a little far from it to the north? I had told you the name.'

'Ursa Major,' Sriman replied instantly.

'Good, now look here,' Bishan pointed his finger a little far from Ursa Major. 'A cluster of six-seven starlets.'

'I don't see them.'

'Look carefully, place your eyes properly on the eyepiece,' Bishan said with irritation.

'There they are. One, two, three, four … yes, seven of them.'

'That's the Pleiades. Remember the name.'

'Pleiades,' Sriman nodded.

'A researcher from Spain has revealed that aliens exist in the Milky Way, merely nineteen light years away from Earth, spread across as many as four planets. But they hardly pose any threat to humanity. They would maintain this benignity for at least another couple of centuries. Scientists are thinking of sending another radio message to outer space, like the one sent in 1974. But the message this time would be simpler, loaded with clues to the construction of the human DNA,' Bishan whispered into Sriman's ears as if confiding a precious secret. He had been increasingly incoherent ever since Jnuiphool's departure.

'Did you understand anything?' Bishan asked, retaining almost the same discreet tone.

Sriman gradually narrated the whole Mintu Pal episode.

Bishan sat in silence for a little time. Then he looked through the telescope again. 'You must learn archeoastronomy … otherwise you won't know how old Giza's pyramid is.'

Giza's pyramid! Sriman could not reconcile it with something as mundane as the desperation hunger can lead to. In the meantime, he managed to steal a glance at the data on the Giza pyramid on his phone.

'Early twenty-six century BC,' Sriman said, based on the information gleaned with the furtive glance.

'Right, long before Christ's birth. The sky then was vastly different from this sky. Sirius used to both rise and set in the east. The alignment of the three Giza pyramids did not match that of Orion's girdle. But we can't deny that the pyramids were born out of this alignment. How far back should we go in time to find the alignment?'

'Good God! The sky too changes?'

'Of course. Twenty-six thousand years from today, the sky will return to its current configuration the movements of the earth, diurnal rotation, annual rotation. Each of these revolutions take 26,000 years to run its course. The appearance of the sky changes bit by bit during these rotations.

'Scientists have utilised the computer to calculate how long the sky would take to return to its present form. It was found that the pyramids had been created around 10,500 BC. This has upended whatever we knew. We have to rewrite Egypt's history.'

'Strange!'

'Nothing can be stranger, even Mintu's hunger is a primordial thing. Insatiable hunger was there in the Vedic Age too, and inequality … man-made evils … the same man later tried to abolish these.

'When the floods on the Nile would bring the construction of the pyramids to a standstill,' Bishan continued, 'the pharaoh would arrange to feed one lakh workers creating a strong bond among them and a massive repository of folk tales; but don't expect this from Yellow Shirts. There can't be any real bonding among you all to shield Mintu nor can you have tales of your own. These companies are destroying all such possibilities. Akashganga is like a fortress, we must assemble here, all of us who want to relocate to the other planet.' Bishan's incoherence was at work again.

'What do you mean?' Sriman was surprised.

'Is it too hard to understand? We must assemble those whom we will be taking to the other planet. We must acquaint them with the sky. The sky is our escape, isn't it?'

That meant he could bring Mrittika and Bubka to Akashganga. Sriman rang Mrittika. Mrittika told her that where Bubka lived did not matter to her. What mattered to her was whether he should be brought out of that house legally or illegally.

Sriman had no answer to this.

Mrittika disconnected the call.

# 11

Lately, Sriman had been hearing a droning sound inside his ears. Though he did not give it attention initially, he had been sensing impaired hearing for the last few days.

The complication became alarmingly obvious last Sunday morning when he was at Harisha Haat. Sriman was a regular there because things were quite cheaper than in other markets. He had become a familiar face there so much so that sellers who sold things only in dozens sold him single pieces.

Sriman picked up a shirt and paid the price. The shopkeeper extended his hand, 'The balance?'

'I gave you a 100-rupee note!'

'It's 170, sir … one-seven-zero! Is anything available at hundred rupees any more?' The shopkeeper smiled.

The man was right, he should have thought of it earlier. How did Sriman hear 170 to be 100? He should have applied common sense. But that was no solution for a complication which was becoming disturbingly frequent. A few days ago, one of his friends was sharing a naughty joke in their assembly at Hatibagan. Though he spoke in a lower than usual tone, for obvious reasons, he was audible to all except Sriman.

After the recurrence of a few more embarrassing situations, Sriman decided to go to Subhra, the nurse.

'What's the problem now?' Subhra looked at him quizzically.

'Would you treat me if I say it's all about the heart?' Sriman tried to give a flirtatious mould to a serious issue.

'Is it serious?' Subhra looked concerned.

'Not at all, it's the ears this time.'

Subhra arranged an appointment with Dr Sunil Ghosh, a renowned and highly in-demand ENT specialist. But with Subhra's involvement, they easily got an appointment on Tuesday morning.

The doctor examined his ears variously. 'Sixty per cent of Kolkata's population has impaired hearing. Welcome to the club, son,' Dr Ghosh said with a smile.

'Strange things are happening in the audible world of late. Twelve per cent of birds have stopped singing. Many of the rare ones that still do, are mimicking other birds. The females of the species are conditioned to identify the male companion from the melody of his song which defines their species. The songs of late are so different that it is near-impossible for the female bird to recognise the male.

'Hard to believe, isn't it?' Doctor Ghosh looked at Sriman who was wondering how this was linked to his problem.

'A male Regent Honey Eater is singing on a eucalyptus tree in a park in Melbourne. His song is a mating call intended to attract a female. But the female does not respond because the notes of the song are alien to her ears. So, you see, son, why the world of sounds has lately become a very strange place. Excessive pollution is the most potent factor behind it,' the doctor paused.

'See, son, people like you spend your day exposed to blaring horns, din of buses and cars, and other damaging noises, right?' he asked Sriman a little later.

'Job hazards, doctor,' Sriman nodded.

'It's very natural that somebody exposed to so much noise will have impaired hearing. Your left ear has borne the brunt of it,' the doctor said kindly.

'And the headache?' Sriman looked questioningly at the doctor.

'That too seems to be linked to your ears. I am prescribing a few medicines and a few tests. Let's see.'

It was 2 in the afternoon by the time Sriman came out after obtaining the medicines. He decided to inform Subhra.

Subhra had wrapped up her morning shift and was about to leave. She stopped on seeing Sriman. 'What did the doctor say?' she asked.

Sriman briefed her.

'If somebody calls you names, just extend your left ear,' she joked.

'Ummm, what if a pretty woman like you whispers sweet nothings into that ear?' Sriman was back in the mood for flirtatious frolic.

'I will whisper into your right ear, don't worry,' Subhra smiled.

'Can I drop you home on the way back?' Sriman was eager to return the favour she had done by arranging his visit to Dr Ghosh. 'Where do you live?' he asked Subhra.

'Beside Srimani Market, on the other side of the street,' Subhra stated.

Sriman offered the extra helmet in his vehicle to Subhra.

It was 3 in the afternoon by the time Sriman dropped Subhra home. 'Why don't you come in and have lunch with us?' Subhra asked politely.

Sriman had lost several orders since the morning to keep the doctor's appointment. A few deliveries would make up for it. Moreover he was starving. He would surely have accepted the invitation but for the order that arrived instantly. 'Some other day, okay?' he said, adding courteousness to his voice.

'Why not tonight?' Subhra wanted to know.

'Suits me ... will confirm the time later ...' Sriman said, before driving off.

The first delivery location on Ultadanga Main Road was a newly built high rise near Muchibazar. The building was yet to have an escalator. So, Sriman had to climb all the way to the eighth floor to deliver the food packet.

The second order that came through the Aladdin app arrived when he had barely come down. A pack of potato chips and organic vegetables were to be delivered to Rainbow apartment at Rajarhat.

The streets of Kolkata were usually deserted in the transitional hours between the noon and the afternoon. It did not take long to reach Rajarhat.

The overcast sky foreboding rains reminded Sriman of his first delivery as a delivery rider. It was a day of torrential rains. All the approaches to City Centre in Salt Lake, the pick-up location, were under water. He had come to pick up a cake from the renowned confectionery on the ground floor of the swanky mall. When he sought the direction of the cake shop from another delivery boy wearing a Yellow Shirts tee, he said, 'Wait below the Metro Railway bridge, you'll get your consignment there.'

On glancing in the direction of the bridge from a distance he saw five delivery boys waiting beneath it. Four of them wore the Yellow Shirts livery, one the Guava tee. Sriman reached the safe sanctuary of the bridge as fast as he could. But the approximately hundred-metre path from the bridge to the mall had no roof. He would be badly drenched if he tried to reach the shop. Soon after, Sriman was pleasantly surprised to see a boy in black tee and an umbrella approaching them.

'Order number 5485?' the boy from the confectionery asked him.

Sriman nodded, 'Yes, that's me.'

'New recruit, right?' The boy verified his hunch with the hint of a smile.

'Yes,' Sriman nodded again.

'The cake is a delicate thing. It will be a mess if it falls. You'll bear the brunt of it, be careful,' the boy explained everything patiently.

Sriman placed the cake in the huge bag and was about to put the key into the bike's ignition when the boy said, 'What's the hurry? Don't you see it's raining?'

'I'll be late if I wait for the rain to subside,' Sriman was feeling restless. 'The app would show delay.'

'No problem. Wait here and just don't hit "pick-up complete" until the rain subsides, okay?'

Sriman agreed.

The confectionery boy stood by Sriman while the world outside was being lashed by the rains. On his very first day on the job Sriman had realised that if workers are united, they can outsmart even the most powerful surveillance.

Bishan-da had laughed out loud on listening to Sriman's experience that night. 'My God, you have launched a virtual class struggle!'

'What do you mean?' Bishan-da's remark was too obtuse for Sriman.

'You have unknowingly taken the first step to an intelligent resistance against the "Big Brother"-ism of the capitalist establishment.' Bishan's explanatory observation hardly made things easier for Sriman. He could not see what was so radical about what he had done. He had simply followed the confectionery staff's advice. Sriman was so deeply lost in his thoughts that he did notice when he had arrived at Rainbow apartment. The main entrance was made up of floor-to-ceiling doors of thick glass, transparent yet impenetrable. The security guard sat on a chair by a desk on the other side of the glass, immediately beside the elevator shaft. A strangely impenetrable transparency, Sriman thought. The guard peeped out through the small inlet next to the main entrance and asked, 'Where to?'

Sriman mentioned the customer's name and flat number.

He was allowed entry only after his details were jotted down in the logbook. The parking lot was impeccably clean. A few astronomically priced cars were parked. He passed by a swimming pool, the water crystalline in its blueness. A door inscribed with the words 'Sports Lounge' could be seen, probably indicating a gymnasium. Sriman's destination was on the third floor. He was about to take the stairs when the door to the elevator opened. A woman, apparently a domestic help, descended. Sriman went in, on making sure that there was no sign forbidding the entry of delivery personnel.

On coming out of the elevator on the third floor, Sriman was greeted by a confounding darkness. He somehow spotted the apartment and rang the doorbell. The door partially opened before he could ring again. Once Sriman's eyes adjusted to the darkness, he saw the human figure partly visible behind the partially opened door.

'Okay, okay,' the man responded.

From the guy's body language, it was evident that he was a domestic help who was desperately putting up a sententious solemnity. 'Please verify the items,' the man commanded.

Sriman opened the bag to hand him the package of potato chips and organic vegetables. Rich brats, mostly obese couch potatoes, gorge on packaged potato fries, while their health-conscious parents have switched to organic veggies. An amusing concoction of the organic and the inorganic, Sriman wondered.

Sriman's phone jingled. A new delivery assignment.

Sriman pushed the glass door, but it did not oblige. The guard was not at his post. In fact, not a single soul was visible nearby. How to go out? Despite repeated attempts, Sriman could not make the door budge. His next pick-up location was seven kilometres away. Would he miss the order?

Suddenly someone appeared on the other end of the glass door, from the street outside. A woman, in her early thirties, dot of vermillion on her forehead. 'Can't open from this side. Please help,' Sriman yelled.

Sriman's voice could not travel through the impermeable glass barrier. He tried physical and facial gestures instead. That worked.

The lady indicated the way out from Sriman's predicament with the movements of her fingers that resembled the agility of a danseuse. Sriman opened the glass door and stepped outside after thanking the lady.

He suddenly met Subhabrata at Ultadanga, on the way to his fifth delivery of the day.

'What's up, boss? How many till now?' Subha asked.

'Not much.' Sriman recounted the reason in all details.

Abir rang around 9 in the night with the shocking news that his food consignment had been stolen near the backside of a hospital at Kalikapur.

'Please come. I have asked Somnath and Jaideb also,' Abir said.

'Jaideb who?' Sriman could not locate the name.

'Jaideb Mondal from Haltu.'

'Okay, I'll be there. Where will I find you?'

'I'll be on the footpath facing Super Food.'

Despite avoiding the main roads and their traffic snarls, it took Sriman almost half an hour to reach Super Food from Esplanade. Alongside Abir, Somnath, Naseem, two more unfamiliar faces, one of them presumably Jaideb, had already arrived. Somnath introduced him to both Jaideb and Vignesh Kumar.

Abir recounted his experience which, in its uniqueness, was frightening for any delivery rider. Abir had reached the destination, along the road behind the hospital at Kalikapur. Suddenly, three men accosted him on an unlit stretch. One of them held a gun to his forehead and demanded all the money he had, while another took away all the food packets he was carrying: three packets of biriyani and two packets of reshmi kebab. The third one forced him to cancel the order on his phone.

'That amounts to a loss of Rs 700!' Sriman was shocked.

'Not exactly. They gave me a 100-rupee note, patted my back, and left.'

'Bastards!' Somnath said angrily.

'Did you inform the company?' Jaideb asked Abir.

'No.'

'*Unko batane se kya fayda*? No point at all. They would neither support nor shell out even a farthing ... *ek phooti kaudi bhi nahin*!' Vignesh said.

'*Woh toh thhik hai, lekin* ... if we inform the company, they might declare it a black zone. That would warn all other delivery partners beforehand, isn't it? Delivery partners *ko yeh jaankari rehni chahiye, hai na*?' Naseem asked.

Somnath concurred with Naseem.

Abir phoned the supervisor who asked him to send it to him in writing. Abir wrote it all and e-mailed it. But the money was gone.

'What do I do now?' Abir was distraught. 'We labour day in and day out yet earn peanuts. Why can't they let us be?'

'Don't lose heart. We are with you. We'll work out something,' Sriman consoled Abir.

'Don't worry, they've given you Rs 100, na? Something is better than nothing,' Somnath said with characteristic cynicism.

'How can you be so insensitive, Somnath?' said Jaideb. 'Can't you see the boy is in a mess?'

'Seriously, what kind of a life is this?' Abir had collected himself. 'We are already at risk of breaking our limbs while carrying delicacies from door to door. Now this nuisance of the consignment being stolen and a company that won't compensate any of it!'

'Right, they won't understand that this is not something that can be done with the click of a button. It takes back-breaking labour and the risk of life,' Sriman said sadly.

'Why just them? The company, the customer, the traffic police, nobody understands. Add to it the low pay,' Somnath remarked.

'The company must be made aware of our issues,' Abir said.

'At least those who are the worst sufferers, must have a meeting. What say?' Jaideb glanced at the others for endorsement.

All of them agreed.

'But where do we meet? We need a place where phone calls won't disturb us.' Vignesh was talking sense. 'The supervisor should not be able to poke us if he notices we are not online.'

Akashganga could be ideal. Sriman mulled over the viability of the venue. The walls there were so thick that mobile connectivity, inside the rooms, was erratic at best.

It was almost 10:30 when Sriman started homewards. It would be inappropriate to go to Subhra's place at this hour. She had called twice while he was meeting with Abir and the others. Sriman had rejected both the calls and sent the template message, 'I will ring back later.' When he rang Subhra on the way back, she mocked him, 'Feeling scared?'

'Should I?'

'Depends on your guts. After all, I am—' Subhra broke into a peel of laughter.

Sriman had called to request her to postpone the dinner to the next day, as it was too late. But Subhra's incessant chatter did not allow him the scope.

It was an appetising spread—egg curry, paneer-capsicum curry, and chapatis. Sriman was floored by the minimalist elegance of the arrangement and the warmth of the host.

Subhra was courteous in her welcome though Sriman had kept her waiting till that late hour.

'Why don't you join me?' Sriman asked Subhra, feeling awkward that he was eating alone while his hosts were starving.

'Of course, I am starving. Also, I've to report for duty in the morning,' Subhra said, sensing his discomfort.

Sriman told Subhra about his family and Bishan-da, alongside Abir's horrific experience as they ate.

Sriman relished every morsel of the humble but toothsome menu. 'Truly delicious. You cooked all of it?' he asked Subhra.

'Nothing doing, sir, not everyone is lucky like you to have a mother,' she jibed playfully.

'Right. Not everyone is blessed with a wife like you either.' Sriman immediately realised that he had goofed up. 'Where's your husband, gone to bed?' he asked before Subhra could tease him again.

'He is out on night duty.' Did he notice a fleeting tinge of sadness in her face? Subhra, however, flipped back to her mischievous normalcy at once. 'Are you missing a wife?'

Sriman was really caught on the wrong foot.

'Tell me, I'll arrange one for you.'

'No way, madam. Can't afford to marry at this moment,' Sriman said shyly.

Subhra broke out into laughter again. Was she camouflaging her sadness too?

'If any of your friends meets with an accident or falls ill, please don't hesitate to bring them to our hospital. I'll do my best. Okay?' Subhra said with a reassuring warmth.

'That would help a lot,' Sriman responded frankly.

Suddenly, Subhra held Sriman in a passionate embrace. Sriman was aghast. Her heady fragrance, coupled with the tremulous nubility of her touch, was overpowering. But Sriman nudged himself back to his senses by recalling Sirius and what Bishan-da had learnt from his Gajen uncle, the necessity of maintaining a self-effacing lightness, along with Sirius's ethereality. He regained his poise as he remembered Mrittika's swarthy face.

'You're a good soul, madam. Never let this sanctity die. Otherwise, I won't be able to introduce you to Mrittika,' Sriman said to Subhra.

'Who's Mrittika? Your girlfriend?'

'No, my pole star,' Sriman told her as he keyed the bike to start.

'When are you introducing me to her?'

'Maybe when she complains of pain in the underbelly,' Sriman smiled.

Subhra broke into a roll of laughter.

# 12

The wanton ways of the weather that have affected almost all places around the world are telling upon Kolkata as well. Sudden spells of shattering rains, or incessant downpours that were limited to the rainy season, have become an everyday affair. It is a nightmare the people of Kolkata are gradually learning to live with alongside other evils that cripple their beloved city.

These unpredictable showers, however, do some good too. They feed the water bodies of the city. The Kolkata Corporation map is dotted with as many as five thousand ponds, including Sendighi, Laldighi, Raidighi, Kamaladighi, Goldighi, Shibganga, Hedua and more. Sendighi, the oldest among these, is located at Boral near Garia, in the southern fringes of Kolkata. Relics of the Pal, Sen, and Maurya eras have been discovered from its vicinity. A member of the Sen dynasty had dug this lake to attain virtuous karma. The ancient temple dedicated to Tripurasundari is nearby, where Sati's left palm is believed to have fallen and, hence, attracts humongous footfalls.

At 6 in the morning, Sendighi was beaming under the effect of the ongoing spell of rains. The clouds had splayed their reflections over the lake which appeared recumbent in peaceful placidity.

Sendighi had an unfamiliar visitor at this early hour: Mrittika. With puddles of darkness below the eyes and a bluish contusion on the lips, Mrittika was a stark contrast to the unblemished elegance of the lake. Residues of sleepless nights, these aberrations hinted at some inner turmoil. Mrittika, for the last couple of days, had been disturbed over the issue of Bubka's custody. The anxiety over the uncertainty of getting her son back had been gnawing at her vitals.

The tranquility of the cloud-clad water was having a restful effect on Mrittika, making her oblivious of her sadness for the time being. Last night, even at work, her mind had been racing back to her son. She had felt like running off to where he was, into that house, at that ungodly hour. She was even ready to don the docile wife's mantle again. But she could not accept the thought of having to share her bed with Supriyo once more.

Mrittika panicked that Bubka would like to stay back with his father. That house pampered him with luxuries that could easily lead him astray—the lure of material goodies, overindulgent adults, none to put pressure on him for studying, and no routine.

Nevertheless, Mrittika was certain of one thing. The day Bubka developed a mind of his own, he would realise the ordeal his mother had undergone, her sacrifices, her love for him. He would invariably come back to her that day. But what if the idleness of his paternal side rubbed off on him by then?

Mrittika had been earning and saving only for Bubka's higher education. She must get him admitted in a reputed college. He may have to go outside this state, maybe overseas, for a job. She was ready to accept even that, to see him established. These were the dreams that her reality thrived on.

With the rains rushing in, Mrittika killed the Fast Move and Quick March apps. Passengers do not book bike rides in the rain. She opened Guava instead. This food-delivery app proved handy during such calamities. She must ensure a steady inflow of money. She must stay afloat, at any cost. For Bubka.

Mrittika hurriedly offered her daily oblation to God. She could not afford to waste time. Piping hot chapatis or parathas along with a delectable vegetable curry from the neighbourhood shop, rounded off with a cup of cutting chai, would make a wholesome breakfast. But she avoided eating at the shop today. 'Madan-da, parcel please, two parathas and veg curry,' she yelled to the owner-cum-cook who ran the shanty.

'Got it,' Madan Barui replied, without lifting his head. 'Will two parathas do?' he enquired, on second thoughts.

'You must have three at least, along with a boiled egg, after an exhausting night.'

'That would be too much, Madan-da,' Mrittika replied, sounding unintentionally brusque to her own ears. The Bubka issue had started to have a spillover effect, she realised.

'Huh, she will run all through the night and vent her anger on me in the morning!' Madan Barui muttered in a voice too low for Mrittika's ears. 'Little lady with giant attitude!' Accustomed to Mrittika's ways, he did not budge from his decision of parcelling three parathas while putting in a banana instead of the boiled egg. Nobody with a sentient heart could miss the oodles of fondness for the hapless girl oozing from the wrinkles of the fifty-something Madan's face.

Mrittika keyed her bike to a homeward start. On the way, she picked up some curd. She would reach home, have breakfast, bathe, and then be bed-bound. She wouldn't get up before dada-boudi called her for lunch. Then, a brief leisure of post-lunch gaming on the phone until sleep took over.

Mrittika was up at 6 in the evening. Paying a hasty evening courtesy to Lord Shiva, she was ready in two shakes. She had earned nearly Rs 500 by 8:30 pm. A handsome profit. A few more deliveries and she would be entitled to an incentive of Rs 300. Almost immediately, a new order arrived, for ten Bull Fighters. The gadget-obsessed, spoilt brats of rich men guzzled this intoxication, particularly on weekend nights. One carafe was enough to keep sleep at bay for the night, setting the body on a whirligig. No matter what you did—play games, watch movies, race along the streets on incredibly expensive motorcycles—sleep would not dare play spoilsport.

Mrittika took the flyover for Bagha Jatin after crossing Dhalai Bridge in Garia. A cellular notification had intimated her that the item was available in the ordered quantity in one of the shops in the plush market on the left at the end of the flyover.

On reaching the pick-up location, Mrittika quoted the order number. 'We don't have ten, you've to manage with eight,' the scrawny guy who came out from inside the shop said.

'But the order is for ten and you had accepted the order because you had the stock, right?' Mrittika felt anger rising within her.

'I was expecting to procure it by the time you arrived,' the man was obviously lying. 'Make do with eight,' he repeated.

'Are you gaslighting me?' Mrittika was furious. But she checked herself and spoke with a pseudo gentility, 'See, mister, this is not done. I must deliver ten. You must arrange for that.'

But Mrittika's insistence had no effect on the man.

Moving out of the man's earshot, Mrittika rang the Bengaluru call centre of Guava, their go-to number in crisis. A man responded in a sluggish voice, garbling something like, 'Let me check', before disconnecting the call.

But Bengaluru did not call back even after half an hour. In the meantime, the customer called. Mrittika explained the situation and requested him to manage with eight instead of ten.

'This is our fun time, why compromise? You are bound to provide what I've ordered, nothing less than ten will do, you understand, bitch?' The man's sozzled lewdness bespoke such toxic derision that Mrittika was mortified. She rang Bengaluru and went the whole hog again. Though colleagues, the people on the other end were machines devoid of fellow feelings for delivery workers like her who sweated it out on the streets. This one too blurted out the stock reply, 'Let me check,' and disconnected.

'Please cancel the order, sir,' Mrittika pleaded in desperation to the customer who had started using expletives.

'Keep your nonsense to yourself. You've already spoilt our night, slut. Wait till I screw you royally,' came the reply in obscene abusive language.

For these men, the delivery rider was a sub-human menial, deserving only the filthiest abuse, particularly so if it was a woman.

Mrittika rang Bengaluru again. After repeating everything again, she told the person on the other end to get the order cancelled, or else, refer a shop where the required quantity of the energy drink was available. 'How can I guarantee the other shop would have ten of it?' the call centre executive reasoned.

It was a matter without any solution. Bengaluru would go on arguing adamantly, meanwhile this shop owner would keep pressuring her to manage with the depleted stock, and all the while she would have to be at the receiving end of abuses from a bunch of spoilt brats. Yet she must maintain courtesy and her cool. Mrittika was sorely missing Sriman. But he too was out on delivery. She did not want to burden him with her problems.

The clock had struck 10. The prolonged deadlock had sapped all interest in her to carry on with the issue. Though Sriman's suggestion had made her lose her cool the other night at Nimtala Ghat, it was now the thing she was ready to give her right arm for. She wanted this nightmare to end as early as possible so that she could head for a profound slumber in the warmth of her bed in the cosy comfort of her home.

Exhausted by anger, anxiety, and annoyance, Mrittika bought herself a soft drink from a shop nearby.

She had barely taken a sip when a sudden sensation at her feet startled her. A couple of kittens were playing there. With a fetish for the female foot, both were snuggling along hers in their sprightly frolic. She was enjoying it, sitting on the uppermost rung of the steps to the shop while savouring the drink. The kittens, emboldened by the indulgent access, had climbed up her knees and nestled on her thighs. She was delightfully intrigued at their confident ease with a stranger. Suddenly, her phone rang. Sriman.

'You'll live long,' she said delightfully.

'What have I done to deserve this curse?' Sriman asked jokingly.

Mrittika narrated the whole thing. 'Be it the company, or the customer, we are nothing better than animals to anybody. I am so frustrated that I have decided to follow your theory, go home and go to bed straightaway. All other things can wait till the morning.'

Sriman was pleasantly surprised at Mrittika's sudden volte face. 'No, I can't be so cool when in such a miserable mess.'

The kittens had begun to fight, emitting angry snarls. Mrittika gave a strong tap on the tail of one of them. It set the cat fuming. Suddenly, it lunged at her and scratched the bare part of her neck. Mrittika sprang up on an impulse, slapped both the kittens, throwing them away from her. They ran off. Her phone dropped down in the commotion. Thankfully, the call to Sriman was not disconnected.

'Hello, hello … are you there? Everything okay? What's that noise?' Mrittika could hear the tinny sound of Sriman's worried voice.

'I've been scratched by a cat. Come at once!' she stated in almost teary desperation.

'My God, how?'

'They were playing nearby … come soon!' Mrittika disconnected the call.

Sriman took a U-turn in the direction of the hospital, after asking Somnath to join them there. Mrittika had received the anti-tetanus injection by the time he arrived. Two more shots were to be given.

'Are the injections essential?' Mrittika panicked.

'Yes, the scratch is deep. Why take unnecessary risk?' the doctor tried to allay her fear with a smile.

'My God, it's paining like hell … ouch!' Mrittika grabbed Sriman's arm with force.

'Be brave, Karate Queen. Just imagine you are landing a powerful kick on the face of the customer who has insulted you.'

Having administered the shots, the doctor left after advising them to wait for half an hour or so.

'Have this, you'll feel strong,' Sriman offered her a *sandesh* from his satchel.

'I *am* quite strong …'

'Is it? Let's leave that for some other day … for now, have this, you'll feel better … forget the incentive,' Sriman advised her.

Mrittika gestured to Sriman, to hand her his water bottle. As he complied with her demand, he could sense that even a gesture as trifling as this was enough to moisten the heart of this girl and bring her out of her hard crust. The most intimate chords of this girl, in moments like this, played a tender symphony. But Sriman was besotted with her ostensible imperiousness too. 'What did you decide about Bubka?' he asked, to conjure Mrittika's arrogant avatar.

Mrittika told him about her plans in detail.

'That's like a level-headed girl. But my Akashganga proposal was to help you have the options you urgently need ... Bubka will like it too, I am sure ... and you'll get to know Bishan-da.' Sriman delineated the delights of life at Akashganga, persuading her to shift to that house.

'Problem, *bhaijaan*? Problem, *behenji*?' Somnath breezed in, Jaideb in tow. Despite his many faults, Somnath had this effortless ability of striking up kinship with rank strangers. Mrittika had become his 'behenji' in the first meeting itself. Not everybody welcomed his overzealous bonhomie, but that hardly bothered Somnath.

Jaideb rushed off to meet the doctor and returned with positive tidings. 'All's okay, doc said.'

'Yes, I am okay, no need to worry,' Mrittika had regained her confidence. 'Let's leave.'

'What about a cup of steaming tea before we start for home?' Somnath proposed on coming out of the hospital. Everyone readily agreed. Sriman sat down on a bench by the tea stall, gesturing to Mrittika to sit down beside him.

Somnath never ran out of scoops. This time it was about Yellow Shirts reducing base pay.

'We're already underpaid. Are they trying to make us work for free?' Sriman asked.

'We won't accept if they cut it down further,' Jaideb was furious.

'I've also heard that Aladdin is acquiring our company for six crores,' Somnath almost whispered to Sriman in conspiratorial confidentiality.

'They're what? Impossible!' Sriman was taken aback.

'It's right from the horse's mouth. Haven't you noticed Horizon's share prices soaring madly of late?' Somnath asked, maintaining the confidentiality.

Sriman was hardly interested in the share market. Somnath dabbled in shares, health insurances too. A single source of income was no longer enough to make both ends meet.

'We must have a joint discussion,' Sriman posited.

'Sitting for a discussion would mean losing trips,' Somnath countered, 'and—'

'Oil prices have risen steeply, but the company is paying us the same old rate. How can we carry on?' Jaideb added before Somnath could continue.

'Accidents too are on the rise … two of our riders have died in the last few months,' Mrittika joined the discussion.

'True,' Somnath agreed. 'The dead can't come to the rescue; their families must be given a one-time compensation.'

'We are glorified as delivery partners, yet we stand almost bankrupt while the company rakes in billions,' said Jaideb.

'Partner, my foot,' Somnath said, 'we are basically pimps!'

'Absolutely. We better learn to live with the reality that we are labourers selling our labour,' Mrittika said ruefully.

'These are strategies to ensure that we don't form unions,' Somnath raised his voice.

'Just imagine,' Jaideb propounded, 'I meet with an accident on my way home after duty. How's the company going to compensate me?'

'They won't,' Somnath said candidly.

'We need to voice these issues at a proper forum,' Sriman submitted.

'Let's decide a date that suits all,' Jaideb suggested.

'We can never have a consensus date,' Mrittika specified. 'Let the interested ones among us sit down first, then we spread the word through small gatherings.'

'Exactly my point,' Jaideb concurred. 'Our kind of work won't allow all of us to gather at the same place and time … so, let's first assemble those who can and then we spread the message.

'All of us wait at some place or the other between deliveries,' Jaideb resumed after a pause. 'We must utilise those breaks for discussion. I often wait at Kantapukur.'

Somnath nodded, 'Yes, I wait at Rashbehari, Sriman at Hatibagan, Anup at Salt Lake.'

'But when and where are we meeting?' Mrittika said.

'Akashganga,' Sriman blurted out spontaneously, eyes fixed on Somnath.

'But is your Bishan-da going to allow that?' Somnath asked.

'Why must he? We would be meeting inside our apartment,' Sriman stated.

'It's done. Let's leave now.' Mrittika got up. Glancing at her phone, she found the Bull Fighter order still pending.

Somnath and Jaideb left.

'I will drop you at your place,' Sriman told Mrittika.

'That would be a lot of help. The pain has recurred,' she said.

'Must buy paracetamol on the way,' replied Sriman.

The roads bore a deserted look. It did not take more than twelve minutes to reach Mrittika's place. They would have reached even earlier if the conked-out truck had not created the snarl at the crossing of Dhalai Bridge.

'Hope you don't have fever?' Sriman enquired.

'Can't say,' Mrittika replied, placing the reverse of her palm on her forehead. 'Could you check? … please.'

Sriman sensed a silent tremor inside. He was startled at his sudden wobbliness resulting from Mrittika's request. As he touched her neck to check the temperature, discreetly though, he could feel his escalating palpitations.

'Is it hot?'

'Bit feverish, nothing to worry. Take paracetamol if necessary.'

'What if I fall asleep?'

'Then it's better to have it earlier. Want another *sandesh*?'

'Are you a sweets-vendor or what?' Mrittika smiled.

'This one would be the last, I had kept it for you only,' Sriman said shyly.

Mrittika took the sweet and the pill together with a generous gulp of water. 'Feeling better,' she beamed.

Sriman smiled too. 'Check your phone, the problem must have been resolved by now,' he said optimistically.

'That would be great,' she began checking her phone hopefully. 'Heehaw! … order cancelled!' she almost leapt in joy.

Sriman guffawed at her childishness.

'You are a godsend!' she exclaimed with eyes moistened by relief.

# 13

The meeting finally happened. Not at Akashganga, but at Mathuresh's place.

The Lunar Pod, the attic of Akashganga, was the initial choice, but was ruled out for its cellular accessibility. The proceedings could not be impeded by phone calls and messages. The sequestered and unventilated storeroom on the ground floor, which Bishan believed to have originally been the labour room, based on its resemblance to the one at Jorasanko Thakurbari, was the second choice. Though mobile phone connectivity was almost nil in the room, it too was precluded because it could not accommodate more than seven people, while ten would be a suffocating jostle.

The room to the west of Bishan's on the first floor would have been ideal with its twelve-inch-deep walls which did not allow the penetration of cellular signals. Bishan would not have objected either. But Sriman did not want their meeting to be an intrusion on Bishan-da's privacy.

'Hold it in the club,' Mathuresh proposed.

'Here!' Sriman made a mental survey. 'What if somebody objects?'

'Why would anyone object? You aren't doing anything objectionable,' Mathuresh reasoned.

'But we would be discussing our demands as delivery partners. We can't refuse a club member if he wants to join, even if he is not a gig worker … can we?'

'I get your point,' Mathuresh nodded. 'It would be awkward for both you and the member concerned.

'Hold it at my place, okay?' Mathuresh said after a brief pause.

'You mean at the workshop where you make idols? That's a lot of space,' Sriman was relieved at finally getting a venue that fit the bill. 'That would really help. But won't that obstruct your work?'

'Now that Jagaddhatri Puja is over, Kumortuli is seeing a lull. We are gradually starting to make Saraswati idols. A two-three-hour meeting would hardly matter,' Mathuresh assured him. 'You may even hold it in our house,' he added, taking a brief breather. 'Yes, that would be perfect. Mobile phones ring inside the studio, but not in the rooms on the north of our house. They have fifteen-inch walls.'

Not ten, but a total of twelve delivery riders, across all delivery zones of the city, turned up. Mrittika was there too, as a mark of solidarity.

'Friends, all of us feel it is high time the company raised our base pay. But how do we convey it to the company?' Nasim Ali, who did not like to mince words, set the tone of the meeting in his booming baritone. 'All of us must raise our voice so loudly that it rattles even the head office at Noida.' The earnestness of feelings, articulated in Nasim's deep voice, struck a chord.

'Petrol has become too costly, but the company hasn't raised even a paisa since the beginning,' Vignesh observed.

'What they are paying per kilometre is less than even the price of a *phuchka* in front of Victoria Memorial,' Somnath had hit pay dirt with his jibe which was greeted with a huge applause.

'We must include the maintenance cost of the vehicle too,' he added.

'*Sahi bola, dada*,' Vignesh concurred, 'you are absolutely right.'

'I travelled from Ultadanga to Joka the other day on a delivery for just Rs 225. Did not get any order on the way back. I could not recover even the cost of my journey,' Anup said.

Anup got a unanimous applause. He was right. Many of them were suffering losses, when the income was so low.

'We are supposed to earn Rs 55 to 58 per delivery, but we hardly get that. Must be some anomaly in the system.'

'Anomaly or scam?' Somnath quipped.

'They've bugged the system to cheat us,' Jaideb remarked.

'We've to counter them tactfully, we must learn how to create apps or programmes,' Anup said. 'We can consult some technical expert.'

'Right, I think we should consult those who know computer programming,' Abir seconded Anup.

'When I had lodged a complaint against a customer's indecent behaviour, no action was taken,' Mrittika recounted her experience. 'Instead, my ratings have been reduced based on the customer's false complaint, without any investigation.'

A few of the members agreed with her.

'We must demand higher wages and fight for it too,' Sriman stressed on a vital point. 'Two of us broke their arms on the way to a delivery last month, and the company did not pay any compensation. This must be the experience of others as well.'

'*Sahi bol rahe ho, dada*! There have been deaths too.'

'They never stand by us,' Sriman raised his voice.

'They are just making money ... *Sirf kamaai ho raha hai, kamaai*.'

'*Kadam uthhana padega, bhaiyon* ...' Nasim urged upon the audience. 'We must take action, brothers!'

'*Uthhana padega*,' came the unified response.

Mathuresh gifted miniatures of Jagaddhatri idols to all after the meeting. 'It's lovely, dada!' Nasim could not help exclaiming.

Mathuresh was glad to see Mrittika. 'Mrittika should be with us round the clock. Our whole existence thrives on *mrittika*, after all,' Mathuresh smiled at his own pun. He gave her a Saraswati idol too, for Bubka.

The three hours of the meeting glided by imperceptibly. Evening had descended by the time the meeting ended. The last vestiges of the twilight had melded with the darkness of the evening. Both Sriman and Mrittika were to set out for their night shifts after having dinner in Shiuli's presence. Sriman had to brief Bishan-da about the meeting before that.

Bishan Basu was watching the sky through his telescope.

'This is Mrittika, she's a driver-partner with Guava, with Fast Move and Quick March also,' Sriman introduced Mrittika.

Bishan watched Mrittika closely, a mystic hint of a smile on his lips. The nuanced grammar of his glance was enough to evince the affection he felt for her in the first meeting itself.

'Look carefully, Sriman. You'll see Sirius, Orion,' Bishan said, placing his eyes on the telescope.

Sriman looked at the sky with his bare eyes which were quite accustomed to recognising effortlessly nowadays.

'Look at the centre, Aldebaran … the Butterfly Cluster … you won't see them this clearly any other time … that's the Capella,' Bishan was naming one astral wonder after another in his excitement.

'Sriman, come, take a look, bring your friend too,' Bishan invited them, moving away from the telescope. 'Come, Mrittika, let's introduce you to the Pleiades,' Bishan was smiling.

'No, I want to begin with the Aldebaran,' Mrittika said.

Bishan looked into the telescope again. He realigned it for a better focus. 'Look now.'

A whole new world opened up before Mrittika. An ocean populated with stars and planets. No one else mattered here, not Bubka, not Sriman, nobody. She seemed to be mesmerised, a whirlpool of names eddying in her head: Sirius-Aldebaran-Pleiades-Orion-Butterfly. They were inviting her. She was caught in a daze even after disengaging her eyes from the telescope.

'How was it?' Bishan smiled.

'Amazing! I was hooked to the Pleiades,' Mrittika said. 'The clots on the moon looked so clear!'

'I think you know the love story of the Moon and the Pleiades?' Bishan asked.

'Never heard of it,' Mrittika and Sriman replied in the same voice.

'Strange! Your grannies didn't tell you this story?' Bishan shook his head with incredulity. 'Okay, listen—'

'Love story of astral bodies! Unbelievable!' Mrittika was genuinely surprised.

'Why unbelievable? If trees, rivers, mountains, jungles, the sun, and the moon can have their stories, why can't the stars?' Bishan was smiling. 'Actually, we humans have been brooding over the elements since time immemorial … Also, before the

TV and the mobile phone, there was boundless time at our disposal. We were procuring fodder for the mind.

'There was a king called Daksha. He was seeking husbands for his twenty-seven daughters who were twenty-seven stars. Who could be a more eligible groom for them than the Moon? He ruled over the night sky, stayed awake and guarded the stars through the night. So, Daksha offered his twenty-seven daughters to the Moon. "Look, son, you have to treat my twenty-seven daughters equally, love them equally," he stated categorically to the Moon.

'All of Daksha's daughters were beautiful, but the Moon was besotted with Rohini, who was the prettiest. He ignored his father-in-law's instruction and spent his time in Rohini's passionate proximity making love to her alone. Deeply hurt by their husband's discrimination, Rohini's sisters complained to their father.

'Daksha warned his son-in-law, "See, son, I am warning you again, love all my daughters without making any discrimination because none of them loves you any less than Rohini."

'But the Moon, besotted with Rohini, was loath to heed his father-in-law's advice. His other wives complained to their father again. Daksha was livid. He gave his final warning to the Moon. But the Moon continued his love life with Rohini with unabashed intensity. "May Plague befall you," Daksha imprecated his son-in-law.

'The Moon started waning night by night. He tried several desperate measures, including holding *yajna*s, but couldn't get rid of the degenerating effect of the curse. The lunar deprecation resulted in the drooping of crops, the loss of vitality among animals.

'When the gods asked him about the reason behind his mysterious fading night after night, the Moon recounted everything. While the gods snubbed the Moon, they visited Daksha to seek pardon for him.

'Daksha said, "There might be a way out. If the Moon stays true to all his wives, and if he bathes in Prabhas, the foremost pilgrimage of the river Saraswati, he'll from now on keep waning for one half of every month and keep growing in the other."

'You'll find this story in the Shalya Parva of the *Mahabharata*,' Bishan said, concluding his narration that had held Sriman and Mrittika in thrall.

'But this is not entirely fiction, it has elements of astronomy and science,' Bishan pointed out.

'Is it?' Both his auditors were astounded.

'Yes, I believe Daksha is the axis of the sun. His twenty-seven daughters are the stars spread around the sun … Ashwini, Bharani, Krittika, Rohini … even the number twenty-seven has its own logic,' Bishan explained.

'You know the Moon rotates on its own axis, from the west to the east daily as the 127th fragment of that rotational cycle … that 127th fragment is the chamber of each of the wives of the Moon,' he explained, trying to make the complex arithmetic as intelligible as possible. 'The moon enters a new chamber every day. Its rotational cycle ends when it covers all those twenty-seven rooms. Each room is marked by the diagram of a star … that's how date and time were calculated in the past.' Bishan paused. He was trying to recall something even as he was explaining this.

'Well, that ablution at Prabhas … Prabhas means the sun in the context of this story. Prabhas is linked to the imparting of light. Who is our ultimate source of light?'

'The Sun,' Sriman answered.

'Absolutely right,' Bishan was glad. 'It indicates that the astronomers of ancient India knew that the Moon's radiance was courtesy the Sun's glow.'

'Yes,' Sriman nodded.

'You will find this story in the Rig Veda. So, we come across a lot of astronomical facts in this love story, isn't it?' Bishan asked one of his rhetorical questions.

'Amazing! Never heard such a story before,' Mrittika said.

Bishan was too engrossed to register Mrittika's remark. 'Many more facts of astronomy can be linked to the Moon-Rohini love story,' he continued. 'For instance, Rahu is the point where the solar and the lunar axis converge, Ketu is the other, but they aren't constant. They are gliding towards the west along the solar axis. I'll explain this complex mathematics later.'

'Yes, Bishan-da, that would be so different from our usual drudgery,' Sriman said brightly.

'Let me tell you another story. This is about the same Daksha and Usha, one of his daughters.'

Sriman's curiosity piqued.

'Usha or Saraswati was exceptionally beautiful. Even her father Prajapati was smitten by her beauty.' The curiosity of his listeners had prompted Bishan to narrate another story. 'Prajapati assumed the appearance of a stag and chased Usha who was running away in the form of a doe. The stag got hold of the doe and forced himself upon her.

'Extremely livid at Prajapati, the gods decided to punish him severely. After a lot of deliberations, they amassed their collective angst and created the strong and valiant Bhootvaan. They had no doubt that he was the right choice as Prajapati's nemesis.

'Bhootvaan, in turn, sought blessings from the gods to make him the ruler of the animal world. The blessing was granted. From then onwards, Bhootvaan came to be known as Pashupati, the ruler of the animals.

'The battle began. Prajapati was killed by Pashupati's arrow. After this, Bhootvaan took refuge in the sky along with Prajapati and his daughter, Usha. Prajapati took the form of a stag on reaching the sky. Pashupati, his assassin, became the hunter-killer of the stag, while Usha became Rohini, the star.

'Actually, the stag-like avatar of Prajapati is the other form of the Orion. The three stars across Prajapati's waist represent Pashupati's arrow. Three bright and two dim stars on Prajapati's waist comprise the star called Ilvaka. The three stars resembling Pashupati's three-pronged arrow that killed Prajapati, point directly at Rohini.'

Done with the story telling, Bishan said, 'The exciting narratives spawned by our saints in Vedic times are a curious blend of science and fiction. They have been repeatedly recounted by generations down the ages, yet they continue to enthral us.'

'How could they have such incredible foresight?' Mrittika was astonished.

'Our Vedic saints, my dear, were the privileged class. They didn't have to engage in physical labour. Nor was there any distraction to muddle their minds, unlike today. So, they had all the time to devote to the realisation of their intellectual faculty,' Bishan explained.

'Another thing,' Bishan felt excited while speaking about this. 'Most of the stories in the Puranas are about the triumph of good over evil. The effort you people are putting in towards redressing all wrongs, trying to bring about a healthy system, that too is a way of defeating evil. You are the virtual gods of today,' Bishan said with a proud smile directed at Sriman and Mrittika.

Sriman was fascinated by Bishan's stories. Why didn't Bishan-da tell these stories earlier? Sriman was surprised. But it was time for him and Mrittika to take his leave.

'We must get going, Bishan-da, call of duty,' Sriman said, sad to interrupt Bishan who seemed eager to embark on another narrative odyssey.

'Oh … duty! Yes, duty comes first,' Bishan replied, seemingly engrossed in a dream beyond everything mundane.

***

The news was made public a week later, lending validity to Somnath's scoop. Aladdin had acquired their company Horizon, for 650 crores. This meant Horizon from now onwards would be adding a wider range of deliverables to its inventory, from veggies to stationery. Horizon had launched its new app Foreman after the acquisition. Another MNC, named Cameron, would be entering the Indian market.

The ways of the new management made the likes of Somnath, Vignesh, Jaideb jittery. They suspected that Foreman was conspiring to cut down the delivery riders' pay.

'What makes you think so?' Sriman asked.

'They are collecting every possible detail of the staff, including their earnings. This is insider news,' Somnath said from the other end of the phone.

'But that does not necessarily mean they are planning a pay cut,' Sriman inferred.

'Not just that, they are on a recruitment drive as well, so when supply exceeds demand, it is bound to affect our income,' Somnath specified the rationale behind their suspicion.

'Just wait and watch how many stay on, and however cruel the company is, it must survive on the labour of people like you and me,' Sriman said.

'Bloody bloodsuckers,' Somnath dissented. 'They've acquired the app, and now they would be banking on the goodwill of the company, only to devour us little by little.' Somnath sounded worried.

'We must be alert,' Sriman heard himself say by instinct, though he was not on the same page with Somnath on the issue.

'They're devising new strategies every day to cheat us,' Somnath continued.

'We too must work out new ways to neutralise them … even the most terrifying zombie has a weak spot,' Sriman tried to breathe hope into his friend.

'Yes, the balls, we must give those a stinging squeeze, ha, ha!' Somnath laughed with unbridled abandon.

# 14

Rumours tend to spread incredibly fast. The news of the meeting held at Mathuresh's place had become common knowledge with greater alacrity than expected. Any delivery rider colleague Sriman came across ever since sympathised with the cause and expressed eagerness to be counted in.

Lately, delivery riders of Guava based in Bally had stalled deliveries there for a couple of days so that their demands reached their bosses. Stationing themselves at all strategic points, they prevented errant colleagues from performing delivery. Any rider found to be flouting the whip was stopped on the way, sensitised against breaching the unity, and made to desist. 'We are no less destitute than you are. When we can wait, why can't you, that too for merely a couple of days?' No political leader was allowed to interfere in the demonstration of disapproval. The whole thing was coordinated over the phone.

Sriman was so very impressed that he registered himself immediately with the Guava app. He now had the option of serving both the apps. In case he missed a Yellow Shirts assignment in the morning, he compensated it with a Guava assignment later in the day.

The team of twelve delivery riders, including Sriman, learnt the deets from the boys of Bally. Their second meeting was arranged at 10 in the morning, in the inner courtyard of a medium-sized factory near Nagerbazar on Jessore Road. Pradip Mondal, a delivery rider of the area, supervised all arrangements.

Sriman had come here two years ago. Back then, it was a factory of spare parts for bicycles. 'When did this become a godown?' he asked.

'Early this year,' Pradip said.

Sriman felt sad. One after another small to medium-sized factories were succumbing to the unhealthy competition in the market. They were either being converted into warehouses of commodities or into skyscrapers.

'Soon, no small or medium factory would be left in this country, the bigger ones will have eaten them up. Otherwise, they'll become storehouses like this, and we'll be carrying their products on our motorbikes,' Sriman smiled sadly at Pradip.

'Right,' Pradip acquiesced. 'A few days ago, the hosiery mill nearby closed down.'

'Let's start the meeting, brothers,' Vignesh signalled the members to assemble. They formed a circle around him in the courtyard of the factory.

'We are in a hurry ... *iss liye, humko* meeting *jaldi khatam karna padega* ... all of us have to go to work ... *ab apna apna* demand *bataiye* ... speak up,' Vignesh ran his glance across all the expectant faces.

'The minimum pay must be raised,' Sanjay proposed.

'How much?' Vignesh asked.

'Twenty-eight rupees ... at least,' came the reply.

'No, it should be thirty-five rupees,' Abir said.

'They won't pay us that much, let's demand a little less,' Anup said.

'They must raise the per-kilometre pay, fifteen rupees minimum,' Sushanta proffered.

'What do you think, they'll give us whatever we demand? They'll grant ten rupees max,' Sanjay said practically.

'Let's keep the demand of minimum pay to thirty-two rupees and per-kilometre fees to twelve, or else, thirty and ten,' Subrata suggested.

Almost all the issues that had come up in the first meeting were largely raised in the current meeting.

'*Dekho bhaiyyon*, we've raised these demands earlier too,' Vignesh said, '*lekin unhone dhyan diya hi nahin* ... since they paid no heed to our demands, there's no other option but to cease work.'

'You have our full support ... Horizon *aur* Foreman *ke taraf se aap logon ko pura* support *milega*,' Nasim declared.

Sriman's thoughts strayed to Mrittika. What would she have said had she not been down with viral fever?

'Well, we can't say that the company is sitting idle. It had arranged vaccination for us during Covid, as well as accident insurance. I hear they are about to introduce a bunch of new facilities for us … but we must make them hear our demands,' Sanjay pointed out.

'So, we should be grateful to the company for the miserable pay? … Don't worry, with the stupendous price rise we're witnessing, that measly amount would soon prove inadequate,' Bikram sneered at Sanjay's loyalty to the company. 'As for the vaccination, it was in their interest … otherwise, customers wouldn't be accepting food packets from us,' Bikram added.

Sriman could not accept Bikram's view. With nerves agitated by nightlong work, he simply could not bear a cockily aggressive attack on the simple and innocent Sanjay.

'Well, Sanjay didn't say anything wrong. He simply spoke his mind. You shouldn't have …' Sriman stopped midway. His uncharacteristically angry outburst had surprised everyone.

Sriman broke the silence himself. 'We must be vocal in our protest against the company's malpractices. We must speak out, but we won't do anything that could make the company withdraw its business from these parts.'

'That's what I had exactly meant,' Sanjay admitted.

'So, should we go ahead with the strike or not?' Vignesh asked generally.

He got no reply.

'Let's convey our demands to the company first,' Sriman said. 'We go ahead with the strike if ...'

'A group of chicken hearts!' Nasim was exasperated.

'As of now, the majority is against the strike,' Vignesh summed up.

'We should send the letter first,' Sriman suggested.

Everybody left for work at the end of the meeting. Sriman returned to Akashganga. He had bathed before leaving. He would have lunch and then a sound siesta.

The carry-home gist of the meeting was that despite their eagerness to fight the company's injustices, boys like Sanjay, Anup, Sushanta, Abir, with a background of work at Yellow Shirts, were more interested in engaging in a discussion over their demands.

Sriman began a hypothetical argument with them.

'What if the company refuses the demands?'

'They're bound to accept, at least some of the demands ...'

'If they don't?'

'That's absurd!'

'In case they don't?'

'We would convey our demands again honestly but clearly.'

'We must make them understand how helpless we are ...'

So, this group wanted an amicable discussion. Sriman might be a little more vocal than them, but he knew that he belonged to this coterie.

What about the other faction? The one that comprised Nasim, Jaideb, Bikram, and probably Somnath as well; those who worked for Horizon and Foreman. Sriman imagined a similar exchange with that group too.

'What if the company doesn't give in?'

'Strike ... strike ... strike ...'

'If they don't accept in spite of that?'

'They must.'

'If they don't?'

'Deliveries stop, godowns and hubs close down ... we give them a tough time.'

Sriman was fast asleep before reaching even the middle of the argument.

An e-mail was shot off to the company mentioning the demands. The foremost demand was for raising the minimum pay to thirty-five rupees and the per-kilometre perk to ten rupees.

The bosses at Noida had reportedly woken up to the gravity of the situation on learning of the meeting. It would be a crisis if deliveries came to a standstill during the festive season. The company could incur huge losses.

The Peoples' Officer, Ramesh Jain, arrived in Kolkata the next day itself. On reaching the Salt Lake office, he wanted to meet Sanjay, Anup, Sushanta, Abir, and Sriman.

'I want to interact with people from my own company, think about their problems. What do I care for the staff of other companies? *Unn logon se humein koi lenadena nahin hai* … they're outsiders,' Jain reasoned.

'But they are with us in this, we've discussed everything with them,' objected Sriman. 'They are already here, waiting outside.'

'*Ho sakta hai, aap sab ek hain, lekin* … they don't belong to our company,' Jain was adamant.

Sanjay, Anup, Abir, Sushanta kept mum. Sriman assumed that they didn't want to create a ruckus over this us-and-them issue. '*Ek minute*,' Sriman came out to inform his compatriots waiting outside.

'Dada, *yeh mamuli issue* … you all get going with the meeting,' Nasim said.

The discussion began with very basic demands: three t-shirts in place of two per year, a raincoat per year, along with gum boots. The last two were essential appendages without which it was difficult to survive the increasingly humid and scalding summer of Kolkata or its waterlogged streets in the rainy season.

'Sir, we need a sleeved vest in the winter … a white one,' Sanjay said.

Abir seconded him.

'We'll wear the sleeveless uniform of Yellow Shirts over it,' Anup quickly added.

Ramesh Jain's impassive face gave away nothing. He was listening to them attentively, occasionally taking notes too. He seemed to be sympathetic towards the demands.

Tea and refreshments were in abundant supply at frequent intervals. But Sriman and the others were finding it hard to raise the crux of the demands.

'Jain ji …' Sriman, increasingly impatient, addressed the PO.

'*Haan, boliye, dada,*' Jain looked up.

'Our minimum pay must be raised.'

'Yes, and the per-kilometre fee too,' Abir, bucked up by Sriman's move, did not waste time to add.

'Must it be raised?' Jain looked surprised, as if he was hearing the demand for the first time. 'Okay, let's see … how much?'

'We had specified everything in the e-mail,' Sriman replied promptly.

'Sorry, dada, *jaldibaazi mein woh parhna bhool gaya* … you tell me,' Jain was evidently trying to bypass the issue by coming up with excuses.

'Here, please take a look,' Sriman handed a copy of the mail to Jain.

Jain pretended to read attentively. As his eyes navigated the content, his brows took on an irritated wrinkle. 'Base pay thirty-five rupees! Ten rupees per kilometre ... *yeh to bahut zyada ho gaya* ... this is too much.'

Another round of verbal duel ensued. Sriman and the others tried to justify their demand, while Jain kept on countering it.

Suddenly, Jain's phone rang. He went outside the room, virtually whispering into his phone.

He had regained his spirits by the time he came back. '*Haan ji, toh hum kya* discuss *kar rahe thhe*?'

Sriman refreshed Jain's memory.

'Yes, base pay ... but the company pays you fifty-five rupees per delivery. Right?'

Vignesh who was trying to be patient so long could not hold it in any longer. '*Arre, Jain sahab, aaplog samajhte nahin kya*? If you can show me that any of us has been paid fifty-five rupees for any delivery in the last six months, we'll withdraw our demands. But you have to promise that you'll accept all our demands if you can't cite any such instance,' Vignesh said firmly.

Jain, dispirited, mumbled feebly, 'You all don't get the fifty-five rupees? ... Glitch in the system?'

'After all, this system too is devised by you people, *hai na*?' Vignesh was in no mood to desist from his verbal onslaught.

'Okay, I'll inform the head office about everything. Tomorrow, we meet again, 10 am sharp. I have to get back to Delhi in the afternoon.' Jain sounded completely subdued.

When Sriman, Vignesh and the others came out, evening had descended over the city. At least a hundred delivery riders of Yellow Shirts had gathered on the pavement on the other side, avidly waiting to know the outcome of the meeting.

Vignesh spoke aloud over the megaphone. 'The outcome is nothing worth mentioning. The more we tried to make him appreciate our demands, the more he evaded them … we have proposed they can send one of them to be with us on our deliveries all through the day, to verify our meagre earnings.'

'Can't say nothing happened,' Sriman said. 'We've driven home our demand for the base pay, though our reasoning was almost ignored. We've told them categorically that we shall be forced to go on strike if they don't raise the base pay.'

Speaking into the megaphone, Vignesh said, 'We must maintain our unity at any cost, otherwise the paid menials of the company will simply crush us down.'

***

'Good news! The company has accepted your demand for three t-shirts … one of them sleeved, for winter; the demand for raincoat and gum boots are accepted too,' Ramesh Jain tried to begin the second day's meeting on a positive note.

Jain surveyed Sriman and Vignesh briefly before continuing. 'I have told the management the base pay given to my friends is too low as far as their inhuman toil is concerned … I have told them if my friends sit on a strike in such a situation, it would be highly justified. My friends have kept the strike call on hold, at my request, and under the condition that their base pay be increased … So, my friends, let me give you the gladdening news that the management has raised your base pay to twenty-five rupees.'

'We protest,' Sriman shook his head defiantly, 'anything below thirty-five rupees is unacceptable.' The others thumped on the desk in support.

Sriman had started to get the hang of Jain's game; he wanted to wear them down by making them speak continuously. He would say all sorts of hypothetical things, without actually granting anything. The whole thing had turned into a war of nerves.

Twenty-eight rupees, that is what Jain agreed to grant at the end of the meeting. Sriman and the others were ready to accept it if it was raised to thirty rupees. But under no circumstances would they agree to a per-kilometre payment of less than ten rupees. Sriman and Vignesh had a confidential conversation with Jain.

'So, you see that we never get the fifty-five rupees for a delivery,' Sriman said. 'We don't need that much, sir, we would make do with thirty-five rupees.'

'We could do with thirty rupees as base pay along with ten rupees as the per-kilometre charge. If you agree to that, I will try to convince my colleagues,' Vignesh said frankly.

Jain called the Noida office again. But in vain. He came back with a long face. 'This is the festive season, so please don't call a strike this month. I assure you, there'll be some action about your demands by the end of the month.'

Ramesh Jain bought time till the month's end, that is, till the 31st. So, Jain was requesting them to do nothing for the next twenty-six days. He hoped to convince his bosses on returning to Delhi to accept at least some of the pay-related demands, if not all.

Vignesh came back after informing everyone waiting outside. 'Okay, we will wait till month end, but we won't sit for any discussion until our demands are granted,' he told Jain.

***

A couple of days later, Sriman learnt of the impending trouble at Foreman. Somnath informed him that the per-delivery incentive of fifty-five rupees Aladdin used to pay its delivery workers had been reduced to twenty-five overnight, since the acquisition by Foreman. The company had been behaving autocratically ever since it had reduced job openings. Two meetings had been held with the bosses, but they were unwilling to increase even a rupee.

'What do we do now?' Somnath sounded helpless. 'They are going to starve us to death.'

Sriman was at a loss.

'We must stay united … but that won't be easy,' he finally managed to say.

***

Another meeting was convened, this time at the massive campus of the company's store at Kantapukur, a suburb in the southern outskirts of Kolkata.

Apart from Nasim, Bikram, Jaideb, and Somnath, a lot of young faces, mostly in their early twenties, appeared on the designated date and time. Kabul Das and Mohammed Nagib from Tangra were proactive, executing the responsibility of assembling all for the meeting either by contacting them over phone or meeting them personally. Vignesh, Abir, and Sriman too were informed.

'Friends, we had told the company that we don't have any new demand, just maintain the per-delivery incentive we used to get … they didn't listen… we repeated the demand,' Jaideb said.

'They didn't listen even then,' Bikram added.

'So, what's the way out?' Kabul asked.

'Calling a strike is the only way out,' Mohammed Nagib replied.

'Stop delivery, close the stores,' Kabul raised his voice.

They soon devised the route map for the strike. Though Vignesh, Abir, and Sriman did not belong to Foreman, they were given the responsibility of monitoring the activities of the Foreman stores across Kolkata.

'Sriman, you know all the Aladdin warehouses in north Kolkata, so please keep an eye on them,' Kabul said.

'Sure,' Sriman nodded.

Deliveries of Foreman had been stalled for the last three days. The bosses at Bengaluru had never expected such a backlash and a huge loss during the festive season. Their Peoples' Officer, Venkatesh Naidu, who had tried to convince the bosses that it was a hoax, received a severe drubbing from the bosses once the strike became a reality. The PO failed to gauge the dynamics of a highly competitive market which is infested with sharks and alligators, ready to sink their teeth into your flesh.

So, Venkatesh was replaced by Swaminathan. Swaminathan met everyone in the same Kantapukur premises. He asked them to provide him with the address of a place that served quality curd rice. Bikram ran and brought him curd rice from Green Leaf.

Swaminathan's flight was in the evening. In the late afternoon, he declared that the delivery riders would get thirty rupees per delivery from now on. The warehouse premises resounded with a big round of applause.

'If one nudge can make them comply, they'll return to the old rate of fifty-five rupees if we can pressure them further,' Bikram said after Swaminathan's departure.

'*Sahi bola*,' both Mohammed Nagib and Jaideb agreed.

Barely after a day of resuming work, they shot off a new e-mail informing the bosses that they would stop work if sixty rupees was not paid per delivery.

Swaminathan was sent back to negotiate. Another round of talks ensued. At the end of the day, Swaminathan declared that the per-delivery pay would be fixed at rupees forty.

Silence prevailed over the meeting.

'We'll inform you of our decision tomorrow,' Kabul said, on behalf of the riders.

'Why … why not today?' Swaminathan asked.

'We need to discuss it among ourselves.'

'Okay, fine. But as your well-wisher, I would advise you to accept the forty-rupee rate and resume work. Otherwise, the management will retaliate.'

The riders sat down for a discussion among themselves. Sriman, Abir, Anup, Vignesh and even Somnath argued for accepting the forty-rupee rate for the time being and resuming work.

'No, we should stick to our demand for sixty rupees per delivery,' Kabul was adamant. So was Bikram.

'They won't give in,' Vignesh tried to reason with them. 'They must have guessed our weak points during the discussions in the last few days.'

'They've complied with our demands twice,' remarked Abir.

'Most of the riders of north Kolkata would be happy to get forty rupees per delivery … I've spoken to them,' Anup informed the gathering.

'If they can be pressured to give in and pay fifty rupees, why would we miss this opportunity?' Kabul refused to budge.

'You are wrong, you should accept the forty rupees per delivery charge,' Sriman insisted.

'Sriman is right, *sahi bola,*' Vignesh said. 'Accept it for now, you'll be at least in a position to fight after six months.'

'*Bhaiyyon*, let me remind you of a proverb … *toofan se jo darta hai usey darpok kehte hain, lekin toofan se jo ladta hai, usse sherdil kehte hain* … the one who dreads the storm is a coward, the one who faces the storm is a hero,' Nasim Ali suddenly said.

'We won't run away from the storm, we won't genuflect,' the chorus of voices chanted. 'Let's call a strike,' the majority demanded. The tornado of emotions had blown away all logic.

Sriman, though an ancillary to the strike, shuddered at the thoughtless decision. The Foreman management was in no mood to accept the demands of its workers this time. They had already threatened to take strict measures. They could even wrap up their business in the city, but under no circumstances would they increase the delivery cost. The management had reached out to workers who were willing to continue at the forty-rupee charge and asked them to communicate their decision as early as possible.

The decision led to a tug-of-war between the striking employees and the staff who did not cease work. Sriman was leading the first group.

No processions, no blockades, no posters. The striking staff devised ways to take the campaign to its height without affecting a bit of their time or earnings. Responding to Sriman's request, a few students of two renowned universities came forward to help. A few social media savvy supply staff were roped in too, as campaigners.

A publicity blitz was initiated. A website dedicated to the strike was launched: www.wethedeliveryriders.com. Facebook, X (formerly Twitter), Instagram, WhatsApp became the ancillary platforms of publicity. A prominent national daily covered the issue. Support in favour of the employees on strike poured in not only from Delhi, Mumbai, Chennai, Patna, Bengaluru but Dhaka, Birmingham, Amsterdam, and Paris too.

The honchos at Bengaluru must have taken serious note. They probably had had no idea that the protest by delivery workers of a city could have so much impact.

Their back against the wall, the CEO of the company declared that they would pay forty-two rupees for each delivery, but only in select stores across the city.

Sriman had opted for the night shift on Yellow Shirts so that he could canvas for the strike in the daytime. He bumped into Anup on one such trip. The Anusri issue came up. It would cost more than Rs 10,000 to set up a shack on the land they had chosen in New Town. Initially, it would cost them around Rs 15,000 per month which would increase in proportion with the growth in the number of clients and earnings. The shack with the highest sales in the vicinity spent Rs 30,000 every month. Anusri must clock a steady profit of at least Rs 15,000 per month to maintain that sort of an expenditure.

'Better set up a cloud kitchen instead,' Sriman rationalised.

'Yes, both of us will be stuck if we have to run a proper restaurant,' Anup concurred. 'But if it's a cloud-based thing, we can easily manage it alongside other work.'

'So, let's get going with the menu,' Sriman was emphatic. 'We'll sit down again in a week's time.'

'Yes, dada … where do we set up our cloud kitchen then?'

'At Akashganga … with my mother Shiuli Barik as the chef-in-chief,' Sriman smiled. Mrittika would help too, Sriman thought wistfully. He must discuss it with her once she recovered. It would be wise to include Srinath too. Sriman made it a point to speak with his elder brother on returning home.

Foreman's three stores in south Kolkata had started operations. The staff serving the stores too were entitled to the forty-two rupees perk per kilometre. The company closed its Kantapukur hub within a week of making these stores operational.

Foreman had blocked the quartet of its employees which had led the agitation from the front—Nasim Ali, Kabul Das, Bikram Saha, and Jaideb Mondal. Their names simply disappeared from the company's database. Other companies too were notified against employing any of them.

# 15

It happened in front of his eyes.

Like other days, Sriman had saved a portion of his breakfast for Munnu, the two-and-a-half-month-old kitten he had lately grown deeply attached to.

Somebody had left the kitten at their door, one of their neighbours perhaps. She was then a fluffy fascicle of fur, dangerously frail and yet to develop eyesight. Sriman had been attending to the kitten ever since. He had switched from his earlier menu of chapati-laddu to puffed rice in milk so that he could allot a part of it to his furry darling. Sriman called her Munnu; Chunnu was Shiuli's name for her. The intelligent kitty responded gingerly to both, conscious that though Sriman fed it in the morning, it had to depend on Shiuli for the two square meals of the day.

Like other days, Munnu gave a mild shake of her head, a reciprocation of affection, after having its bit of breakfast from Sriman's share. It detected a movement on the other side of the road … a rat? The kitten ran fast. That very moment, a three-wheeler van, packed with enormous plastic vessels brimming with water, came rushing.

'Munnu, stop!' Sriman had yelled. The kitten had even halted for a moment to look back, only to resume its course within a fraction of a second. She was helplessly puny to resist the overwhelming magnetism of impending death.

The front wheel of the van passed over Munnu's downy belly.

Shiuli came running, 'Chunnu, Chunnu … oh God!' She broke out into an inconsolable fit of tears.

A couple of neighbours came running. Sriman was hardly registering anything. The only action on his part was to stop one of their neighbours from hustling the van puller who was not responsible for the accident.

Munnu's mouth quivered. The proverbial nine lives, that is what Sriman desperately wished Munnu to have at that moment. He rushed back with a jug of water. Did the ounce of water go down Munnu's mouth? Moments later, all movements stopped.

Sriman did not feel like going out to supervise the operations of the cloud kitchen, for which he had switched to night shift latterly. He and Mrittika were to meet in the afternoon. He cancelled that too, texting her the reason. He lay idle all through the day. Nothing went down his throat except glasses of water.

'Get up and go to work!' The steely urgency in Shiuli's voice compelled Sriman to shed his grim hangover and begin preparations for going out.

'Sit down. I have made hot chapatis, have them with molasses,' Shiuli said, fully aware of the void that her son was gaping at inside.

Sriman got dressed immediately after having the food. That very instant, an order arrived on his phone.

Whenever Sriman discerned stern insistence in his mother's voice, he knew she was upset. Shiuli was no less affected by Chunnu's death, but experiences had toughened her. Life had taught her that grief has a shelf life, it should not be indulged beyond a certain limit.

Since switching to the less profitable night shift—from 7 in the evening to 4 in the morning—Sriman was apprehensive of a slump in his earnings. To make the most out of it, he was desperate to perform as many deliveries as possible from 7 to 10: the magic hours. Thereafter, it would mostly be an idle wait. Yet this was the schedule that suited him the best at the moment. It allowed him the scope to carry out the huge amount of work to make Anusri functional.

The menu of the restaurant had to be decided and uploaded on all the food delivery apps. The menu must offer the customer a wide variety of choice to order from. Except for the cooking, everything about the kitchen would be virtual.

Shiuli would cook all the ordered food at the abandoned garage in one corner of Akashganga. As soon as an order was placed, it would pop up on Sriman and Anup's phones. The delicacy would be ready in time and reach the customer shortly.

Sriman knew that once the project kicked off, it would run smoothly, but this initial stage of arranging things was crucial. It was funny that he and Anup were co-owners of four virtual restaurants. This is the era of virtuality. One can float even an institution as humongous as a university which would entirely function online. But they must be cautious. That was why Sriman kept his mornings vacant.

Sriman had observed a curious thing since beginning night duty. Orders that arrived between 7 and 10 pm were mostly selfsame. But after 1:30 am, it was a fusillade of an astounding variety. Mutton rolls, biriyani, kebabs, chicken momos, tandoori rotis, parathas, all at 4 am.

Had Kolkatans grown gluttonous overnight, Sriman wondered. What was particularly interesting was the customer profile of those who ordered these indigestible dishes during the graveyard shift. They were mostly young boys and girls, habituated to working through the night from the confines of their home: a legacy of the pandemic. Many returned home early in the morning after working a sleepless night shift, ordering the food on the way back. But not all orders were from people at or returning from work; these nocturnal clients included night owls as well as those who spent their nights watching movies or web series. Often, he heard snatches of sounds emerging from the living-room TV while delivering an order, that included orgasmic groans, leaving nothing to the imagination.

Once he got a delivery assignment of chicken butter masala and paneer tikka to Ganganagar. It was 2:15 am when Sriman started his motorbike. He activated the GPS and inserted the ear pods to follow the vocal prompts to stay on course on the unfamiliar terrain.

Driving at night is a breeze through empty roads devoid of the deafening decibels that assault the ears in the daytime. Around 2:45 am, Sriman reached a wilderness near the delivery location, uncannily deserted and pitch dark. As Sriman walked a little into the area, he faced a temple, its sanctum wide open. His heart skipped a beat at the menacing massiveness of a gigantic idol of Goddess Kaali, her tongue lusting for blood.

Ultimately, he decided to give the customer a call. The route the latter suggested was different from the one suggested by the GPS.

'But, sir, the route shown on the phone is different,' Sriman said.

'Yes, that's the shorter route, but avoid it at night, follow my directions.'

The customer repeated the instructions. Compared to the previous one, this was a decent route, amply lighted. Sriman had to take a brief detour, though. It was 3 am when he reached the location.

The forty-something gentleman opened the door with a smile to receive the parcel.

'If you don't mind, could you please tell me why you advised me to avoid that route? Because it was dark?' Sriman asked before leaving.

'Yes, that was one of the reasons ... actually, there's a graveyard nearby, a primitive one, no electric furnace, corpses burn over wooden pyres ... no habitation in the vicinity,' the gentleman clarified.

Sriman shuddered inwardly. 'But it doesn't show on the map!' he said.

'It won't until it becomes a crematorium,' the man smiled. 'A graveyard has to cremate a thousand corpses to be eligible to become a crematorium.'

Sriman was unaware of this, though he had lived near two well-known crematoria. This is what he loved the most about his job: this interaction with people and the enrichment it brought.

Another day. Another dead-of-the-night delivery. It was 2:30 am when he arrived at the apartment complex at Dum Dum Park to deliver the package. The iron gate was closed. No security guard in view. He called up the customer as many as three times in quick succession. No response.

Sriman was successful on the fourth attempt. An aged man picked up with drowsy disgust. 'Why are you bothering me so late at night? I've cancelled the order, my money has been refunded, don't disturb me again.' The line was disconnected.

Sriman was astounded. The company had not notified him about these developments. Sriman texted the company. The supervisor called soon after. 'What happened?' Sriman explained everything. 'Wait a little,' the supervisor hung up.

The supervisor rang back twelve minutes or so later to confirm that the customer had cancelled the order.

Earlier, in such instances, the rider had to return the food to the restaurant from where he had picked it up, but now the undelivered food became the rider's property.

Despite that, Sriman had suffered a huge loss. He had lost precious time which he could have utilised in delivering at least a couple of other orders. Nor did he get the whole amount that a rider was entitled to when an order was cancelled, probably due to some technical glitch. The company had started cheating the riders at every given opportunity.

'However swanky your company might look, Sriman, it surpasses the medieval slave owners in cruelty … they killed their slaves physically, your company starves you to death!' Bishan-da's words resounded with a prophetic tenor.

The ninth order entered while he was delivering the eighth. The delivery location was Nagerbazar. Kachori and jalebi from

Vansidhari's shop at 3:30 in the morning! But the shop did not open so early. Sriman peeped in through the pores of the iron shutters of the shop on reaching it. The staff were fast asleep. In two minds whether to wake them up, Sriman noticed two delivery riders of Guava waiting two shops away.

'Hi there. Kachori-jalebi pick-up from Vansidhari's?' one of them asked with a smile.

Sriman nodded. 'Do they make these things all day long?'

'This is the company's cloud kitchen … the packet bears their name, but the hands are different … take a look,' the other delivery rider said, pointing at the interior of the shop they were stationed before.

The name, Vansidhari, was splayed in haphazard hand across a rectangular piece of paper on the door of a minuscule kitchen which apparently measured not more than 10' / 15'. A teenage boy could be seen inside, knee-length shorts, napkin wrapped around a soiled vest. A notebook and a mobile phone lay on a table. The little boy ran the entire business at these strange hours—from preparing the food to packing it to handing them to the rider concerned on verifying their respective number. He meticulously kept note of every transaction in the notebook.

'Does Vansidhari's name stamped on the packets guarantee that the food has his unique flavour?' Sriman asked his two companions.

'The name is everything, boss. The average customer hardly has the ability to discern the taste … even if they don't like it, they'll say it's good only because the brand name is there,' the first of the delivery riders said with a chuckle.

The packets were ready within fifteen minutes. Sriman was done delivering his consignment by 4:10.

Sriman loved to drive on Jessore Road, VIP Road and E.M. Bypass. These roads are smooth glides. Ma flyover is a biker's paradise, particularly for those who have a fetish for bike racing, though accidents are quite common there. B.T. Road is the best place for driving at night. The road ahead, looking like an open field, lures the rider to speed over it. Despite the frequent red signals, the unbarred expanse allows the rider to manoeuvre his motorbike and deliver the food in no time.

Jessore Road is comparatively middle-class, mundane, and mild in character. Sriman had developed a rapport with this highway. Wherever his destination might be, he did not waste an opportunity to take this road at some point or the other. Sriman had also learnt to love the numerous craters and bumpers that dot Jessore Road. They are like asinine members of your joint family, whom you might detest, but ultimately must learn to live with.

Tonight, too, Sriman took Jessore Road on his way back as usual. Though the darkness of night had lightened, it was reluctantly yielding place to the light of day.

Sriman was approaching Lake Town, when a bizarre sight startled him. A middle-aged lady, clad in a nightie, was walking in his direction exactly along the middle of the road. He blew the horn, but that could not dissuade her from her stride. As Sriman drew closer, he discovered that the lady's eyes were closed. An ambulance whisked close by her. Suddenly, a two-wheeler emerged from inside Lake Town. This was surely going to hit her. Sriman brought his bike to a screechy standstill. The two-wheeler dodged her by a few inches. 'Fucking madwoman!' cussed the driver.

'No, definitely not a "madwoman",' Sriman muttered to himself. He caught hold of her when she was about to trip over a hole. 'Open your eyes, ma'am!' Sriman screamed.

The lady opened her eyes the second time Sriman yelled. The volatility of the eyes indicated they were still in a stupor. She was about to fall asleep placing her entire bulk on him.

'Where do you live? Why are you outdoors all alone at this awkward hour?'

'Kalindi Housing,' she mumbled.

'Apartment number?'

She gave no reply. Sleep had taken over again. She must be under the impact of drugs. He somehow dragged her to the traffic police post nearby.

The post was abandoned, but it had a chair. Making the woman sit, Sriman rushed out of the cubicle. He must locate a policeman. He did not have to go far. Two policemen were chatting at the next crossing. He related everything to them and brought one of them to the traffic police post where he had left the woman, but she had vanished.

'What's the matter? Come clean … Is she related to you? Don't hide anything,' the cop said with an aggressive gruffness while skimming him with suspicion.

Sriman had already told the cop who he was. He produced his ID card this time. 'If you don't believe me, just ring the number given here … and the lady is none of my relations, but one can't afford to turn a blind eye in such a situation,' he told the cop frankly.

'Hmmm, so, what do we do now?' the cop asked in a tempered tone.

Suddenly, Sriman located the lady, approximately 300 metres ahead.

Sriman started his bike with the policeman riding pillion.

They managed to stop her midway.

On being prodded by the cop, the lady blurted out the specifics, adding her name this time, Sabita Dutta Bhowmik. She lived with her husband and mother at flat number 4A of Block C of Kalindi Housing Estate.

The first light of dawn had suffused its soothing presence all around by the time they entered the housing complex. A sizeable crowd had gathered before one of the apartments. Eyes turned on their entry.

A fair complexioned, diminutive man rushed towards them. 'Good God, Sabu, where had you been? I was searching for you everywhere, calling people. I was so worried!' The man sounded rattled.

The elderly woman who had followed the gentleman to where they were standing, waved her hand at the lady. 'Sabu dear, come, let's go upstairs.'

The elderly woman's calming voice seemed to have brought the lady back to her composure. She was glancing around, shocked. 'How did I come here, Ma? When?'

'Come with me, I'll tell you everything,' the mother assured her daughter.

The women went inside.

'What's your relationship with her?' the policeman asked the gentleman, indicating Sabita.

'She's Sabita, my wife, she teaches in a college … thank you, sir.' The man looked relieved. 'By the way, I'm Jyotirmoy Bhowmik. I teach at Science College.'

'Why was she out on the road all by herself at such an odd hour? Husband-wife tiff?' the cop asked.

'Nothing of the sort, sir. Actually, my wife suffers from somnambulism, she walks in her sleep.'

'Why don't you keep the door locked?' the police officer asked.

'Sir, I forgot to do it last night as I was busy with other chores. I didn't notice when she had slipped out.' The man ran his hand through his hair, a gesture that insinuated embarrassment. 'But I must thank you, sir … please come up and have a cup of tea, if you don't mind.'

Sriman was about to get onto his two-wheeler after the police vehicle had departed the precincts when Jyotirmoy stopped him, insisting he join them for breakfast.

He had almost failed to recognise her when Sabita Dutta Bhowmik came in with the food, clad in a muted handloom saree. Bright eyes, a liberal dot of crimson, hair finely combed.

'Please have some food, brother,' she politely requested. The cordiality of her tone moved Sriman.

Sriman had a gratifying breakfast with bread and butter and sweets, rounded off with tea.

The old lady entered when Sriman was about to leave. 'I won't forget what you've done for my daughter,' she said in a tone moistened with gratitude. 'It's a rare virtue, son … stay blessed.'

Gliding smoothly through the sparse early-morning traffic, Sriman reached Shyambazar shortly via Duttabagan and Belgachhia. Akashganga was five minutes away from

Shyambazar. The blessings from the lady warmed the cockles of his heart, infusing a sense of contentment.

On reaching home, Sriman told Shiuli about it. A hint of a smile crossed her face. That was the optimal effect Sriman's account could elicit from her. Shiuli was one of those in whom the surfeit of sorrow had deadened the capacity to enjoy things. Happiness scared her. The moment it arrived, she could sense sorrow crouching round the corner, ready to pounce on her.

But unlike his mother, Sriman had an unrelenting faith in the goodness of life that prevailed unless deflated by circumstances. He had tried several times to make his mother see things differently, but without success. Whenever he had wanted to know the reason behind her attitude, she had given him the same reply. 'The moment I began to believe in your father, he was arrested for smuggling drugs. I tried to believe that he was the only man who truly loved me, but soon he was caught sleeping with another woman.'

Sriman walked towards the Ganga to relieve nerves frayed by the immense pressure he had endured last night. The mildness of the morning air soothed his mind. Like other days, Sriman sprinkled water on his face and over his head while descending the stairs, the old lady's words reverberating in his ears.

Sriman had barely seated himself on his bed after relishing a cup of tea when his phone chimed. A new message from the company. Yellow Shirts had blocked him for a month.

# 16

Why now?

The question was bothering Sriman more than the action taken against him by Yellow Shirts. What took them so long to take the step?

Mrittika came to Akashganga in the evening. She had something to discuss with him, in person. Sriman did not feel like poking her about the issue. He asked her to have dinner with him so that they could have an affable conversation.

But he could not restrain his emotions when she arrived in the evening. 'Yellow Shirts has blocked me. Can you imagine?'

'What?' Mrittika was stunned. 'Why?'

Sriman gave her all the details, including the uproar over Foreman, though he had already briefed her about it.

'Someone must've ratted against you,' Mrittika said grimly. 'Who could it be … Jaideb—' she stopped midway.

'Might be,' Sriman nodded with incredulity. 'Somnath is often so jealous!'

'But why? The company hasn't penalised him,' Mrittika could not figure out Somnath's motive.

'Not yet, but as I said, he is envious of people. Maybe he wanted to punish me for poking my nose into the affairs of their company.'

'But you don't work for Foreman, yet?'

'Why not? I had the audacity to stand by the striking employees, help the strike in north Kolkata … Foreman must have sent the information to Yellow Shirts. They are all hand in glove,' Sriman observed with a smile that oozed sadness.

'Forget it, you're registered on Guava too,' Mrittika tried to console him.

'Oh yes … thanks for reminding me.'

Sriman activated Guava. But despite repeated attempts he could not enter the app. 'I think Guava too has blocked me,' he said to Mrittika.

'Is it?' Mrittika could not think what more to say.

An uneasy silence prevailed between them for some time.

'Forget it, what do you want to discuss? I was waiting to hear from you, but this sudden development left me confused. Sorry,' Sriman said, breaking the silence.

'Everything's okay … besides, what I wanted to discuss was not that …' Mrittika broke off.

'See, the worst has happened … now I must try and stay afloat.' Looking outside the window, Sriman continued,

'I'm thinking of something, but before that, let's hear from you.'

'I've decided to bring Bubka to stay with me permanently,' Mrittika said after a brief silence. 'He has stopped studying, his grades at school are falling, the school has intimated me that they would give him a transfer certificate if he doesn't improve.' Mrittika stopped as if to collect herself. 'No, I must bring him out … seems his folks aren't willing either to keep him any more,' Mrittika said to herself, as if oblivious of Sriman's presence.

'That's great,' Sriman said. 'They were unwilling to give up his custody so long. But now that the situation is beyond their control, they want to wash their hands of him. But see the positive side. You'll now be able to keep him with you, feed him as you like, take him anywhere, anytime.'

'True,' Mrittika smiled. 'But I am worried about his schooling. His present school is near the Bhupen Bose Avenue and B.K. Pal Avenue crossing. How would he travel such a long distance every day from Garia?'

'You should shift here.' Sriman was astonished at the impulsive effortlessness with which he said it. The spontaneity of the proposal made it clear that it had been incubating inside him for quite some time. But Bishan-da must be informed, Sriman thought. The mercurial man would invariably refuse.

'Let's go to the terrace,' Sriman suggested.

'I haven't seen Cassiopeia this bright in the last fifteen years ... take a look,' Bishan said, shifting his eyes from the telescope.

'So very clear! ... I can see why it's called an archer, ready to shoot with his bow and arrow,' Sriman was mesmerised.

'Why deprive yourself, partner?' Bishan said, turning towards Mrittika. 'Come and take a look.'

Sriman came to the point before Bishan could be back in the celestial sphere. 'The company has struck off my name from all its registers, dada, as if I never worked for them.'

'This is the modern method of murder,' Bishan said after a brief silence. 'You were sad that you were spared while your friends were being punished. The score's even now ... But how'll you make ends meet? I can help.'

'No, Bishan-da, it's enough that you've allowed me to stay here. This is my personal battle, I'll fight it alone,' Sriman said with gritty determination.

Though Bishan was worried about Sriman, he was evidently satisfied with Sriman's determination. He was probably feeling happy that Sriman was finally evincing the backbone which was the essential eligibility for entry to the new planet.

Sriman summed up Mrittika's situation to Bishan-da. 'Dada, I've told her to shift to this house with her son, without taking your permission.'

'I get it. But who'll take your son to his school? One has to think before accepting a responsibility.' Bishan-da's response astonished Sriman. Did he not approve of Mrittika shifting to this house?

'I will take him to school every day. He will go alone once he grows up a little,' Mrittika chipped in fast.

'Will you be able to manage it after working nights?' Bishan wondered. 'Otherwise, Sriman will reach him to school. Won't you, Sriman?'

'No … I mean, yes, I can go,' Sriman fumbled at Bishan's abrupt ask.

'Say it louder!' Bishan roared. 'This job of carrying lifeless commodities has muddled your brain. You've forgotten how to take the responsibility of a living human being … you should resume your swimming classes immediately.'

'I'll take him to school and back,' Sriman cleared his throat. 'I don't have much to do in the morning.'

Sriman's mind was racing even as he was talking. The cloud kitchen must be made functional as early as possible. Earnings must be augmented. Only then can everything be okay.

'Very good,' Bishan was upbeat again. 'When my manager has assured you of his services, can I dare refuse you, ma'am?' he winked at Mrittika. 'You can shift in today itself, if you want. The room in the corner of the first floor would be yours. Welcome to Akashganga.'

Sriman had never expected things to work out so smoothly. He felt relieved.

Mrittika thanked Sriman in a voice choked with emotion as they descended the stairs.

'That's enough!' Sriman felt uncomfortable.

'When do we bring Bubka here? Day after tomorrow, or the day after?' Mrittika was impatient to have her son with her. Sriman said nothing. He wanted Mrittika to take the call. 'If we bring him on Saturday, we'll have Sunday to organise things,' she went on, undeterred by his silence.

'Okay, I'll get the room cleaned tomorrow,' Sriman said, without replying to her question. 'By the way, I think it's more or less clean. Our first meeting was supposed to be held there,' he added.

'You mean the meeting which was finally held at Mathuresh's?'

'Yes.'

The mention of the meeting brought them back to the upsetting awareness of Yellow Shirt's punitive measure against Sriman, while invoking the names of Jaideb, Somnath and the others. One of them must have snitched on Sriman to the bosses. Mrittika tried to dilute the issue. 'When did it occur to you all that a joint discussion was necessary?'

Sriman closed his eyes briefly to recall the date. 'It would be easier for me to recall it as that time when you and I came closer than ever … It's true that we had a consensus on the urgency of the joint discussion, but not all of us were on the same page on the issues we discussed. If there's largely unanimity of objective, there will be dissenting voices like Jaideb and Somnath too,' Sriman went on speaking almost to himself. 'Both electrons and protons exist at the centre of an atom.'

'I agree,' Mrittika said.

Sriman, too absorbed in his thoughts to heed what Mrittika was saying, continued, 'There might be electron-protons of contrary opinions within us, but we can still work together when the objective is the same. Because we must stand up in protest!'

Mrittika felt that Sriman was bleeding inside though he was trying to put up a brave face.

Mrittika had decided ever since learning of the punishment imposed on Sriman that she would give at least ten to twelve thousand rupees every month to him. With the small earnings of his mother and brother added to that, all of them, including her and Bubka, could somehow thrive on. Mrittika wanted to tell him about her decision but could not find the right words for it.

'It would help if we stayed together, particularly Bubka … But I won't stay for free,' she said while reccing the room on the first floor.

'Who would let you stay for free? I'll be at your door at the end of every month to seek the rent,' Sriman smiled.

Mrittika was relieved to see Sriman smiling once again. She wanted to stay a little longer with him. 'Wanna accompany me on duty?' she asked.

'No choice, ma'am … can't let my folks assume that I've been suspended.'

With Sriman on the backseat, Mrittika felt no need of ferrying people. Instead, she activated Guava. Together, they negotiated the city of the night. Sriman would rush in to hand the package to the customer on reaching every destination, while Mrittika would wait on her bike.

Most of the deliveries fetched her good ratings, raising it to 4.7. She would earn a bonus of Rs 500 and above if she maintained a rating of 4.5 or above. Mrittika anticipated her total earnings for the week to exceed Rs 5000. The money would help her meet the miscellaneous expenses on the cards, of shifting to Akashganga with Bubka, buying a tiffin box, books and stationery for him, maybe even a new white shirt for his school—plus, she had to set aside a part of it for Sriman. He might refuse, but she would insist. She would be happy to be of help when his life was in the doldrums.

The tenth order came around 3:30 am: pick-up from the idli-dosa joint at Tala Park. Though this cloud kitchen stayed open overnight, it got crazily active from around 3 am, serving mostly passengers of early-morning flights who flocked here to have a quick breakfast or get their breakfast packed.

The parcel of masala dosa and medu vada was handed to Mrittika at the right time. Mrittika carefully verified that the chutney and the sambar were included. The customer would suspect the delivery person if either was missing.

The GPS showed the destination to be located on the lane facing the ATM near the airport, Gate No. 1. Sriman surveyed the vicinity on alighting the bike but found no ATM nearby. It was 4 in the morning and the surroundings were mired in darkness and a mystic veil of mist. Sriman felt he could not locate the ATM due to the impenetrable darkness. They would probably have to take any of the three lanes that entered the locality.

Sriman asked Mrittika to ring the customer.

The customer responded on Mrittika's third attempt.

'Sir, I'm calling from Guava, I've reached your location, but can't make out which lane to take … could you help please?'

'Take the lane next to the temple,' the customer instructed.

Mrittika, after some serious attempts, located a minuscule temple with a tiny deity on the footpath. They did not have much of a trouble locating the destination after that. The customer, R. Srinivasan, lived on the third floor of the four-storey building.

The staircase to the apartment was mired in pitch darkness. The elevator was not working. Nor was there a soul in view. Two stray dogs were blocking the approach to the staircase, making it impossible for anybody to set foot on the stairway. 'Give me the packet, I'll somehow convey it,' Sriman said.

'Why take the risk? You might slip in the darkness. What if anybody thinks you are a thief?'

'Thief!' Sriman smiled sarcastically. 'Why not? We delivery riders are easy targets.'

Mrittika rang Srinivasan. 'Sir, we are in front of your building. But we can't take the stairs, they are so very dark. Could you please come down and receive the package?'

Srinivasan disconnected the line.

Mrittika called up customer care. Briefing the person on the other end, she said, 'Please request the customer to come down and collect the parcel, he is not cooperating.'

'Okay, you ring the customer again, I am on the line,' the customer care personnel replied.

Mrittika patched Srinivasan into the conference call. 'Sir, you probably didn't hear what I said, the stairs are dark, if you please …'

'No! It's *your* duty to deliver the package to my door, you are paid for it. So, cut the crap and deliver my order,' Srinivasan sounded utterly rude.

The customer care personnel disconnected himself from the call, probably on sensing the complication. Mrittika placed another call to them and repeated the whole episode. 'Whatever you do, just remember that the customer cannot be displeasured,' the customer care professional uttered the stock advice in a voice as mechanical as a robot's.

'But do you have a solution?' Mrittika was losing her cool. The person on the other end disconnected the line without a reply.

'Enough is enough. Let me take the package to him,' Sriman had lost his patience.

'But it's so dark!'

'Not to worry, darling, I'm switching on the torch on my phone,' Sriman was smiling.

Srinivasan gave such a miserable review that Mrittika's rating plunged to 3.25. Along with it was gone her dream of earning an extra Rs 500. The niggardly Srinivasan would never know how desperately Mrittika needed that amount.

Dropping Sriman at Akashganga in the morning, Mrittika returned to her Garia house. She must make a list of things to carry into Akashganga. She would have to prepare for bringing Bubka on Saturday after fetching all those things.

As is natural after a sleepless night, Sriman fell fast asleep in the afternoon. He was suddenly awakened by the loud knockings on the door around 3 pm. Who could it be? Sriman opened the door with sleepy eyes to four strangers staring at him. A gawky man was carrying a letter from the bank. Beside him, stood a fair, rotund, serious-looking gentleman, ID card hanging from the lanyard around his neck. Along with them stood two brawny ruffians.

'Whom do you want?'

'Srinath Kundu.'

'Yes, that's my brother, but he is not at home ... anything urgent?'

'He hasn't cleared his EMIs. We tried to contact him, he neither returned the calls nor met us,' the fair-complexioned gentleman replied. 'We had informed him of the last date of payment, two days have passed since then ... we've come to take away the car, give us the keys.'

The burly twosome stared at him all along with unblinking, deadpan eyes. Sriman felt they were bloodhounds in human flesh, raring to pounce upon him.

Sriman neither had the physical might to take on the rowdies nor could he even think of repaying the debt. He decided to give it one last try to tackle the issue for the time being.

'My brother may have defaulted on the EMI, but I can assure you that he'll resume paying them regularly from the month after next, if not from next month itself. Please keep my number, contact me whenever you need.'

The sudden confrontation had robbed him of his siesta. He changed his clothes and went out to meet Anup.

'We've got the trade license, right?'

'Yes, dada,' Anup confirmed.

'Yes, what about the food and fire license?'

'We've got the food license, I had applied for it on their

website … hope to get the fire license this evening, will fetch it as soon as it's ready.'

'Good. Let's start the cloud kitchen from tomorrow itself,' Sriman was determined.

Anup had learnt to read Sriman's pulse in the last few months. Sriman's growing desperation for an alternate source of income since being blocked by Yellow Shirts had not escaped his scrutiny. Every minute mattered to Sriman now. Anup felt he must impart hope to Sriman.

'The menu card is more or less ready, just take a look and I'll upload it as soon as you approve it … our menu will be available on both Yellow Shirts and Guava,' Anup informed Sriman.

'So, I'll need at least a couple of days more to get it going … just spread the word about Anusri on as many apps as possible … I'll start the Facebook promotions this evening itself,' Sriman was dead earnest.

'That would be great,' Anup said.

It was not before the next day's afternoon that everything was finally ready. Rwitaban Basu, the boy next door who had of late become an online sensation for his posts on Facebook, visited Anusri's kitchen on Sriman's invitation. Impressed by the taste of Shiuli's puri and aloo dum, he lavished praise on the food, even going so far as to call it the best of its kind in Kolkata on his Facebook page.

The first order, for twenty-five puris and aloo dum, came in on Sunday morning, to be delivered to Madan Mitra Lane near the Vivekananda Road-Bidhan Sarani crossing. Packing the food into disposable white plastic containers, Sriman and Anup went off to deliver it.

The GPS led to a jaded three-storey house. The black nameplate on the green door mentioned 'Mihir Debnath, Advocate' in large grey letters. Sriman rang the doorbell. A middle-aged gentleman opened the door.

'We are from Anusri,' Sriman said.

'Great!' the gentleman was enthusiastic. 'Your puri and aloo dum is here!' he yelled to someone inside the house.

'Oh, it has arrived! ... Jhimli, dear, go and fetch the food from your father,' a female voice responded from within.

Sriman could sense a festive mood in the house. But a festal feel is not quite uncommon in north Kolkata households on Sunday mornings. The negativity of the gig economy is yet to affect these households, Sriman thought.

Sriman and Anup rushed to the market on Tarak Pramanik Road to celebrate their first earning with a couple of kachoris and a cup of tea each. From there, they headed to Bagri Market to collect plastic containers stamped with the Anusri insignia. Jaiswal-ji had called in to inform that the consignment was ready.

# 17

Life is an interplay of binaries: ebb and tide, dynamism and inertia, enthusiasm and apathy.

The Facebook page of We the Delivery Riders was no exception. During the outcry over Yellow Shirts or the uproar surrounding the strike at Foreman, it was buzzing with activity—the number of followers soared by the hour, news of delivery riders poured in from all over the country, there were regular posts by Jnuiphool Roy Corbyn, and a deluge of comments.

That enthusiasm had ebbed since. The deadline of twenty-six days within which the Yellow Shirts bosses were to declare their decision on base pay and per-kilometre payments had long passed. Yet there was no update from Ramesh Jain. More surprising was the silence of the delivery riders on the issue. Should it be called collective oblivion or something else, Sriman often wondered.

Sriman did not get much time to toy with his phone nowadays. His nights were consumed by work related to

Anusri, while for the greater part of his waking hours, he was too busy managing the security of Arcadia Apartments. At best, he could afford a covert glance or two at the screen.

Arcadia was a massive residential complex. Fifty-two cars were parked across its massive premises. During the day, the cars, one after the other, left the complex. Six of them kept coming and going. The large iron gate had to be opened and closed constantly in quick succession. The same routine repeated itself in the evening when the big shots returned. When Sriman returned home at the end of the day, his back and shoulders felt like lead. Bone-tiring and unbearably monotonous, this was way worse than a delivery rider's job.

Yet Sriman was grateful for the job at a time of crisis: dada's income had come to zilch, ma had lost one of her domestic help jobs, and Mrittika had just shifted to Akashganga with Bubka. Incidentally, Brindaban Das, the security guard of the huge complex in the locality, had gone on a month's leave around the same time. Sriman, an able-bodied young man of the neighbourhood, had been the first preference as Das's temporary substitute. The moment he learned of the vacancy, he went directly to Prakash Agarwal, the chairman of the residents' body. Agarwal took a shine to Sriman. He sent him to the secretary, Manoj Jaiswal.

'Mind you, it's a back-breaking job, 6 am to 6/6:30 pm,' Jaiswal had warned.

Sriman had heard that working hours cannot stretch beyond eight hours, but these people were unabashedly declaring it a twelve-hour job. Take it or leave it. There was no dearth of job seekers.

'No problem, how much will you pay?' Sriman was desperate for the job.

'Eight thousand, and a little extra during the Pujas … not a bonus, though,' Jaiswal had clarified, laying emphasis on the word 'bonus'.

In the anchorless situation Sriman was in, Rs 8000 seemed a princely sum. He would get a chance to turn around even if Yellow Shirts and Guava revoked their suspension after a month. But that, Sriman knew, was a fat chance, given the nonchalance with which the companies had been dragging their feet beyond the twenty-six-day deadline. Sriman was dwelling over all of this stationed in the security guard's cubicle at Arcadia.

The workload somewhat lessened in the afternoon, once all the cars were out. It was then that Sriman could afford a peek at his phone on the sly. He had to be careful lest the retired men, the self-appointed guardians of the complex, raised an uproar—'Were you given the job to play with your phone?' 'Raise your royal derriere from your throne, and take a walk round the complex, will you, sir?' 'Would you please take the pains to check if somebody is trying to break in?' Sriman had often been subject to such sarcastic commands.

Of late, Sriman had changed tack in dealing with these faultfinders. Nowadays, he saluted and beamed at them before they could speak: 'Good morning, sir, how are you?' The strategic greeting was responded to with a toothy grin of complacence before the respondent walked off to the other side to perhaps join a game of cards. It was during these brief reprieves that Sriman checked his phone.

The only person to stay consistently attached to the Facebook page of We the Delivery Riders was Jnuiphool Roy Corbyn. Since the inception of the page, she had been constantly writing about the plight of delivery workers the world over.

Yesterday, she wrote about John Estrada of East London.

Food delivery riders of London felt demoralised. They did not have job security, the right to take leaves, me-time or even money. At times, they had to wait for forty to forty-five minutes for an order to arrive. Hence, they were compelled to work for ten hours per day only to ensure a semblance of a decent existence. Their per-delivery base pay was being curtailed every year. It now stood at a measly £3.

Thirty-year-old John Estrada of East London said, 'I've never experienced a job as lawless and anarchistic as this. It makes my blood boil. We face extreme scarcity of space for parking bikes on Ashwin Street and Kingsland Road, the two locations from where we pick up most of our orders. If by chance we park the bikes in a wrong position, we are charged a fine of £65. When this happens several times in a day, which is often the case, we are left with almost no savings. One other major issue is the acute crisis of toilets on the streets; nor do all parking lots have toilets. We often have to park bikes far away from the restaurants. This, quite obviously, reduces the time at our disposal as well as our income.

'Although we delivery riders keep the restaurants alive and thriving, they do not bother to show us the minimum fellow-feeling. We are made to wait under the open sky on our bikes or scrounge for shelter around the dumpsters of the restaurant when it rains (and rains are too common in London), until the restaurant hands the package to us. We are always apprehensive that a customer might spot us in such an embarrassing situation because that would be a slur on the reputation of the restaurant. Friends, do note that the flexitime you hear we delivery riders enjoy is simply a hoax. I have been in this job barely for the last six months and I am already so very disgusted that I am joining the Independent Workers' Union of delivery riders today. You will find me among the agitators in front of the burger joint on Kingsland Road next week.'

Jnuiphool had posted again early this morning. Followed by another, which came a couple of hours later. The first one was about the predicament of the food delivery riders of New York.

Food delivery riders of New York were paid a paltry $3.90 per delivery. Most of them alleged that the customers were extremely rude. 'If I worked as a mason in a house,' one of them said, 'the owner would greet me good morning, even respectfully address me as "sir", but if I arrive at the same house as a delivery rider, the same owner treats me like a dog.' Many of the food delivery apps active in New York no longer mentioned the minimum pay issue.

Jnui had shared Cynthia White's post. Cynthia was a female food delivery rider. 'I have been delivering food across New York over bicycle, for the last five years. Ever since joining this job, I have learnt that new methods of deception have flourished in this era of sophisticated technology, alongside the opulence of low-pay, menial jobs involving cheap technology.

'The app through which I delivered food to Byram Hills had guaranteed me $6.85 per delivery. The woman who had placed the order opened the door in a multicoloured bath robe and tipped me $3, through the app. But what I finally got was nothing more than the fixed amount of $6.85, the $3 tip included. Funny, isn't it? Had the lady not paid me any tip or had handed me $3 directly, instead of paying it over the app, the company would have paid me the full amount of $6.85. But as soon as they got to know that I had been tipped $3, they backed out of their promise and paid me $3.85. So, the lady, instead of tipping me, had actually tipped the company!'

Delivery riders all over the world were facing the same exploitation and ignominy, realised Sriman. Seated in his room in Akashganga, on the cusp of the departing afternoon and the approaching twilight, Sriman witnessed darkness gripping the world. He could see John Estrada manoeuvring his bike through the streets of East London in the midst of heavy rains, dressed in a waterproof jacket, gloves, a bulky helmet, and dark glasses.

Cynthia was headed to deliver a parcel of egg sandwich on her bike. The greetings pasted on the package made it obvious that it was the birthday of the recipient. Cynthia arrived at the address ahead of the expected time. The woman who opened the door was wearing a dress that befitted a gala occasion like a birthday. 'Good morning, Christina,' Cynthia greeted her.

Christina responded with a bland 'Good morning'. In keeping with the celebratory mood, Cynthia sang 'Happy birthday to you'. The woman mumbled an insipid 'thank you' as soon as the song ended, while retreating to close the door. She did not even bother to tip Cynthia.

Sriman's heart went out for John and Cynthia.

The other post from Jnuiphool was shorter. According to Maria Figueroa, the head of Cornell University Workers' Union in Manhattan, the delivery worker is in the bleakest position in this era of digital labour, holding on somehow in an extremely difficult struggle for existence.

Sriman was pleasantly surprised at the massive readership of Jnuiphool's posts that exceeded 50,000. But the gladness fizzled out as soon as he dwelled on the general silence maintained by his delivery rider colleagues of Yellow Shirts over the non-action of the management. 'Why are we silent about the assurances given by Yellow Shirts?' Sriman wrote on the wall of their Facebook group.

Sriman had barely posted it when he heard an approaching car. Dipesh Chatterjee was back. He returned at 7 pm, but today he was back at 5. Sriman opened the gate and saluted Chatterjee seated in the rear of the car; Chatterjee acknowledged the salute.

Sriman glanced at the screen of his phone after closing the gate. Sanjay, in reply to Sriman's post, had commented. 'I understand, but should we force them if they don't want to come to the negotiating table again? Should we call a strike again? What will be the result? They would sack a few of us again. Nothing more. We can't let that happen. Yet, we must carry on the fight, but how?'

Sriman did not think it right to answer on the public platform of Facebook. Instead, he wrote in their fifteen-member WhatsApp group and added, 'I don't have any answer to your question now. But all of us must think over it because our situation is worsening by the day. Moreover, while the Yellow Shirts honchos are unwilling to work on the assurances they had given, we too are to blame for our amnesiac carelessness.'

'Absolutely right. Are we suffering from amnesia?' Mrittika wrote in the group.

Mrittika's shifting to Akashganga had been of much help to Sriman. She took Bubka to school at 7 in the morning, returned to have her meal and set out for work at 10. Mathuresh fetched Bubka from school in the afternoon. Bubka spent the afternoon with him. Mrittika was relieved because Bubka was in Mathuresh's company. Sriman had advised Mrittika to work the morning shift until she became familiar with the nooks and crannies and the residents of the neighbourhood. So, Mrittika could now devote the night to the management of the affairs of Anusri, after helping Bubka with his studies.

Contrary to Mrittika's apprehension, Bubka was quite happy to be in Akashganga, though nobody here had a pocket as deep as his uncle who pampered him by buying anything he demanded.

Bubka went to the terrace in the afternoon with Mathuresh to fly kites, waffled frankly with Bishan-da, unabashedly demanded an omelette from Shiuli. Everybody here was eager to keep him happy, particularly Sriman, with whom he shared a special intimacy. Bubka knew that Sriman kaku would be at his disposal if his mother was busy. Bubka seemed to have matured ever since coming to Akashganga.

Mrittika suddenly had a bout of breathlessness while driving her motorbike one fine morning. She suspected it to be long Covid. Thankfully, she never left without an inhaler in her bag ever since her first brush with breathlessness during the pandemic. Though Mrittika tried to ignore it, she felt increasingly uneasy. Bringing her vehicle to a standstill, she took two consecutive puffs from the inhaler. The overwhelming sense of fatigue made her stop for the day.

The complication continued for the next few days. Mrittika tried to avoid dust and pollution, but these are inescapable hazards a delivery rider can hardly shield themselves from.

When Sriman consulted Subhra about Mrittika's complication, she arranged an appointment with Dr C.K. Sen, the renowned pulmonologist, at 10 in the morning the very next day.

Sriman requested Mathuresh to go with Mrittika to the doctor's chamber.

'I am sorry, this is incurable,' Dr Sen said without mincing words. 'Lungs are the worst casualties in people like you who travel through this heavily polluted city. Still, I would recommend that you keep an inhaler handy.' Dr Sen prescribed a new inhaler along with a few other medicines.

Mathuresh procured the medicines as fast as possible. Mrittika opened her purse, offering to pay, but he politely refused.

Despite the preoccupations of a security guard or the functioning of the cloud kitchen, Sriman could not shrug off his attachment with the astral bodies. Both he and Bishan Basu, who had induced the astral preoccupation in him, could not imagine surviving without gazing at the night sky. The visual enabled both to forget the pains and ignominies suffered during the day.

'Look at the Pole Star closely,' Bishan said.

'Hmmm … strange, isn't it, Bishan-da?' Sriman asked. 'It does its job silently, fixed at its position, helping find directions, but nobody knows its story.'

'The Pole Star has quite a story … in the *Vishnu Purana*,' Bishan replied a little later, exactly the allusion-rich response that Sriman had expected.

'Priyabrata and Uttanpada were the two sons of Manu, bravehearts both and religious scholars,' Bishan continued. 'Uttanpada's dearest wife, Suruchi, gave birth to Uttam. His other wife, Suniti, gave birth to Dhruv. But Uttanpada had no affection for Dhruv. One fine day, Dhruv found his brother Uttam seated on their father's lap who was petting him affectionately. Dhruv went to his father and demanded that he caress him as well. But Uttanpada refused him because he did not feel any attachment for his mother, Suniti.

'Dhruv came crying to his mother. Suniti tried to subdue her son by telling him that it was all due to the karma of his earlier birth. Uttam was entitled to the affection of his father with the good karma of his earlier incarnation. Dhruv had collected himself by then. "This is wrong, and I will prove it, Ma. I will achieve the greatest glory in this birth itself," he said in a calm but forceful voice.'

The rest of Bishan's tale was about Dhruv's successful pursuance of an ascetic life away from home as suggested by the Seven Sages. 'The *Vishnu Purana* describes Dhruv as the harbour of all heavenly bodies. His position is above the sun, the moon, the stars, and the Ursa Major,' Bishan added. 'There is no such thing as a previous birth. You sow as you reap in the only birth you have been given,' he smiled at Sriman.

Sriman was about to say something when Mrittika stepped onto the terrace. 'I need a father,' she was yelping.

'Another Uttanpada story is about to begin,' Bishan smiled mischievously.

Mrittika was in a quandary. Bubka's school wanted both his parents to attend the first parent-teacher meeting. Mrittika did not want to take her near-divorced husband with her. So, she had asked Mathuresh, but he had refused.

'You were wrong, madam, to ask him in the first place,' Bishan said. 'How could you expect a clay model maker to assume the responsibility of a living being?'

'Actually, I couldn't think of any other person ... Sriman can't go, he goes to work in the morning,' Mrittika justified her decision.

'Sriman will go with you, Mrittika … if not as the dad, then as the uncle,' Bishan said with a perky smile.

With parents of all students in attendance, the school hardly had time to verify the parental identities. Sriman had butterflies in his stomach. But he had to perform this role-playing as Mr Sen successfully. Mrittika's prestige was at stake. Bishan-da too was relying on him.

'Akashdeep is doing well. He is very well-behaved. So, we were worried that he was a bit inattentive recently,' the teacher looked at Mrittika and Sriman. 'But he seems to have overcome it. We understand you take much care to ensure that. Please keep it up.'

A message arrived in the rider group while they were on their way back. 'Why don't we take out a bike procession and stage an agitation in front of the Yellow Shirts office on the 25th?' Vignesh had written.

'Only agitation won't help,' Nasim had replied. 'Enter the office, vandalise it. Let's create a stir.'

Sriman sensed the foolishness of the idea. 'That would set the police after us,' he wrote.

'We don't care if they arrest us. The company should realise that we are hard nuts to crack. Plus, we would get the attention of the press,' Bikram countered Sriman.

'A peaceful agitation would be enough if getting press coverage is the concern,' wrote Sriman. 'If the popular dailies don't feature it, there's social media.'

'I agree with Sriman. The delivery riders of London have agitated in front of a world-renowned restaurant,' Sanjay wrote.

'Photos of the agitation have been posted on our Facebook page too,' Mrittika informed.

'Right, if there is a stir over Yellow Shirts in the press or media, the company is bound to take notice. They won't want their image to be tarnished,' Sanjay wrote again.

Finally, it was decided that they would continue pressuring the company one way or the other. In other words, they would follow the course of action suggested by Vignesh.

Preparation began on a war footing for the grand congregation. The Facebook page of the Riders was abuzz with activity again. The workers wanted to tell Ramesh Jain that if he kept his promises, they would keep theirs too. To it, was added the latest slew of demands.

Sriman would not be able to attend the meeting. Mrittika would. The procession would start at 3 pm sharp from the Sector II bus depot at Salt Lake and head to the Yellow Shirts office at Sector V.

Mrittika felt a sharp pang of hunger on completing a delivery around 1:30 pm at Esplanade. There is no dearth of eateries here. Parking her scooter at Corporation Place, Mrittika took the elevator to the third floor of the building. She had a quick but filling lunch. She had barely sat on her bike, when an order arrived. She had to pick up the order from the renowned biriyani shop exactly opposite of where she was at the moment. The delivery location was one of the apartments facing Bagmari bazaar, which would be on her way to Salt Lake. She accepted the order.

But unlike what Mrittika had anticipated, it was a bumpy ride. The bumper-to-bumper traffic was moving at a snail's pace. Mrittika tried to keep her cool. It was 2:50 pm by the time she was done with the delivery. She was already running late for the meeting. While approaching Kankurgachi crossing, where traffic signals take time to change, Mrittika was fervently praying that the light stayed green until she passed it. She stepped on the gas. She was barely 100 metres away from the crossing when the light started blinking amber, foreboding its imminent switch to red. Once that happened, Mrittika would have to stand still for at least five minutes. Each second was costly now. Mrittika accelerated her vehicle. She would be turning left and then make a semicircle.

That very moment, a bicycle crossed her path. 'Rascal!' Mrittika muttered while stepping on the brakes. But she could not avert the disaster. The cycle rider was thrown on the ground. Mrittika too was on the ground, the bike landing on her left leg.

A trio of students from a private engineering college nearby was chatting on the footpath. They came rushing. One of them pulled up the bike. 'Thank God, no serious damage,' the boy heaved a sigh of relief.

Mrittika stood up with the help of the other two boys but amidst immense pain in her left arm and left leg. A bone had broken, she was sure. 'Didi, place your arm on our shoulders, let's take you to the shoe store there,' one of the other two boys said.

'Will they allow me to sit there?'

'They have to. Nobody messes with college students,' the boy on the right smiled. 'You sit here, didi. Let me fetch some ice for you.'

'Where's my bike?'

'It's in front of the shop.' One of the boys handed her the keys. Mrittika inserted them in her pocket.

'Call home, else we can call the police and tell them to send a vehicle,' the boy on whose shoulder Mrittika had balanced her left arm, said.

'No need to inform the police, I am calling home,' Mrittika nodded. She called Sriman.

'I am coming at once,' assured Sriman. 'Wait there.'

Luckily, for both Sriman and Mrittika, the plumber who came to the tea stall facing the complex in the afternoon was sitting idle today. Otherwise, Sriman would not have been able to come to Mrittika's rescue leaving his security guard's post.

With Mathuresh in the passenger seat, Sriman reached in half an hour's time. Anup had reached the Sector II bus terminus. He too arrived on his motorbike along with Vignesh and Nasim on learning of Mrittika's accident.

Mathuresh and Anup held Mrittika cautiously. But as she was unable to walk, they carried her and placed her gently on the bike behind Sriman.

'I am driving slowly, you just hold on to me, carefully,' said Sriman. He had intended to take her to Subhra's hospital, but Mrittika was in too much pain. 'Can't bear it any more,' she shrieked in pain. Her arms and legs had swollen up. Sriman decided to take her to the nearest government hospital. Mathuresh was following them on Mrittika's bike and Anup was driving his own bike. Sriman gestured both to stop. 'Let us go in. If they refuse to admit her, we'll take her to Subhra's clinic.'

'Yes, let's go in. I know someone on the staff here,' Anup replied.

Mrittika was admitted. The X-ray report revealed a crack in the wrist joint of her left arm. The shin bone of her left leg had been fractured too. A metal rod had to be inserted. The attending doctor, while bandaging Mrittika's left arm, said, 'She must stay here for four-five days and then a month's bed rest at home, absolutely no bike driving.'

The company was briefed about Mrittika's accident. She sought reimbursement of the medical expenses of her treatment based on the company's policy regarding on-duty accidents. But the People's Officer at Guava refused her demand on the ground that the accident had occurred after the delivery, not on the way to it.

These companies know nothing other than making money. They have no humanity, no sympathy. What Mrittika finally got was a virtual card from the company in her inbox. 'Get well soon' were the three words it carried.

# 18

'One step at a time ... that's it ... very good ... your feet are moving again.' Subhra was helping Mrittika to slowly walk on the terrace one evening. 'See, I've brought your Pole Star back to normal again!' Subhra said with a smile to Sriman who had come up to the terrace. 'Keep walking ... slowly.'

'This is a miracle!' Sriman was excited. 'A bit of evening walk on the terrace, a little climbing the stairs along the day, and you'll be doing karate, judo, kickboxing again,' he tried to pep Mrittika up.

'Back from work already!' asked Mrittika. 'Bit early today?'

'The night duty replacement reported earlier than usual,' Sriman said, happily.

Sriman owed his job as watchman to Brindaban Das. The vacancy had been created by Das's sudden absence. Sriman retained the job because Das continued to be AWOL. Mrittika had volunteered to prepare Sriman's lunch before he left for work. It gave her a tingle of excitement to imagine Sriman feeling the warmth of her touch while having his lunch.

Thereafter, Mrittika relaxed a little once Bubka left for school. Mathuresh had been taking him to school and back since her accident. She then went to the ground floor on a brief recce of the activities of Anusri's kitchen. A little later, when Anup too was convinced that all was okay, he left for work. By then, Srinath took charge. Mrittika had become habituated to this diurnal quotidianness of life.

Yet, could one say Mrittika was at peace with her circumstances? Probably not. Although Bishan-da had specified on the first day itself that she should feel free to enjoy all amenities available to her as a denizen of Akashganga, it beat her that she was unable to contribute anything financially. But what she missed more was her dynamism. For a delivery rider, on the move round the clock, it is a curse to sit idle at home. It increasingly dispirited her. Moreover, one of the benefits of her job was making new acquaintances every day. Some of these people are so precariously lonely that they feel relieved even to interact with a rank stranger like a delivery rider. For them, the rider is the link to the outside world, while the rider too feels happy to dispel the darkness that surround these helpless souls.

Mrittika had been feeling a renewed surge of confidence since she began walking on the terrace and the daily rounds of climbing the stairs. It would not be long before she took to the roads!

However, it was not Mrittika's accident but Bishan's viral fever that had brought Subhra to Akashganga. Bishan had a sudden bout of vertigo while watching the night sky a couple of weeks ago.

The constellation appeared uncharacteristically bright that night.

'Crystal clear!' Sriman had delightfully exclaimed on glancing through the monitor of the telescope. Earlier that night, Bishan had already reoriented Sriman on the Marichi, Vasistha, Angiras, Atri, Pulastya, Pulaha, and Kratu—the stars of the Saptarishi constellation. 'By the way, Bishan-da,' Sriman said, 'isn't that Arundhati, the little star very close to Vasistha? Look,' Sriman moved away from the telescope.

Bishan promptly looked through. 'Very good, yes, that's Arundhati.'

Bishan felt he was standing underneath his childhood sky over Rajnagar. He recalled his Gajen uncle, who had acquainted him with the same Arundhati among other things.

'That sky, those stars are no more,' Bishan said to himself. Despite his low voice, it reached Sriman's ear due to the lucidity of Bishan's pronunciation. 'Can't be, Bishan-da! Things can't change so radically in forty-fifty years that you won't recognise them,' Sriman dissented.

'No, dear, I fail to recognise this country, its people,' Bishan said ruefully. 'Everything has changed. Students today don't like to study; they mug up things before examinations. Youngsters don't bother to look at the sky, identify the stars.'

Sriman now realised which sky or stars Bishan-da was referring to. 'Is it? I thought you were saying that the Saptarishi had changed,' Sriman said.

Bishan thought of something and nodded to himself. 'This Saptarishi constellation won't look the same after ten millenniums, its stars will follow a different configuration,' he remarked with a sigh.

Suddenly, everything turned dark before Bishan's eyes and he collapsed on the floor of the terrace. He would have injured his head had Sriman not caught hold of him at the right moment. Bishan was running a high temperature.

Carrying Bishan carefully to his room on the first floor, Sriman somehow laid him on the bed. The neighbourhood physician, Dr Biswas, who usually treated Bishan, was not in town. Who else would agree to pay a visit at 1 am? Sriman could only think of ringing Subhra who was working the night shift.

'Give him a paracetamol 650 for the time being … let's wait till tomorrow morning,' Subhra advised.

Sriman fetched the drug from the medicine shop at Shyambazar that stays open round the clock. Half an hour after having the medicine, Bishan seemed to be responding.

Sriman touched Bishan's forehead lightly. 'Is it you, Jnuiphool?' Bishan responded to the touch, still in the stupor of somnolence. 'When did you …?'

To hell with your Jnuiphool! Sriman felt like shouting out. He regained control, with a tinge of embarrassment. Why was he holding Jnuiphool responsible for Bishan's condition? Bishan-da had never spoken ill of her nor had she denigrated him ever. Still, why did he have this animus towards her?

Subhra had the next day off, as a routine transition between shifts. She brought a trainee doctor along with her to Akashganga. Sriman was out on duty. So Mrittika took Subhra to Bishan.

'Mrittika, dear, your leg has been cured!' Bishan exclaimed delightfully in a singsong voice. He glanced curiously at the two unfamiliar people who stood by her side. 'New faces?' he asked.

'This is Doctor Bappaditya Nath and this is Sister Subhra,' Mrittika introduced them. 'Sriman had requested them to come,' she added.

'Yes, I've dragged the doctor here,' Subhra smiled. 'Actually, Sriman sounded so worried! I know your stories of stargazing, your expedition to discover the new planet,' she added enthusiastically.

'Oh, I see, you are a stargazer!' Dr Nath sounded pleasantly surprised.

'Yes, his planetarium is open to all every night,' Mrittika smiled.

'Not fair, Mrittika, dear, you're spilling the beans of our secret society,' Bishan said in mock anguish.

'My God, he's still running a high fever. Just see how swollen his face looks.' The doctor was checking Bishan even as he spoke. 'Hmmm, there's congestion,' he said grimly as he placed the stethoscope on his chest and back.

Subhra was startled as the thermometer read 102.5°F. 'It's impossible to guess you have such high fever!' She shook her head in disbelief.

Doctor Nath looked at Subhra. 'Seems like viral fever. I am prescribing medicines. Let's watch for the next seventy-two hours. We'll run blood tests if the fever persists.'

Subhra was about to leave along with the doctor.

'Sister Nightingale, you too are leaving? Let me give you your memento,' Bishan said.

'No, uncle, I will be back after seeing him off,' Subhra replied.

Subhra had been coming to Akashganga ever since. She spent hours with Bishan every day after attending to her hospital duty. Bishan needed company. The bout of viral fever had left him feeble. Subhra regularly sponged him with warm water before sprinkling powder on his frail body. But Bishan would not allow her to do anything more. He had received a drubbing from Sriman for trying to walk up to the terrace alone.

'If you try this again, you'll surely end up on the pyre instead of the terrace,' Sriman had warned him without mincing words. Bishan had laughed aloud to that. 'Well said, from the Lunar Pod to the electric furnace.' He was not allowed to go to the terrace alone; either Sriman or Subhra accompanied him. Mrittika too lent a hand if she was at home.

On mornings following night shifts, Subhra visited home briefly before coming to Akashganga. Though she avoided speaking about it, Sriman sensed her queasiness about her fraught relationship with husband Rajesh. He did not force her to come or stay here. But Bishan was adamant. 'No, Nightingale, you must come. Who else would sponge me? Who else would I talk to?' He kept on pestering her like an unreasonable child.

Old age has been rightly defined as a second childishness. The old man, just like a child, craved attention, affection, and love. He was irrationally demanding and refused to see reason. Sriman often wanted to explain to Bishan-da Subhra's complicated situation owing to her marital discord. But when he proposed the same to Subhra, she vehemently refused. 'He will stop asking me to give him company if you tell him that. I too like to chat with him, and besides who would acquaint me with the night sky?' Sriman agreed. 'True, the acquaintance with the sky—' Sriman stopped abruptly.

But Subhra's return to her home was delayed because Mrittika met with an accident the day she was scheduled to go back. Although Bishan himself had recovered, he wanted Subhra to keep coming to help Mrittika. 'Nightingale, would it be impossible for you to stay back for another week or so?'

How could one refuse such an ardent request? Plus, Bishan paid her Rs 500 per day. That too was not a negligible sum. And it was also true that she did not want to abandon Sriman and Mrittika in such a crisis.

With Subhra's help, Mrittika regained the ability to perform a few essential personal chores on her own within a week's time.

***

Subhra loved to watch Mrittika recovering. It gave her so much pleasure when a patient recovered. She was holding Mrittika's hand while walking on the terrace. 'So, Pole Star, will you remember me when you resume karate, kickboxing and all?' Subhra asked.

'Of course,' Sriman replied before Mrittika could, 'because the first kick would invariably land on you.'

'My God, you people are dangerous!' exclaimed Subhra, grimacing in pretentious anger. 'And I thought you all to be my own!'

Bishan appeared on the terrace. 'All of us are close to your heart,' he said. 'You can't avoid us. Our hearts have been wired to yours.'

Mrittika looked stumped, while Subhra maintained a confused smile.

Bishan placed his eyes on the telescope.

'What's holding you two back?' Bishan said to Mrittika and Subhra without removing his eyes from the telescope. 'This star won't be there forever! Don't miss this chance. They are our true friends, friends forever. We were born from them. The sun and the solar system were created from the gases that spilled into the space following the explosion of stars.

'Organic life was born of inorganic matter,' the man at the helm of Akashganga continued to spill the mystery behind the creation of life. 'But I can't pinpoint how and when highly complex protein molecules were born of a few ordinary chemical ones, that bred the organic cells spread across our body.' Bishan stopped abruptly while his audience waited eagerly for him to continue.

'Know something, our relationship with inorganic matter dates back to billions of years.' He pointed at Mrittika's left leg, 'What's inserted there?'

'A rod,' Mrittika replied.

'What's that rod made of?'

'Stainless steel,' Subhra replied.

'Right, unblemished steel, specially designed for use in the human body,' Bishan nodded. 'At times, a metal alloy is used by mixing inorganic elements, or a metal like titanium.'

The three of them nodded assent. As Bishan continued, every single strand of the creation of life was peeled layer by layer before the eyes of Sriman, Mrittika, and Subhra. 'We are related to the stars since time immemorial. This is how we are bound to one another.' Bishan's observation lingered in the air briefly before melting into the distant galaxy.

'Bishan-da, could there be another earth like ours?' Subhra asked.

'Of course, Nightingale. We may not have spotted it yet, but once we find it, all of us will shift to it together.'

'Our astronomers haven't discovered it yet?' Mrittika asked.

'Mrittika, American scientists have found an earth-like planet and named it Kepler 452B,' Bishan replied. 'It's one and a half times bigger than earth, 1400 light years away from here, each a 385-day year … that's all I know,' Bishan raised his hands in simulated surrender.

'Someday there will be a bridge linking our planet to theirs and we'll be flying there on spacecrafts wearing Yellow Shirts or Guava gear to deliver chicken butter masala or mutton biriyani,' Sriman said wistfully.

'The woodcutter never forgets his axe,' Bishan wisecracked.

***

Subhra went home seven days later.

Though Mrittika had regained the strength in her feet, she could not resume bike riding right away. Sriman suggested she should keep it in abeyance for the time being and think of acquiring a little more strength with a few more rounds of climbing the stairs. Mrittika agreed quietly. But the act of sitting idle was getting on her nerves.

'Why so sad?' Sriman asked.

'I feel so worthless that I can't contribute anything!' Mrittika could not keep her emotions in check.

'Is money everything? You're managing the kitchen, supervising the deliveries, also maintaining the accounts at the end of the day on the computer,' Sriman was trying desperately to instil positivity in her.

'All's well, but the call of the road is irresistible,' Mrittika expressed the typical home-confined delivery rider's quandary.

'Can't deny that,' Sriman shook his head in agreement. 'Okay, rest for a few days more and then, if you feel ...' Sriman paused. 'Why don't you join Mathuresh's studio? They'll start making Durga idols from February. You can go there, observe how they work and learn their skills. I was so very fascinated with it when I was a child!' he added as an afterthought. Sriman related myriad stories associated with idol-making leaving Mrittika excited.

***

Mrittika was taken aback on entering the artisan's chamber at Mathuresh's place. The room, no less than 800 square feet, had an uncommonly high ceiling, which breathed old-world architecture. The cemented floor had a rugged surface. Two bamboo scaffoldings were attached to two parts of its walls. The one on the western wall was a bit high, nine-ten feet from the floor.

The scaffolding attached to the southern wall was comparatively lower, yet no less than seven feet from the floor. Both platforms were supported by sturdy pieces of wood because the walls would not be able to provide that support. Two separate ladders of different heights were attached to the platforms. The frail ladder leaning on the higher platform could easily be used to climb up the lower platform. For Mrittika, habituated to stringent measures to make ends meet, the second ladder was simply redundant.

A heap of straw lay in one corner. On the other end, an idol stood half made, a virtual scarecrow, impossible to discern which god or goddess it was intended to be moulded into. That explained the pieces of straw scattered all over the room.

Components strewn all over the floor made it evident that the artisans had spent their nights in the room, probably on the scaffolds.

***

As arranged, Mathuresh came to Akashganga every afternoon to accompany Mrittika back to his studio. Bubka went with them at times. Bubka finished his homework at Mathuresh's studio. Mrittika watched and listened to everything carefully.

One day, Gurakesh oriented her on the character of clay. He taught her how to identify and use sticky clay and sandy clay, how to change the character of sticky clay by adding straws to it. Mathuresh taught her how to meditate on the goddess before making the idol, to mould with clay the exact representation of the image as she appeared in the artist's imagination. He described how such an exact representation could be very difficult, yet how, at times, incredibly easy.

'Very good. Imagine the goddess with all your soul, then create her idol with dollops of clay … don't forget that they too are delivery riders like us,' Sriman said, hearing everything.

'What nonsense!' Mrittika said in pseudo indignation.

'They come down from the skies to deliver things we humans order: education, knowledge, prosperity, success. We pray for it and down they come. Laxmi, Saraswati, Ganesha, finally comes Ma Durga, answering our prayer of conquering evil,' Sriman explained, with a wink.

Mrittika smiled at his absurd but unique humanisation of divinity.

'And you are above the gods …' Sriman smiled.

Mrittika did not get it.

'We say the gods have created us and you are *mrittika*, the mud that moulds the gods,' Sriman explained.

'Okay, I'll make Saraswati first and then—' Mrittika said.

'*Asur*,' Sriman quipped, completing her statement.

'What? *Asur*!' Mrittika was caught off-guard by Sriman's joke.

'You won't have to think too much, just remember my face,' Sriman laughed at his own joke.

'Stop kidding!' Mrittika said, punctuating her loud laughter with an attempt at solemnity. 'Why would you be a demon? You are my dearest Shiva, my beloved Bholanath, whom I worship every morning,' she said, with a gentle peck on Sriman's cheek.

She held him in a passionate embrace. 'You are my graveyard friend from that strange night, remember?' she whispered in a voice brimming with passion as their bodies melded into each other's. Sriman could hear magical chants, as he yielded to the overpowering fragrance of Mrittika's breath and the tantalising urge to unveil the mysteries of every corner of her swarthy frame. His rigid defences collapsed one by one, while he silently chanted, 'Sirius, Sirius, Sirius.' The star, seated in some faraway frontier of the firmament, worked its spell and the seed of the protein molecule melded into inorganic matter.

# 19

Sriman had never expected everything to fall into place so smoothly. It was not easy to assemble thirty to thirty-five people under the same roof to discuss their respective issues. But, finally, the impossible was made possible and Sriman felt happy.

The idea was Bishan-da's brainchild. He came up with the advice one fine morning. 'Sriman, why don't all of you sit down together? Not just Yellow Shirts, delivery riders of Guava, Fast Move, Quick March, Foreman, Cameron, Horizon should also be there. It would be a pleasant experience to exchange thoughts with one another. If not anything else, it will be a grand rooftop picnic.'

'But the cost of a picnic … also, arranging the refreshments and all,' Sriman felt iffy about the mammoth task.

'It shouldn't be your headache alone. Distribute the responsibilities among your friends … this get-together is as important to them as it is to you. You must make them realise this,' Bishan reasoned.

'You're missing the point, Bishan-da, no one is ready to do anything beyond what serves their interest ... maximum eight to ten would turn up,' Sriman said, disheartened.

'If you can assemble even four people from each company, that would make forty. Even if it's three, it makes thirty.'

'Won't be that easy, Bishan-da.'

'This is the problem with you, Sriman. You accept defeat even before entering the battlefield!' Bishan thundered.

***

The drubbing served its purpose. Things took on a momentum after that. First, the date was fixed, the first Monday of the next month, as decided by Bishan-da. Time: 11 am to 4 pm. Venue: the Akashganga terrace.

'But can we arrange everything in just fifteen days?' Somnath sounded chancy.

'If you can't assemble thirty people in fifteen days, you won't be able to do that in thirty days either,' Bishan said, matter of factly. 'The date will remain unchanged ... let's discuss other things.'

Somnath was silenced by Bishan's no-nonsense baritone. 'How do we arrange the food, awning, mats, loudspeakers in such a short time?' he mumbled nervously.

'Keep me in the loop, everything will work out. You just get the attendees,' Bishan said reassuringly.

Sriman and Somnath prepared a list. Fifty people from ten companies. Invitations were sent over the phone. The message was taut and crisp: all of us are facing the same issues. We must sort them out in an open-minded discussion. Not a meeting but an informal get-together that would acquaint us with one another while sharing our respective concerns with one another.

Nasim, Vighnesh, Kabul, Anup, Abir took the initiative for contacting people personally. People invited over phone were invited again, face to face. 'We'll have lunch together that day—jeera rice, dal, brinjal fry, chicken curry, dessert. Tea in the afternoon. Contribute whatever you can, if possible. Feel free to come even if you cannot contribute. Remember, the first Monday of next month. We'll remind you again, three days before the event,' they were told.

The formal announcement appeared on the Facebook page of We the Delivery Riders: the city was going to have its first conference of delivery workers to discuss their demands. The declaration was followed by the date, time, and venue of the assembly. The schedule of the conference was posted on Instagram as well.

The message spread like wildfire. From the city, it spread to the outskirts, from there to other states, reaching the major cities across the country. Delivery riders of Delhi were the first to send in their best wishes for the success of the meeting. Best wishes from the big cities were followed by the deluge of similar messages from smaller ones like Guwahati, Bhubaneswar, Jamshedpur, Ranchi, Patna.

'Had they sent cash instead of wishes, we could have made it a lavish treat,' Bishan quipped.

Jnuiphool had sent her best wishes. Her students from the universities of Berkeley and Indiana too had wished good luck.

'You've worked a miracle, my dear Sriman!' Happiness oozed from Bishan's voice. 'Don't be surprised if you start getting invitations to international conferences. Get in touch with your Jnui madam, start writing papers and all,' Bishan smiled.

***

At around 10 on the morning of D-Day, Sriman was checking whether everything was going according to the plan, standing beneath the flimsy canopy on the terrace of Akashganga. Everyone had contributed their humble mite to Somnath. It escaped Sriman how Somnath could make such a huge arrangement with that paltry amount. Bishan-da had chosen the right person to collect the funds, Sriman thought.

The details of the programme must be written down. After that, photocopies of the same must be made. Sriman rushed to the stationery shop nearby and bought a notebook in which contact details of all attendees were to be noted down. On his way back, he got photocopies of the programme made. He got Subrata to sit at the desk near the door. He would jot down the contact details of every attendee the moment they set foot on the terrace. Each of them would be handed a copy of the programme after their details were noted down.

'Who will write down the minutes?' Sriman looked at Somnath.

'I shall be busy arranging for the refreshments … ask someone else,' Somnath said.

'Okay, I'll ask Mrittika,' Sriman said.

Mrittika gladly agreed. She was in low spirits for the last few days following her accident. She was back in the groove since starting to learn idol-making. But today's excitement had surpassed everything. Her poem on delivery workers which had been posted on the Facebook page of We the Delivery Riders would be sung at today's meeting.

The team from north Kolkata had been at work from the morning; the south Kolkata coterie of Nasim-Vighnesh-Kabul-Jaideb-Bikram had also arrived. The number of attendees had reached thirty-five. Would the food suffice if some more attendees arrived? Somnath rushed to the kitchen of Anusri. Srinath and Anup were managing the kitchen. Mathuresh was supervising the arrangement for laying out the spread.

'We had initially thought that the attendees would be below the expected number. But now … ' Somnath sounded anxious.

'Don't worry, we'll manage,' Srinath assured him.

'Why not?' Mathuresh smiled. 'We will have our lunch a little later than the others … What say?'

'We won't get to have the lunch after working so hard?' Somnath asked. 'Okay, if you all say so … '

'Don't take it so seriously, bro, Mathuresh-da is joking,' Anup said, 'none will be deprived of lunch, there's provision for forty people.'

The smile was back on Somnath's face. 'Okay then, I thought … ' Somnath went back to the terrace leaving the sentence hanging in the air.

'I welcome all of you to this grand get-together,' Sriman began his welcome address. 'Let's begin our historic meeting with a song written by our dear friend Mrittika. Noted singer, Shuddhabrata Mazumdar, a student of medicine, will lend his voice to it.'

Shuddhabrata started singing before the applause could die down …

Scurries aimlessly, day and night, delivery boy,
Carries the load, day and night, delivery girl,
Night and day, day and night
Thankless tale, relentless fight.
Patience, guts and grit,
Sleepless streets roll under fatigued feet.
Lights blink green, amber, red,
Dawn to dusk, bike to bed.
Enacting the hackneyed script of a jaded plot,
They bear their inscrutable lot.
Don't question don't doubt,
Just navigate the ruthless streets,
Day in, day out.
Wheels roll, wheels ply,
Tears drip, tears dry,
Dreams grow, dreams die.
Yet, new dreams burgeon
Across the mind's valley,
Street to lane, nook to alley.
The delivery rider, the new-era mail-bearer,
New peddler of commodities, the 'now' labourer,
Delivery rider delivery worker delivery rider …

A big round of applause greeted the singer even before the song ended. 'Wonderful, just mind-blowing, doctor!' Bishan-da's enthused voice rose over the clamour. 'You should seriously consider a career change and regale us with songs! … Brilliant writing, Mrittika dear!'

'Now it is the turn of the attendant delivery riders to voice their issues,' Sriman made the formal introduction. 'All the demands voiced here shall be compiled and edited to sum up a comprehensive body of general demands—friends, it is a tough time for us who earn our livelihood through honest labour. Our back is against the wall, but we can't do anything. As soon as we stand up to protest, we are silenced … they take away our livelihood. In such a situation, we must prepare a unanimous list of demands. These demands shall be posted on our Facebook page too. Whenever any of our friends sits down with the bosses of their company, we hope, they'll raise the same demands.'

'*Ekdam sahi baat* … very true. It's a pretend rivalry that our bosses project. All of them are hand in glove when it comes to harassing us,' Mohammed Nagib stood up.

Sriman felt encouraged by Nagib's words. 'If they can unite to harass us, party together to heckle us, we can make them realise that we too can sit down together to discuss our problems. We must first decide what we exactly want. Whoever wants to speak out, please raise your hand, we'll call upon all, one by one,' he said.

Nasim was the first to raise his hand, with a body language that evinced nervousness. Nasim was not a seasoned speaker.

Their family business of tanning had run into rough weather. Nasim had joined the profession of delivery rider only to bring his family out of the doldrums.

Nasim began in a shaky voice. '*Saathiyon, aap sabko mubarakbaad.* Like Sriman bhai, I too urge upon you to frankly express your demands. The companies are exploiting us in whatever way they like … brothers, don't let them do this.' There was a new enthusiasm in Nasim's voice. 'They can't block us simply because it suits their whim, without judging the situation a delivery worker is in, without letting the worker speak.'

The meeting resounded with applause.

Vighnesh said, 'It's inhuman to work for twelve-fourteen hours at a stretch. Yet, most of our friends are forced to undergo this torture every day. A delivery worker must have Rs 700 to 800 at hand at the end of a day, excluding the per-kilometre incentive, to sustain at least the decency of a lower middle-class existence. A company must ensure that its delivery partners get this sum.'

'The companies should not gaslight us by calling us "delivery partners",' Kabul said. 'We're nothing more than daily wagers, we would be happy to be called so; we want to build our union as daily wagers.'

Bikram seconded Kabul's view. 'We must have our own union. The company policies are ambiguous. They keep changing under the autocratic diktats of a few people. The policy for bonus changes, the incentives change. A rule once implemented must be valid for some time, say, two years at least. There must be a specific, uniform rule.'

Mrittika raised her hand. 'In case of a rider's accident on the way to work, their family must be treated with compassion,' she began. 'Financial help, adequate compensation must be arranged as early as possible. Why won't the company do anything if a rider meets with an accident while returning from work? The delivery rider wants security, the guarantee that they don't lose their life in the rush to reach the destination on time. The company must ensure this.'

Another huge round of applause followed.

Nasim stood up again. '*Ekdam sahi baat, didi*, you've spoken my mind. We know, none from the company responded when you met with your accident … When Sriman had his accident, he knew the company won't do anything, so he called Somnath. The company is scared of us because we stand by one another. Friends, we must keep the fear alive.'

'Another point,' Subrata joined in. 'We need decent working conditions, safe parking places everywhere, and a resting place with a lavatory and access to drinking water.'

Vighnesh stood up. 'You have our full support, Subrata. We fully agree with what you've said. Neither the customer nor the supervisor understands the problems we face on the way every day.'

'Don't forget the traffic sergeants,' Nagib added.

'Right,' Vighnesh said. 'The company is aware of the harassment we face on a daily basis. They can arrange permit cards for all of us.'

'Why not?' Somnath said. 'Aadhaar card, Voter card, PAN card, Health card … it's the age of cards, after all!'

'I am serious, Somnath,' Vighnesh snubbed him. 'We won't need to fuss over parking our bikes if we have the card.'

Somnath was about to poke fun again, but Sriman gestured to him to stop. 'It's time for lunch now. We shall regroup exactly forty minutes later,' he declared. 'Some more of our friends will express their views after the break. Then the president of the meeting, Bishan Basu, without whose encouragement and support nothing would have been possible, will share his valuable insights. We are eagerly waiting to hear him. So, friends, eat to your heart's content, but eat fast.'

Sriman was pleasantly surprised to find that additional sweets had been added to the menu. Must be Bishan-da, he thought. But where was he?

He found Bishan-da in the latter's room. 'Bishan-da, why are you sitting alone here? Lunch is ready.'

'Oh, lunch … okay, let's go.'

Sriman could sense from Bishan-da's voice that something was wrong. 'What's the matter? You look a bit off ... Aren't you feeling well? Is it the blood pressure?' he asked.

'Nothing serious, I haven't been keeping well ever since the viral fever ... feel so tired every now and then,' Bishan said.

'Should I fetch your food? ... I'll bring it in a jiffy.'

Bishan was in two minds. 'No, I can't miss the pleasure of eating together,' Bishan smiled. 'Just hold me if I lose balance while descending the stairs.'

The inspiring optics of so many people dining happily filled Bishan with a new vigour. He seemed transported back to his childhood in Kakdwip. What bliss it had been to taste the fresh fish and the fresh vegetables!

The couple of speakers who spoke post-lunch mostly repeated what had already been said. Sujoy was the only one to add a new angle. 'If we set up a union, it must not dance to the tune of any politically biased trade union. We don't want to dress ourselves in any particular colour. Our union should reflect the independent spirit that we bear.'

Sujoy's views received a huge applause.

'Now the president will address us,' Sriman declared.

Bishan Basu began his address. 'I salute all of you. I specially mention Sujoy for being the only one among you to have thought of setting up a new, independent organisation. You are right, Sujoy, the mode of protest has changed, we can no longer think like the traditional trade unions. Technology is the means with which the companies dominate us now, the means for the boss to remote-control his business.'

Bishan paused to clean his glasses. 'Let me tell you all clearly, whatever sector you are working in, particularly those in the business of serving people, it will come under this remote-controlling. Information technology, data science, marketing finance are already into it, others too are following suit. The 9-to-5 job will soon be outdated. Most workers will become gig labourers. Temporary jobs, freelance work will rule the roost. A large section of American workers make ends meet by working multiple jobs. Our country is not far behind. It's better to accept the new order instead of wasting time over its merits and demerits.

'It feels heartening to see that you too are utilising technology to assemble yourselves against them, spreading the word through Facebook, Instagram, WhatsApp, Twitter. So many of you have assembled at such short notice … this is no mean feat.

'They are using the system to torture you. If you want to resist this repression, you must raise your voice against it besides understanding the system. Approach the students of leading institutions. With their help you might be able to set up a system that would expose the inhumanity of the companies, stem their duplicitous practices.

'It will enable you all too to launch a counterattack, a cyber-attack … that is probably how you all have to carry on the fight …'

Bishan started hyperventilating before he could complete what he was saying. Something seemed to crack inside his head. Darkness engulfed him.

Luckily, the ambulance arrived soon. Sriman phoned Subhra before heading for her hospital. Somnath and Anup accompanied them.

The others too were eager to go. Mrittika stopped them, 'No need to create a crowd. I'll keep you all posted.'

'Let me know if blood is needed, I am ready,' Vignesh said.

'Anything for dada,' Bikram said.

The doctor diagnosed brain haemorrhage. Bishan would be kept under observation for the next seventy-two hours. Sriman informed Jnuiphool. She was in New Zealand. But she assured him that she would try to come as early as possible. She told Sriman to get the best doctor in town without thinking of the expenses. She would take care of that.

That night, Jnuiphool called on Sriman's phone. 'Please let me speak to Bishan.'

'He's in the ICU, madam. They don't allow phones there.'

'Okay, patch me in when he is out of danger …'

***

On the fifth day, the doctor assured them that Bishan was out of danger. A paralytic trend was diagnosed in the left cheek, arm, and leg. The doctor told them that things would take time to normalise. In the meantime, physiotherapy must be continued.

Sriman stood by Bishan's bed. Bishan opened his eyes slowly. The eyes bore a smirk, but there was no hint of it on his lips, due to the paralysis perhaps.

'See, I've fooled time again,' Bishan said in a slurred voice. 'Wait and watch how long I can manage it … What about you all? Found any new stars?'

Sriman rang Jnuiphool and handed over the phone to Bishan-da. 'Jnui ma'am is on the line.'

Bishan lifted his head a bit and spoke feebly into the phone. 'I am good, quite good; the show has reached its climax, the arc lights are on … I am so close to the exit!'

Bishan had inadvertently activated the speaker. Sriman could hear Jnui madam saying, 'Bishan, I must tell you something I haven't said before.'

'I know …' Bishan responded in a composed tone before disconnecting the call.

# Epilogue

Two months had passed. Yellow Shirts was yet to revoke Sriman's suspension. They might never take him back. But he was yet to outgrow the habit of opening the Yellow Shirts app every morning. Was it so easy to sever the emotional bond with the company one had served so long?

However, Sriman was happy that he had utilised this hiatus to his advantage. He had allotted time to issues that had long been demanding his attention. He had managed to streamline Anusri's sales mechanism. The Anusri menu now occupied a pride of place across all food-delivery apps, including Yellow Shirts.

Shiuli, Mrittika, and a newly recruited chef currently managed cooking at Anusri. Shiuli was an expert in cooking homely Indian dishes. Mrittika excelled in Chinese cuisine. The chef took care of the continental variety.

Sriman, Anup and Srinath got into action once all the items of an order were in place. It was their responsibility to pack the contents into containers embossed with the Anusri logo. Srinath had given up his regimen of the post-lunch siesta. He now spent wakeful afternoons in the kitchen to ensure that everything ran smoothly.

Earlier, dishes were outsourced from famous eateries and assembled in the Anusri kitchen before being despatched. But that was too much hard work while the profit was negligible. Hence, the decision in favour of in-house cooking.

Crimson, having acquired Ready Mart, had forayed into the market with renewed vigour. They had approached Sriman thrice during their recruitment drive. Sriman's earlier stints at Yellow Shirts and Foreman and his experiences therein were not a deterrent for them to choose him. Brijmohan Kapoor, the company head, was glad to interact with Sriman. 'We are looking for forthright, honest, and brave boys like you,' he had said. By the time Sriman was back on the streets for Crimson and Ready Mart, the cloud kitchen was learning to stand on its own, with the wobbliness of a toddler.

Mrittika had found the person she had been searching for at Akashganga. For her, Bishan Basu was the epitome of the ideal human being. Bishan was the ultimate human for Jnuiphool, Sriman, Subhra, and Mathuresh as well. Somnath, Nasim, Vighnesh, Kabul too had become his fans. Bishan had the rare ability of effortlessly gathering hordes of admirers. What attracted people even more was the impenetrable miasma of mystique that surrounded him. His mercurial nature and unpredictability made him an enigma. Recently, he had stumped Sriman by expressing his sudden whim of spending a night at Sonagachhi with the most educated sex worker there.

'At this age? … Look at you!' Sriman had not been able to conceal his shock.

'Why? Have they introduced age limits nowadays?' Bishan had replied agitatedly.

After overcoming the initial shock, Sriman did away with all his inhibitions and returned to the lanes of infamy in search of an apt companion who would agree to spend her night with a mercurial nonagenarian. Ratrimani Choudhury, a middle-aged courtesan, agreed. Hailing from a well-off and respectable family, she was pursuing her master's when a familial feud compelled her to join this profession. Though a resident of Sonagachhi from her early thirties, she maintained a distance from the actual nub of notoriety. She lived on the second floor of a house nearby and taught music to young girls of the locality. Occasionally, some whimsical fellow visited her quarters. But Ratrimani was no less quirky. She wouldn't admit a bloke unless he suited her fancy.

From the moment Sriman left Bishan inside his room, a strange restlessness had been throbbing in his chest. He lay awake, his mind tossing like a storm-tossed boat.

By the time he rose, dawn was still a long way off. At half past two, under the deep hush of night, Sriman found himself before that door. He thought of knocking, but the thought dissolved at once. A faint gleam was already spilling out through the half-ajar frame. He lingered, torn between curiosity and shame, when a sound unfurled—soft, tremulous, unmistakably a woman's voice. It drifted like mist, a melody from the forgotten 1950s, heavy with sorrow, soaked in longing.

Sriman had not discussed the matter with anybody else, not even Mrittika, lest they misunderstood Bishan-da. Only he knew that Bishan-da was a human being who could not be defined by mundane sensibilities.

Ever since shifting to Akashganga, Mrittika had found both a man of interest in Bishan-da and a job of her liking. She had involved herself real time in idol-making following Sriman's suggestion who had recommended it to pull her out of the quicksand of dejection she was sinking into.

In some obscure recess of her mind, Mrittika had always been harbouring the dream of becoming an idol maker. Sriman laid before her the roadmap to achieve it while Mathuresh helped her bring that dream to fruition. She had become a sensation in the sphere of idol-making in a matter of a few months, nothing short of a whiz kid. Popular as Mrittika Senpal now, she made one idol per year. She decided to which club or puja committee the idol should go to. This year, it was a club from Chandernagore.

Although Mrittika had shifted base to Mathuresh's place, she had not given up her room at Akashganga. She occasionally stayed there, relishing Sriman's proximity on those occasions.

Mrittika occupied Sriman's thoughts night and day, especially when he went to sleep every night. At times, he felt a numbing pain. She had wanted to live with him, as his family. 'You are aware of the situation we delivery riders are in. You know the condition of my family. How can I plunge everybody in such uncertainty? Is it possible to even think of running a whole family with my scanty income? If not anybody else, I need to think of Bubka at least,' Sriman had reasoned with her.

Sriman was gazing at the stars with these recollections hovering across his mind. He remembered Ratrimani touching Bishan-da's feet while he was about to leave Sonagachhi that night. 'Please come again,' she had appealed. Bishan-da had kept his hand on her head. 'I will, keep this charm alive till then.' The man would remain unintelligible to him forever, just like that remark.

Dragging footfalls made him aware of Bishan-da's approach. Bishan-da could not walk without the help of a stick since the haemorrhage. Despite leaning on the stick, he had to drag his feet. But his will power was dauntless as ever, he must come to the terrace to watch the evening sky. Even when Sriman went down to his room, he sat on, deep into the night, looking through the telescope. He trailed the trajectory of the stars, tried to locate the potential havens of aliens across the Milky Way, while scribbling complex calculations in his notebook.

'Abhijit is burning bright tonight,' Sriman said, to the footsteps that were drawing closer. He could discern Bishan-da's footfall.

'How are Deneb, Dhanishtha, and Shravana? Is Uttarashada keeping well? Haven't seen her for a long time,' Bishan blurted out mechanically like a holy man counting beads.

Sriman had learnt the mathematics of the sky, thanks to Bishan-da's affectionate guidance.

'You're my teacher,' Bishan told Sriman smilingly. The very next moment his voice assumed urgency, 'I must teach you the science of sending radio signals too.'

***

Jnuiphool had returned to Akashganga after a long time. Ever since, Bishan had been exuding an ecstatic enthusiasm as on all such occasions.

Jnuiphool had brought a sophisticated gift for Bishan: an ultramodern telescope equipped with a tracker and a camera capable of taking pictures of the space.

'This must have cost you a fortune! … My God, Jnui, what have you done!' Bishan exclaimed on looking at the telescope.

'So, Sriman, which star do you want to see?' Jnuiphool asked while powering on the telescope and the tracker.

'Sirius,' Sriman heard himself saying.

'Type Sirius into the monitor,' Bishan said to Sriman.

'Now press "Enter",' Jnui instructed Sriman.

The telescope started whirring as soon as Sriman pressed the switch. It raised its neck to face the sky, then turned its head to the left.

'Now, Bishan, place your eyes on the eyepiece,' Jnui said once the telescope came to a standstill.

'Unbelievable, Sriman!' Bishan yelled. 'You must see this … your Sirius, our Sirius!'

Bishan lifted his eyes from the eyepiece. 'Sriman, don't miss this opportunity! Capture a full-fledged picture of your Sirius as a part of Orion … This gadget is a miracle! We can spot the familiar stars in a matter of moments … and if the sky is clear we might even spot the Milky Way, our Akashganga, and even the Andromeda galaxy!'

Bishan's enthusiasm had infected Sriman too. With Jnuiphool's instructions, he powered the camera on.

'Brilliant! Jnui, you've given me the best gift of my life,' Bishan exclaimed in a voice that was suffused with enthusiasm tinged with gratitude.

Jnui had brought a treasure of Māori folk tales with her this time.

'Māori tales! Is it? Let's hear some of it,' said Bishan interestedly.

'There's a plethora of tales surrounding the Māori exodus to New Zealand. Some people believe they belonged to central Asia. From there they scattered themselves across the islets on the Pacific Ocean through the Malay peninsula before settling down in the Hawaiki Island.' Jnui paused briefly. She smiled at Bishan before resuming her account. 'No one knows better than you that souls smitten by the adventure bug can't stay indoors. They set out on a new voyage in search of a new land. They finally settled down in the islets of New Zealand.'

'Wow, highly interesting!' Bishan remarked enthusiastically.

'Let me tell you one of the many folk tales associated with that expedition,' Jnui continued. 'Sometime in the tenth century, Kupe and Nage, brothers, reached Cape Terawhiti or the North Cape on two boats. Through a stunted journey along a frail strait, they reached the North Island. Both the brothers were fascinated by the beauty of the island. The soil of this new land was much more fertile than that of the Hawaiki.

'Kupe returned to the Hawaiki with the glorious tale of the discovery of the new land. The brave ones among his folks joined him in the expedition to the new land across the choppy waters of the Pacific. Driven by the dreams of a golden future founded on a rich harvest, they set out on the voyage on three sturdy vessels built specifically for this purpose.

'Days, weeks, months passed, yet there was no sign of land. Kupe could feel the growing desperation of his people. Although they did not say as much, they were having doubts whether Kupe was taking them in the right direction. He checked again and reconfirmed that he was following the same course that had earlier led him to the newfound island.

'The intensifying ashiness of Kupe's face had started to dampen his wife's spirits too. The naturally jovial girl had forgotten to smile. Every morning, she would be staring wistfully at the horizon, in fervent anticipation of spotting the desired land.

'On one such early morning, soon after the first light, with the east the blend of a golden glow and a crimson radiance, she stood on the prow of the boat, stretching her vision to the farthest horizons. Was she seeing a whitish piece of cloud floating over the water? She rubbed her eyes a couple of times in sheer disbelief. No, she was not wrong, it *was* a piece of land, resembling a fragment of a cloud. Unable to suppress her excitement, she yelled to her folks.

'Kupe's vessel followed by the other two arrived at the large cloud-shaped island. Kupe and his folks started rejoicing on stepping on it. They named the island Aotearoa, which in Māori means the land of the long, white cloud.

'End of story,' Jnuiphool smiled.

'This is not a story, this is history! This isn't a fable. It does not have a—' Sriman said with a hint of desperation.

'Yes, this is not a fable. But you can still extract a moral from it if you want,' Bishan replied. 'For instance, you can say that the industrious and the bold are rewarded for their resilience, they ultimately reach the new land they set out for just like us who are searching for a new planet. This is *our* story!'

'Right, absolutely right,' Sriman was convinced.

Jnuiphool was smiling. It was the smile of contentment.

Whenever this lady came, she stayed for a few days and left, draping Bishan-da in a cloak of intense grief. Sriman wondered why. Was she too heartless to realise the saddening impact of her departure on Bishan-da?

Jnuiphool this time had brought a pipe from Havana for Bishan apart from the folklore. She had brought tobacco and a boxful of cigars too. Bishan was over the moon. He had got things from Havana after a long time. He recalled 10 July 1959, when he had accompanied Che Guevara to show him the jute mills of Agarpara during the latter's Calcutta trip. Che had gifted him Havana pipes on that occasion. Che loved taking photos. He clicked a solitary cow at a rain-splattered Dalhousie Square.

Bishan was brooding as he recollected the events of that day. He lit a cigar and an invigorating aroma permeated the room.

'It feels rather strange, Sriman, that Che didn't bother to meet any communist leader of Bengal on that occasion … I don't know—' a severe bout of cough took over Bishan. The cough was so acute that it almost crippled him. His eyes turned red and were watering. Sriman fetched him a glass of water as fast as he could.

Such sudden and severe bouts of cough had become a routine with Bishan, exacerbated by shortness of breath. The doctor had advised a battery of blood tests, but Bishan refused to get them done. Sriman had tried his best to convince him. Mrittika, Somnath, Mathuresh had tried too, but to no avail.

'What's the objection in getting the tests done once?' Mrittika said.

'Do you have any idea? It will leave me poorer by five to six thousand rupees,' Bishan had cited his bizarre logic.

'I'll never understand you, dada! You had no issues shelling out seven to eight thousand rupees during our meeting, but now you can't spend a lesser amount for your own well-being … ' said Somnath.

'No, Bishan-da, you must get them done. If it's a question of money, we'll help you out,' Mathuresh said emphatically.

'Be quiet, will you … Were yesterday's calculations correct? Sriman, could you check?' Bishan asked.

Sriman could very well sense that it was Bishan-da's ruse to change the channel. 'Yes, I will,' he said to console Bishan. He gestured to the others to leave.

How could one drag an able-bodied but unwilling nonagenarian to the hospital? Only Subhra could manage Bishan-da. He was too feeble to withstand the valour of her tongue.

Sunday night witnessed familiar optics on the Akashganga terrace. Sriman at the telescope, Bishan at his side. 'Delphinus looks so bright in the northern horizon tonight!' Sriman was enthusiastic.

'Let me see!' Bishan was restless to take a look. 'Hmmm, splendid! Notice Cepheus and Hercules too, you won't spot them so easily at any other time … ' Bishan counselled Sriman.

'Do you see them?' Bishan enquired.

'Yes, Bishan-da, the view is fabulous!' replied Sriman.

'Never forget these stars, Sriman. Always keep in mind that the new planet is inside the Milky Way itself, our own Akashganga! I have taught you a lot, now it's your turn to teach your friends,' Bishan said.

***

Monday. Bishan was writhing in excruciating pain. Despite this, he was saying, 'Sriman, can't you all carry me to the terrace?' They should have ignored his plea, but they could not help responding to his helpless urgency. Sriman and Mathuresh carried him to the terrace on a chair. He stayed there till the dead of the night. 'No more, dada, you'll catch a cold. Let me take you to your room,' Sriman pleaded.

Running a high fever since Tuesday morning, Bishan began hallucinating. Sriman suspected it to be common cold. Jnui had called in a doctor who diagnosed it to be dengue. Bishan's blood work confirmed the diagnosis in the afternoon. The platelet count was alarmingly low; a further dip would be risky. The doctor instructed them to make provisions for infusing platelets.

Jnui was to fly to Delhi on Tuesday evening. She was to present an experimental paper on the folklores of various countries at the history congress on Wednesday. She had assured Sriman that she would fly back on Wednesday night, else early the next morning.

Sriman initially thought of requesting her to cancel the trip. But he refrained on second thoughts. No point requesting her when she had taken the decision despite the graveness of the situation. 'Wish you a safe trip, madam. I've already informed Subhra, she will probably—' he said to Jnui.

'Excellent, that would really help,' Jnui replied.

Subhra was at Akashganga by the evening. 'Not to worry, uncle, I'm here. Your platelets won't go down any more. I've got the update from the doctor. Will give you a shot, if necessary,' she declared in a forced tone of joviality.

'I'm absolutely alright, Ms Nightingale,' Bishan jibed. 'I was missing you. I had to have you by my side. Couldn't think of a better excuse.'

At night, the fever soared along with hallucinatory fits. 'It's a full moon night. Can you see the tidal waves?' Bishan kept saying such things through the night. Subhra was awake all along, giving him paracetamol, applying cold press.

Bishan was back to his senses next morning. He called Sriman to his side. 'Never forget, this Akashganga is a sanctuary for delivery riders from now on. Whoever loses work would not have to worry for a roof overhead … a sky speckled with stars,' Bishan said.

'Look, Sriman … the Orion, the Great Bear … you must see this … Sirius, Alkaid, they haven't looked this clear before!' Though Bishan had shrieked in his dream, the groans of a sleeping man were too feeble to wake up anybody nearby.

Bishan saw his Gajen uncle of Kakdwip, in his dream. 'See, Bishan, Akashganga above, our own Akashganga below, the Ganga nearby, incredible!' Gajen uncle was saying.

Bishan could sleep no more. He felt a deep yearning for the Sirius that had appeared in his dream. He sat up, recalling the sky of his past, the sky that used to spread over him, canopy-like, in his childhood in Kakdwip. The sky was beckoning him. How could he resist the call? He glanced at his watch: 3:35 am. Sriman was fast asleep on a camp bed in the corner of the room. He had returned late. 'Let him sleep,' Bishan said to himself.

Bishan lit a cigar. An edifying aroma! He was reminded of Che, of his rebuff to his assassins, 'Shoot me, you cowards, one man, that's the maximum you can kill!'

Bishan Basu climbed to the terrace cautiously with his walking stick.

Sriman had a sudden awakening. He turned towards Bishan's bed. It was empty. He was probably in the toilet. It was an old habit with Bishan to perform his daily ablutions early in the morning. Subhra must be asleep beside Mrittika in the latter's room.

Sriman liked going to the terrace on such rare early mornings when he had time to spare. He loved to look at the sliver of the Ganga visible from there. The air at the crack of dawn felt divine.

Sriman's heart skipped a beat as soon as he stepped onto the terrace. He had never anticipated to see Bishan seated in his armchair in that bizarre posture. Bishan's eyes were staring at the void. A penetrative stare, chilling in its poise. His arms were spread across the twin hand-rests of the armchair, one of them firmly gripping the corresponding hand-rest. The telescope stood on the right. On the left, sat the stool with the notebook and the pen and a pipe.

Sriman kept observing Bishan from a distance. The innocently impish rays of the early-morning sun were caressing his forehead. His dishevelled hair, days-old stubble, lips slightly ajar, reminded Sriman of Bishan-da's smile on meeting Mrittika for the first time.

Sriman was so shocked by the unexpected sight that he had not noticed the *neelkanth* that was perched on Bishan-da's shoulder. So that was why dada was abnormally still, lest the bird flew away. Strange man indeed! Sriman tiptoed towards Bishan. But the bird fluttered away much before he could reach the spot.

Only on drawing close did Sriman notice the uncanny imperturbability of Bishan's eyes. He touched him. A deathly chill raced down his spine making him wrench his hand away.

Everything felt unreal. Had the bird, which he had seen barely moments ago, been there at all, or was it a numinous appendage to the surreal scenario? Was Bishan-da dead, or was it one of his macabre pranks? Sriman fervently wished Bishan would explode in a guffaw any moment and say in a mischievous singsong 'Didn't I scare the living daylights out of you?'

Moments passed. Bishan did not stir.

Like the emerging light of the day, reality gradually dawned on Sriman.

He must wake up Mrittika and Subhra. He must inform Jnui madam right away.

Sriman fished out his phone from his pocket.

At once, an order arrived.

A food delivery order, from Yellow Shirts!

# Glossary

*Abhijit*: The Sanskrit equivalent of Vega, Abhijit is the brightest star in the northern constellation of Lyra

*Aldebaran*: A giant star with a ruddy hue, also called the 'bull's eye', belonging to the Taurus constellation

*Ashwini*: The first *nakshatra* (lunar mansion) in Indian astronomy

*Bharani*: The second *nakshatra* in Indian astronomy

*Bhetki*: Bengali appellation for the Barramundi/Asian Sea Bass, a migratory fish

*Butterfly Cluster*: An open assemblage of stars in Scorpius, the southern constellation

*Capella*: A star in the constellation Auriga, also called Alpha Aurigae, the sixth brightest star in the sky

*Cassiopeia*: One of the prominent constellations in the northern sky, bearing the shape of W

*Deneb*: The most luminous star in the constellation of Cygnus

*Krittika*: The open star cluster analogous to the Pleiades of western astronomy

*Lotte*: Bengali name for the Bombay Duck, a species of lizardfish

*Mejda*: The Bengali equivalent of the second brother or middle brother, the brother between the eldest and the youngest

*NEOWISE*: NEOWISE, the acronym of Near-Earth Object Wide-field

Infrared Survey Explorer, is the first bright comet visible to the bare eye from the northern hemisphere since the mid-1990s

*Pleiades*: A cluster of stars in the constellation Taurus visible in the winter sky

*Rohini*: The *nakshatra* which is equivalent to the Aldebaran

*Sandesh*: A dessert made of *chhena* (curdled milk) and sugar, one of Bengal's legendary contributions to the sweet tooth

*Phuchka*: A mouth-watering and extremely popular street food; Bengal's equivalent to the *paani puri* or *gol gappa*

*Sattu*: An energy boosting healthy drink made of roasted gram flour, consumed mostly in summer

*Shravana*: The 22nd *nakshatra* in Indian astronomy, belonging to the constellation of Makara (Capricorn)

# Acknowledgements

When I decided to write an account of food delivery riders, I was a bit hesitant—would it really strike a chord? The only person who unfailingly encouraged me to take up the project was the one who has been fuelling my whims for over 40 years—my wife, Shovona Mukherji.

During my evening strolls, I met a couple of food delivery riders who, in turn, introduced me to some of their colleagues; a few of them were women.

After conducting a ground-level survey—including rides on their pillions—I gained a fairly good understanding of their daily lives: their challenges, joys, and sorrows.

My heartfelt thanks to all 50 bike-borne gig workers who supported me and shared valuable insights—even when my questions sometimes tiptoed on the edges of their privacy.

My friend, Prof. Tirthankar Roy, has written a wonderful foreword. I would be ungrateful if I didn't thank him.

After reading the original Bengali version of this novel, Goutam Ghose, the acclaimed film director, sent me a text: *I can see a film in it.* He readily agreed to write a few words about the book, which now appear as the blurb on the back cover. My thanks to Goutam-da as well.

And last, but by no means least, is Niyogi Books, who stepped forward to publish this work. How can I not thank them?